Swift

ISBN 978-1-61434-519-0

Published in the United States by Booklocker.com, Inc., Bangor, Maine.

This novel is a work of fiction and the product of the author's imagination. All historical characters and organizations are used fictionally. Any other character resemblance to real persons living or deceased is entirely coincidental.

Printed in the United States of America on acid-free paper.

Booklocker.com, Inc.
2011

First Edition

Swift

By
Ed Henson

The legend claims men under the leadership of Captain John Swift were mining silver ore in the wilderness west of the Allegheny Mountains in mid 1700's. History records two of Kentucky's earliest pioneers, Daniel Boone and John Finley in the same region during the very same time yet neither ever mentioned the legend. The current historical accounts are favorable to Boone but have little regard for John Finley. This was an unfortunate omission. While the silver mines have never been discovered there is no proof they don't exist.

Forward

For more than 240 years the oldest folk story in Appalachia has fascinated people, encouraged treasure hunters, puzzled historians, and been told and retold time and time again by elders. My grandmother first told me the story, weaving it with a tale of my great grandfather finding a vein of lead near the top of Pine Mountain.

Ed Henson takes a new approach to the tale, weaving a story of a connection between the historic figures of Daniel Boone, John Finley, John Swift and others and connecting them in a way many treasure researchers and historians have suspected.

For some time there has been a belief that Boone followed Swift into the Kentucky wilderness and that John Finley knew both men.

Along side this interaction Henson offers contemporary characters that chance upon clues and carvings that might lead them to the Swift treasure. Whether you believe the lost treasure legend or not the interplay between past and present is well done and very interesting.

The Henson family have a long-time link with the Swift Silver Mine legend, both in searching and researching the legend, a tale that stretches from West Virginia all the way to Northern Georgia and Alabama. Most of the "Swift Buffs" focus on the area of Kentucky that Henson writes about and follow similar clues. Hundreds, if not thousands, of people either believe in the lost treasure or consider it possible. The idea of taking the story and bringing it up to date is brilliant. The idea that it should be written by Ed Henson is appropriate. Whether you are a "Swift" treasure hunter or not you will enjoy this good read. It flows very well and by page two you become captured by this new and engrossing tale. As someone once said a good story "is more than a yarn, it's a fabric."

Michael S. Steely
Author of "Swift's Silver Mines and Related Appalachian Treasures"

Acknowledgments

Any project of this size cannot be the sole contribution of one individual. No simple way to accomplish such an effort is possible without others providing input, completing tasks and help. This book is no exception. So, let me express my appreciation to those who provided me with all the necessary help at the appropriate time along the way.

First, my thanks to Lorin Hancock for her skillful eye in the early edits of the book, though she didn't agree with me on the ending (don't read it yet!) she, always the professional, encouraged me to keep it *my* book. I want to thank my wonderful wife, BeLinda for her hours of editing and suggesting creative changes. I'm grateful to my daughter Allison for providing me with ideas, approaches and corrections on my writing journey and my daughter Sarah for all the coffee she supplied everyday. I can't express appreciation enough to the first test readers, Clara Henson and Doug Lewis for their reviews and support of the project. Thank you, Michael Steely for your encouragement and the nice forward. My thanks go to Byron Crawford, who suggested I write the book in the first place. Thanks to Chase and Cassie for their input and help. Of course I must thank and remember the late Michael Paul Henson, who, I believe to be *the* person of the twentieth century that kept the Swift legend alive by writing the first book about the subject. And finally to those who listened to me rattle on about this story, thank you for your wonderful patience.

Table of Contents

One:
The First Clue

The summer the air was hot and stagnant. And without a breeze, the humidity was so high every breath was like drinking. This had been one of the hottest summers on record. Why Will Morrow picked this day to hike up the rocky slope of the mountain remained a mystery to his companion, Jennifer. Yet, trudging up the steep mountain trail offered a new adventure. The climb, nearly too much even for Will, prompted him to wonder about Jennifer. He reached the bottom of the massive cliff and perched himself atop a large boulder to rest and wait until she, perhaps a hundred yards behind him, made her way up the difficult climb.

"We're at the base of the cliff, so the tough part is just ahead," Will teased as she huffed the last few paces towards his resting place. Jennifer offered no comment, precisely because she was using every available sticky breath to take in oxygen to sustain her arduous climb. Will studied Jennifer from his seat as she walked the winding path to meet him. Her auburn hair flowed regally against the luscious green forest covering the mountain slope, and her deep blue eyes provided such striking contrast that had always captivated Will. He thought her to be among the more beautiful women he'd ever seen at the bar where he worked. Jennifer never considered herself pretty. She never really meditated on her physical appearance much at all. Jennifer's pride was her independence, which made her all the more attractive to Will. She stood toe-to-toe with Will, or anyone else, when discussing nearly any subject. A voracious reader, she loved to learn about anything scholarly, being more prone to peruse the non-fiction aisles of the library over the New York Time's Bestsellers selection.

"My God, Will, we're going to have a heat stroke," Jennifer complained as she arrived at Will's resting spot, a little red in the face and dripping with sweat. She dropped to the ground, amid the dried leaves and pine needles, on the opposite side of the trail from the boulder.

"Here, have some water and cool down a bit," Will said as he handed Jennifer a bottle of water from his pack.

Jennifer more than welcomed the rest from her difficult climb of Pilot Knob. Though famous in the region, no one recalled for sure how the mountain had gotten its name. It was the last great peak on the western edge of the Cumberland Plateau, which covered the eastern third of Kentucky, and the grand geologic feature marked the end of the rugged terrain of Eastern Kentucky, Virginia and West Virginia. Here the highlands suddenly ended and gave way to the much more benign bluegrass region of Kentucky. The view from Pilot Knob was spectacular, and held the unique distinction of being the point at which Daniel Boone, noted pioneer, had first observed the impressive "levels" of Kentucky's landscape.

The smells of the deep, rich woodlands had now given way to the fresh scent of the small Virginia pines growing in abundance on the cliff tops. Will had learned many of the indigenous tree species and identified them along the way. He always enjoyed trying to name them during his many trips into the woods. This trail was well defined and obviously used by the many hikers who made their way each year to the top of the famous knob. Although a little winded, he still maintained enough stamina to make such climbs, and quite often would go on weekend explorations around the region. As a boy, he loved to hunt for Indian relics and pretend he had found the most priceless of treasures. As he grew in years, he continued his hunting forays, minus the imagined treasure, and one of his greatest pastimes was to walk freshly plowed fields each spring searching for arrowheads. He used to find lots of broken flint pieces, pottery shards and on the lucky occasion, bone tools. Nowadays, the law had changed to protect artifacts from being removed from their original environment and Will, having fostered a certain respect for the history such artifacts provided, abided by those laws.

Will Morrow, 26 years old, stood tall and strikingly clean cut with dark brown hair and eyes to match. Trim and fit, he looked the part of the dashing adventurer, and his love for the outdoors left him with a perpetual tan. Having never developed much of an interest for golf and other "modern-men" activities, he preferred to spend his free time fishing and exploring off-beat trails around the region (no doubt a result of his relic hunting days.) Time for these simple joys had lost ground to the demanding responsibilities of life, making this particular trip more fervent.

Will worked as a bartender at the Brick Yard, a popular bar and night spot in downtown Frankfort and the hours had turned him into a bigger night owl than he would have liked. Being a bartender hadn't been part of his original plan. He had started college ripe with sincerity and on track to study Geology, but had dropped out his second year when both parents became ill. His older sister had married a rancher and moved out to Wyoming and was unwilling to shift her new life back home to care for their sick parents. They agreed Will would be the caregiver since he still lived at home. Over the course of several years, his parents' health continued to decline until each died within the same year. He had intended to return to school someday and get his degree but his interest had waned over time. Will attributed his temporary educational disinterest to the stress of these events and had every intention of finishing his education. With both parents gone, the family farm and a substantial inheritance belonged to him and his sister; and since she had no desire to return to Kentucky, the farm passed to Will. Working outdoors and maintaining the farm suited his disposition, and he found solace taking care of his parent's horses, dogs and assorted chickens. After taking control over the farm he had assumed a variety of jobs, all of which postponed his schooling. But tending the bar at the Brick Yard seemed liked a good fit. Bartending meant odd hours and long nights, but it was more than balanced by the tips which provided a means for Will to pursue his daytime hobbies. Most days, he was content just to mind the farm, and make a little time for his girlfriend. Jennifer Morgan, his latest love interest, recruited him as her guide this hot Saturday in August.

Will had been to Pilot Knob before and agreed to take Jennifer to the top of the landmark so that she could take scenic photographs of the Bluegrass to the west. She frequently sold her pictures to local interest magazines and newspapers. Jennifer, a beautiful 24 year old, had completed college and graduated from the University of Kentucky with a major in journalism. Although a good writer, she positively loved photography. It had become her passion, and she never went anywhere without her camera. She excelled at her crafts, and consistently won top honors at the Kentucky State Fair for her lush landscapes as well as the Hearst Award for journalistic excellence. She specialized in landscapes and scenic vacation spots and she had always wanted to go to the top of Pilot Knob and take photos of the area in hopes of selling them to a nature or tourist magazine.

"Are we ever going to reach the top?" Jennifer whined as she reached the small rock overhang at the base of the main cliff towering above them. This particular cliff was massive, made of trillions of grains of sand and quartz pebbles cemented together by iron ore and other minerals in a concrete concoction of nature. Will moved off the well-defined trail to find a rock bench.

"We're nearly there. Just got to get to the top of this cliff."

"How much farther?"

"Tell you what, let's walk along this ledge for a ways and see if we can find us a gentler climb to the top if you're tired," Will suggested. He figured the statement would fire her up and she would refuse, allowing them to take the straight-on-up direct route and get to the top quicker. She surprised him this time.

"Okay by me, let's do it."

For the next few minutes the two hikers eased along the ledge following the base of the cliff looming above them. It was not pleasant going, climbing over boulders and negotiating thickets of Mountain Laurel clinging to the rocks and meager soil. The laurel bushes with their small spoon shaped leaves filled in every nook and cranny of the hillside; and in the summer there was always the danger of rattlesnakes around these dry cliff areas. Will navigated the underbrush and disappeared around a corner.

"Look at this!" Will yelled out.

"Look at what? What is it?"

"A tiny hole in the cliff."

"Well, so it is!" Jennifer exclaimed after she came around the point of the rocky mountain ledge.

"A tiny natural arch! I guess wind and water keep carving away at this soft sandstone rock and these strange formations happen," Will conjectured.

"I am going to take some pictures," Jennifer said, already hunching down to find the best angle in relation to the afternoon sunlight beating down on the them and the cliff.

"I've been here on this knob more than once but never aware of this formation up here," Will admitted. "Well, I've never actually been around this way before on this side of the mountain. Just goes to prove there is always something to be found."

While Jennifer took several photographs of the unique rock structure Will continued exploring further and discovered a rather prominent overhanging ledge past the arch formation. The massive cliff above them jutted out to form a roof like structure often referred to as a rock shelter.

"Nice rock shelter," Jennifer said as she arrived.

"Sure is," Will said, secretly impressed she knew the correct terminology. "I've never bothered to come around this way before and check this area out."

The rock shelter was in two levels and contained obvious signs of campfires being built here on more than one occasion. Numerous boulders lay strewn about on the floor. Some large, some small and each presumably dislodged from the main rock formation many years ago. Will imagined violent earthquakes shaking so hard the boulders simply fell away from the cliff. The floor of the rock shelter was sandy with bits of charcoal scattered about. In one or two places, heavier concentrations of charcoal indicated places large fires were burned. On the softest part of a rock wall, near the edge of the shelter, the carved names of previous visitors to the site glared out like a garish visitor's registry.

"Hey, smile a little and face at me," Jennifer surprised Will and snapped a shot. "Got to at least record this accomplishment."

"What say we eat lunch? It's nearly 2:00 o'clock and I'm hungry," Will grumbled.

"This is as a good spot as any, right here under this cool ledge." Jennifer said. The two settled down to rest in the breeze beneath the overhang, using a large boulder as an improvised table to lay out their assortment of high energy trail food. Nothing fancy, just granola bars, raisins and some water comprised the meal rations. "This would be a nice place to bring a real picnic," Jennifer suggested.

"Depends on how much food you plan on packing up this mountain!" Will joked.

Satisfied they began to explore around the rock overhang kicking around the sand and dirt hoping to find a hidden treasure but knowing years of use by local teens, hikers and tourists guaranteed they'd find nothing.

"Take my picture." Jennifer handed the camera to Will and showed him what button to push and scrambled up next to the cliff to pose. "Okay, I'm ready," she said as she backed up against the rock wall. "Go ahead. Look through the viewfinder and make sure I am in the right lower quarter of the picture. Hold your breath, and push that button I showed you, okay?"

"Okay, let's see here. Okay, I see you good, good. Here goes," Will said, dramatically demonstrating he was holding his breath.

"Uhhhhm… I think you closed your eyes and I'm not sure I framed it right. Let me try again, just in case."

"Oh, so you're an expert now are you, Mr. Morrow?"

Ignoring Jennifer's sarcasm Will very intently held the camera still and peered at Jennifer through the view finder.

"What the hell?"

"What?" Jennifer yelled. "Something wrong with the camera?"

"Behind you, on the rock wall, I see something." Will gently dropped the camera to his side holding it with one hand and stared intently at the rock cliff behind Jennifer. Jennifer had already turned, following Will's gaze to the rock cliff behind her.

"What is that, some kind of marking?" Jennifer asked.

"It sure does look like something's carved on the rock," Will exclaimed, getting excited. The way the light hit the back of the rock shelter, it highlighted the lichen covering the carved markings, making them visible. The peculiar angle at which Will had positioned himself relative to the rock caused a slight shadow to appear over the surface of the back of the rock shelter.

"That is the damnedest thing. I'm sure something is carved in the rock." Will passed the camera to Jennifer and moved immediately to the rock wall for a closer examination of the strange markings. The lines, symbols and other crude carvings resembled nothing like he'd ever seen, though they inexplicably reminded him of turkey track shapes. Will rubbed his hands over the strange markings, tracing them, gently feeling the stone surface trying to make sense of the unusual discovery.

"I'm going to set my tripod up and take a detailed picture," Jennifer yelled over her shoulder. She headed back to the lunch rock to unpack her equipment. The simple grooved markings appeared to be gouged in the rock. The longest and deepest, two straight lines, started at a slight angle from about six feet high on the wall sloping down to the left, almost to the ground. About midway and to the right side of the lines another line intersected the them near the top. This line ran almost vertically to the ground creating an off-kilter triangle. To the left of this intersecting line one of the markings reminded Will of a turkey, or other bird-like track. The other markings, which resembled x's, circles and more anonymous bird tracks, fell inside the triangle portion of the drawing,"

"You know, this sort of looks like a map," Jennifer mused.

"Could be…although I've never heard of any such thing around here. You know what it might be? Maybe it's an Indian carving of some sort. Heck, this might even have been a burial or camp site," Will continued. He had become familiar with some of the petroglyphs left long ago by the prehistoric people who hunted and lived in this region. These markings appeared completely unfamiliar, though. After a while of scratching around in the dry sand, no signs of Indian habitation appeared and they moved on to even higher ground for better angles for Jennifer's photos.

Jennifer took some magnificent photographs from the top of Pilot Knob. Being especially excited about taking a shot southward of the escarpment where it meets the Bluegrass Region, she hoped this might be another picture that would end up published. On the way home that evening Will and Jennifer pondered the day and the strange carvings they discovered on the rock.

"This might be something worth checking into," commented Jennifer.

"Oh, I don't know. Probably some prank…kids goofing off. Local kids play up around those rocks, I'd bet," Will thought out loud.

"Are you kidding? Kids these days don't get fifty feet away from a computer or a video game. I'd bet this is something real. Real or not, I'll bet it's old."

"Still, I don't know what the thing means. Really, it doesn't make much sense. I've never heard of Indian rock carvings on this scale." Will thought about his buddy, Ray Deevers, a self taught expert in the rock carvings, folklore and history of the region.

"I know someone who might have a thought about this or have some information. His name's Ray Deevers. He might be able to tell us something about this. I'll give him a call tonight," Will added.

"I'll have the pictures ready for you tomorrow. I'll print them out tonight and drop them off at Brick Yard tomorrow afternoon, okay?" Jennifer offered.

"Great!"

As soon as Jennifer gathered up her equipment and packed away they started their trek back down the mountain. The walking proved to be much less strenuous except for extra pressure on their legs going down. They followed the clearly defined trail placed to allow visitors to see the wonderful site and leave the least amount of impact on the environment. Getting off the defined route, like they did, was continuously discouraged by the numerous signs posted along the way. The carvings might not ever been discovered if they had stayed on the trail. Perhaps the discovery overshadows their infraction of the rules.

In one fourth the time it took to reach the summit, they returned to the parked truck alone in the now deserted lot. The drive home relaxed them both as the evening approached. He drove straight to Jennifer's apartment hoping he could talk Jennifer into going out later for dinner. She agreed and they choose a place to go after they both cleaned up from the day of hiking. They didn't often get to eat out because he worked most evenings. This made the day together even more special. Will headed home, fed the dogs and jumped into the shower. In short order he was ready for an evening with his girl.

As soon as the waiter took their order, Will flipped out his phone and called up his friend Ray and told him what he and Jennifer discovered. Ray couldn't recollect ever seeing rock carvings around the big mountain, but seemed interested. He didn't want to sound too excited, but to Ray Deevers, such a discovery was akin to parking a beer truck in the driveway of an alcoholic.

"I'll have some pictures tomorrow Ray. Can you stop by the Yard and give me your thoughts? I can tell you these carvings are strange and someone took some time to make them. They are water worn now and must be pretty old,"

"Sure, I'll run by after work on the way home. As good an excuse as any to have a beer I suspect."

The next afternoon, Jennifer dropped by with the pictures as promised and Ray showed up around 6:00 p.m. Will showed Ray the photographs Jennifer took of the strange rock carvings. She also had drawn a crude replica of the carvings on thick parchment paper based on her photos which emphasized the curious markings.

"These photos show exactly the way it looks Ray, right there carved into the base of Pilot Knob," Will explained.

"I've been to Pilot Knob a lot of times but never saw any rock carvings. You sure they're old carvings?" Ray questioned.

"I'm pretty sure they are old. They sure appear to me that way."

"Well, being close to the Indian Old Fields, maybe these are real Indian markings," Ray noted.

"What are Indian Old Fields?"

"Oh, just the last great Shawnee Indian town in Kentucky. It was called Eskippakithiki. That was the Shawnee name but since most of us can't ever pronounce it right, I guess people just started callin' it 'Indian Old Fields' People used to find arrowheads and ax heads out in those fields years ago."

"Never knew that," Will had to admit. Ray knew a lot of local history and interesting yet obscure facts.

"Sure enough, Indian Old Fields is a famous place, I reckon."

Ray Deevers was Will's best friend. They attended the same high school, played on the same ball team, and made countless hiking trips together. Though he had the classic Irish ginger complexion and shocking red hair, Ray had no real Irish heritage. His freckles were overpowering compared to his pale skin tone and he never got the girls quite like Will did. While Will had at least attempted a run at college, Ray never did, but he did complete a couple of years at a trade school to learn about mechanics and had quite a knack for repairing cars. He loved to fix just about anything with his hands, and was quite handy around cars, lawnmowers and pretty much anything with an engine. Even though Ray and Will took different paths after high school, they managed to pick up where they left off as best friends after Will finished his brief stint in college. Early on Ray had worked as an hourly mechanic at one of the local dealerships but because of his skills, he eventually went to work at a very well-known auto shop in town. Customers knew and trusted him with their cars and he never ceased to entertain them with random trivia.

"Tell you what, why don't the two of us go back up to Pilot Knob and look around. I'd like to take a look at these carvings myself. Maybe I'd get a better fix on 'em," Ray offered.

"Sounds good, what are you doing next Saturday?" Will asked, hoping that would be a good day off for Ray.

"Far as I know, nothing. Saturday would be fine."

"I'll bring Jennifer, too, since she took the photos and knows about this. That'll be okay with you won't it?" Will added.

"Who else knows?"

"Just you, me and Jennifer…why?"

"Just a thought, but what if this has something to do with some kind of devil worshipers or something?

Two:
John Finley

In the summer of 1752, John Finley arrived by a crude river raft at the Great Falls of the Ohio. John Finley, along with seven other men, made the trip from the spot on the river destined to be named Fort Pitt, searching for greater fortunes. An oddity formed by up thrust Devonian shelving, the Falls provided an obstacle to boats and river-crafts but, during dry times, this spot was easily crossed. 1752 happened to be one of those rare dry years. The raft landed on the north shore of the river with a thud. The old raft captain had chosen this location because of the smooth beach, though to deny the role of chance would be disingenuous. Camps sprang up on both sides of the river and people crossed back and forth at the falls. Had the raft landed on the opposite side, John Finley would not have needed to wade the river. Since most of the men's destination seemed to be the north prairie country, the north side was the obvious landing site, and even before the raft hit the sandy shore men began jumping off, grateful to be on land once again.

"I believe I owe you this amount. That's what we agreed on," John Finley told the raft boss as he stepped from the ramshackle water craft.

"I thank you very much."

"Here's my pay too, and thanks for takin' me on," added George Mundy stepping off right after Finley.

"You boys be careful around them falls, you can get hurt, swept away real quick," the tough old raft boss warned both men. A captain of sorts, inasmuch as he owned the raft, he collected from every man on board. On vessels like these no one was entirely in charge. But it was the quickest, most economical way to get into the wilderness and best hunting grounds.

"Looks like the water is down a lot. Good, it'll be easier. I sure wish he'd landed on the south side of the river though. We wouldn't have to get wet," remarked George.

"You've crossed here before, haven't you George?"

"Not crossed, but I have landed here on the south side."

They set out in a brisk, westerly walk. Late afternoon came upon them and both men wanted to get across the river before dark. The river was susceptible to drastic, momentary changes. Even though it had been an unusually dry year all across the country, rains in the east just a couple of days ago could turn the river into a monster. George Mundy knew they should get across as soon as possible. The raft had safely landed several hundred yards above the falls. Those wishing to go farther down the river would have to wait at the raft landing site, soon to be made into a long term river camp, and await the inevitable rise of the river.

George Mundy was experienced in this particular wilderness; familiar with the natives, and spoke their language quite well. He claimed to be going hunting but John wasn't sure exactly what George was hunting, as he was traveling light and with only a little gun powder. Anyone knew it took a lot of powder to do a lot of hunting. The two men had become good friends in the few days they spent together on the raft. Even though John Finley was quite an industrious fellow, this area of the wildness was totally unfamiliar to him.

"You decided where you're going to end up?" George inquired.

"Don't know. I hear the hunting is pretty good about anywhere south."

"You know John, you should come along with me to do your huntin'. That's where I'm headed."

"Works for me George. Makes no real difference to me, and heck, I might learn a thing or two from an old timer like you."

John Finley, pure Irish and a roustabout, dabbled in whatever enterprise suited his fancy on any given day. John had planned to make his way into the wilds, do some hunting and fur gathering to make money. Furs had become popular in Europe and the demand seemed never ending. With this new profitable enterprise more men tried their fortunes on hunting the furs in the wilderness and making huge profits back east. John, now by mere accidental good fortune, had a personal guide of sorts and one who he would soon learn knew the natives very well.

John Finley had with him a pack full of trinkets including small metal tools such as punches, awls, knives, glass beads, yarn and some other small utilitarian items. These amounted to about all he might carry along with his long rifle, powder and mini balls, the bullets made of lead. The clothes he had on his back and his trusty long rifle were everything he owned. He brought along the few trade items in hopes they would get him out of a jam with any hostile Indians. He was quite certain they would be on the same hunting grounds.

"Let's cross here, John."

"Lead the way, George. If you go I'll be right behind you, I guess."

The Great Falls had proven to be the demise of many river travelers. A giant ledge about thirty feet high dissected the river, and formed a practical ford between the two shores of the Ohio River under dry conditions. Here the Devonian limestone was exposed, presenting the interested observer a glimpse at strange fossilized creatures, many resembling sea shells. These fossils exposed in great numbers scattered throughout the limestone bedrock and certainly left many of the explorers puzzled as to their origins. The ledge would occasionally have a broken or missing section, resulting, no doubt, from the endless onslaught of the rushing, scouring current of the river. But during certain times, with care, people and animals could negotiate across the ledge in the shallow water, gaining access from the prairies of the northwest to the savannas and wilderness of the south. The two men stopped intermittently to marvel at the many exposed fossils embedded in the water worn rock.

"Ain't that something," John remarked. He would stop every few feet to look over the many petrified sea creatures.

"Yep," George answered, desensitized from having seen these fossils on previous visits. John thought they looked to be some type of stone animals, sea shells perhaps frozen in the stone for reasons he never begun to comprehended. They reminded him of shells from the oceans back east.

Near the center of the river the men had to wade through water deepened to about four feet. The water became deep enough the two travelers had to hold their rifles and powder high over their heads as they negotiated the swifter river currents. The Great Falls crossing was a busy place on some days with people crossing the river in both directions. The Shawnee and Mingo knew the place well and used the crossing to move in and out of the Kentakee wilderness. Other tribes also were aware of it, but the Shawnee in recent years used the crossing most. There were always encampments on both sides of the river. Most of the camps were Shawnee, trappers, and traders. Once across the stream the two men neared a small camp of five Shawnee. One of the Shawnee directly approached George Mundy and greeted him. They named one another in their greetings.

The Shawnee dressed in skins and loin cloths, bare-chested except for beads and ornaments around their necks. They carried small deer skin bags and each Shawnee had a bow and quiver with carefully fashioned arrows. John studied the Shawnee warriors. The discussion between Mundy and his counterpart ended suddenly.

"Hard headed bastards," Mundy swore under his breath as he walked up to John.

"What, are you makin' a trade with those Shawnee?" John asked.

"Nah, I'm trying to purchase my way to travel with this group. Kind of hitching a guided and safe passage if you know what I mean. They're headed for Eskippakithiki ('S-kip-pa-kee-ta-kee') located east of here. It's only about a day and a half from here and that is exactly where I want to go."

"What is, Esskipi-ah-thi-ki, I mean, what is that?" John asked.

"Ah, a town, a village, whatever you want to call it. Eskippakithiki is located on the Warriors Path. It's one of their biggest settlements in the whole area. Biggest one I know, anyway. There must be five hundred Shawnee living there. I've been there a couple of times. It's a big village," replied George, having no real incentive to offer much more information.

"And you want to go to this place?"

"Well, don't you think a bunch of Indians would have plenty of furs to trade and already located some of the best hunting grounds in the territory? If they ain't going to kill me then I sure aim to find out their best hunting places."

John nodded understanding, but remained skeptical the two men were discussing just a tag-along trip to a village. The discussion seemed to be somewhat plaintive on Mundy's part; at least it appeared that way to John. Nevertheless, John Finley found himself alone in a strange country with, as far as he could tell, only one casual acquaintance. Now that the Shawnee were in the mix, John did not feel completely comfortable with the initial invitation on the other side of the river. The dynamics had changed.

"Say George, I wonder if I might come along too. Would you consider that?" John inquired.

"Well, I already invited you once today, but seein' how I have now hooked up with these Shawnee you'll need to work out your own deal with them. That probably won't be too hard; some of those glass trinkets you're carrying there would cinch that deal, I expect. They're crazy about that kind of stuff."

The fiery sun settled on the horizon and another day in the wilderness along the great river was coming to an end. A deal was made with little fanfare. John approached the warrior, held out some beads while gesturing to himself and pointed east. The message was understood and with a nod the warrior approved the deal. Everyone hastily settled down and prepared to have their evening meal. The Shawnee ate jerky they had carried in their packs and did not build a fire that night. There was little talk among the Shawnee warriors as they sat near each other, consuming the jerky and some berries they had collected somewhere earlier in the day. George built a nice fire on the river bank on the edge of a thicket. The abundance of dry drift wood scattered about the rocky bank offered a good supply of fire wood. Since George and John had traveled the river they had not had the opportunity to hunt fresh meat for their meal and they, like the Shawnee, had to rely on dried jerky and the few dried other items they'd brought with them. John still had some hardtack biscuit bread he shared with George. Tomorrow morning the party would leave for Eskippakithiki.

The next morning as the light swelled upon the horizon, the party set out. The early morning air already thick with humidity, typical of this time of the year, promised to bring a hot and sweltering day for the travelers. The group of seven people was comprised of five Shawnee warriors, George Mundy, and following behind, John Finley. The travelers moved along briskly on a flat terrain with few streams. For the most part they followed a bison trace or trail heading off in a southeast direction. Once or twice they came to places where the trail would fork into different directions, but the party tended to head in an easterly direction, which John concluded by keeping track with the position of the sun.

By early afternoon the traveling party reached the headwaters of a stream. At the rest stop George started up a conversation with the same Shawnee man from the day before. By now John knew this was the leader of the small band of travelers. He watched without being noticed, pretending to cool off at the creek bank. George pulled something out of his pack and handed the item to the Shawnee, who examined it carefully. John wondered what George showed the Indian that interested him so much. After a few minutes of silence the Shawnee agreed to a bargain and slid the item into a deer skin bag. The deal was made, whatever it was. The Shawnee leader veered off and drank water from the stream, then gave a signal to the other Shawnee, who collected their things. Mundy did the same. Sensing the departure, John hurried, refilling his leather water pouch, and filed behind the now moving group.

The traveling party followed the stream towards its mouth. Since the area was in the midst of a drought, most of the time the party could travel in the middle of the stream bed on the flat and smooth bed rock. In a matter of two hours the group reached the mouth of the stream. Here the clear, shallow stream flowed into a larger stream, large enough to be a river. The lead Shawnee picked up a river bank trail and followed it along the edge of the river while the others followed behind him. John Finley remained in the last position about a hundred feet behind Mundy. In short order the Shawnee led the men to a ford in the river. Rocky shoals scattered and stretched two thirds of the way across the river. At the crossing John noticed a wide, worn patch coming off the hill down to the shoals on both sides of the river. Bison and other animals crossed the river here back and forth to grazing and breeding grounds. John considered hunting would be good in this area and noted landmarks he might come back to in hopes of good hunting.

"How about them mud banks there?" George pointed out to John.

"This must be a main crossing point for animals."

"Buffalo. They cross here by the hundreds on some days. Cold weather up north will bring them south huntin' for good grazin' pastures."

"I'd guess they've been crossin' here for years."

"No doubt about that. These Shawnee figure the bison are up north or they'd be all over the place here huntin' them." George concluded the brief conversation and the party quickly made their way across the shallow shoals of the river and continued east. The evening arrived when the party made the night's camp. The camp was along a small stream appearing to boil up from the earth. The great spring provided a favorite stop for the night by the Shawnee who traveled from the Great Falls crossing. The fresh limestone water and the small depression afforded both water and protection from the winds seemingly forever blowing across the vast savannah. The abundant, lush grass in the region with giant burr oaks standing alone scattered about the open plain appealed to John. During fall months the grasslands would be dotted with buffalo in various herds grazing. Most of these herds would have made their way to the general location the same way this group of men made their way.

The Shawnee had a fire started before John had even arrived. Keeping to themselves from the two white fellow travelers they exhibited no hospitality, no discussion, basically no contact. George and John started their own campfire and situated themselves into the positions they would rest for the night. John stepped to the water and filled his water flask. Another night of jerky lay ahead of them. George scouted around a bit before dark and found on the bank a small stand of sassafras saplings. After a few minutes digging around the roots of one of the small trees, George retrieved some of the roots and brought them back to the campfire.

"What do you have there George?"

"Sassafras, I'm going to make us something to drink." George took his knife and shaved the bark off the roots he'd previously washed in the creek. George then took his tin cup, scooped up some water and brought it back to the fire John was tending. George put the root back in the cup and set the cup in the fresh coals of the fire. There was no time, really, for setting up a good cooking fire since the men would all be asleep in a little while and up in the early hours headed east.

"Now, let those get good and hot then we'll have some tea shortly," said George, quite proud of the idea.

Eventually the cup of water boiled and the water turned amber. After the drink cooled for a short time, George took a sip. He shared his tea with John and they passed the cup back and forth until it was empty, at which time George shaved some more bark from the remaining roots and started the brewing process all over again.

The Shawnee had already settled down and most were asleep. John and George discussed the day's trip and conjectured on what tomorrow would be like. George tried to explain to John what Eskippakithiki was like but could not prepare John Finley for what he was about to see tomorrow.

Three:
Arrival at Eskippakithiki

The site of the Shawnee town shocked John Finley as they crossed over a low hill and the entire levels of the town came into full view. They had already greeted others along the path coming out from the town and observed other small parties of five and six hunters moving out in various directions. As they made their way into the village, some took notice but seemed apathetic to the arrival of the group containing two white men. The people of the village assumed the warriors would not have brought trouble to their town.

Eskippakithiki was positioned on a level plain near the foothills tapering outward from the mountains further to the east. The village was a scattering of long bark houses, the kind of permanent house typical of most southeastern tribes. Several poles were set in a general rectangular-shape, stockade style with smaller, flexible rafter poles arched across the top of the structure as roof supports, and mud, moss, leaves, dry grass and bark were mixed in random fashion to cover the entire structure. Despite the unusual materials, the long bark houses provided watertight protection, a necessity in the, often, rainy climate. Numerous cooking fires dotted the camp and sent straight columns of smoke into the blue cloudless sky. Flat fields of green grasses and crops cultivated by the Shawnee hugged the village and made the two strangers feel more welcome. At least one notable stream meandered nearby supplying a continuous fresh source of water. A well-worn path led from the village, westward to the long hill, then downward to the meandering creek. Women and children traveled along the path carrying skins and pots of water to their various homes in the town. Hunting was likely to be good in every direction, with bison located north, south, and west of the town while deer and elk were plentiful east in the mountains. A good source of flint outcropped nearby in the mountainous area. Flint, a precious resource, provided the raw material for practically every tool needed for day-to-day life. This group of Shawnee had begun to acquire metal objects including axes and knives. Rifles had recently become accessible from the French.

John Finley and George Mundy were ignored by their traveling companions as each hunter separated off to their own house and waiting families. The hunters brought back numerous trade items but they never divulged their origins to either John or George. The two strangers moved right though the village and, though were stared at by the inhabitants, they exhibited no hostility. John Finley moved to the eastern edge of the town. He found a big Burr oak tree in the hot savanna plain well outside of the town at the edge of the woods and adjacent to a well used path. John assumed the path to be an old bison trail but later would learn it to be the Warrior's Path. John discarded his heavy pack and set about making a hasty temporary camp. He gathered firewood, built a cooking pit from stones and made ready for his first night's stay in a big town. George Mundy rested under the shade of the big oak tree, watching John hurry about setting up camp. Some of the Shawnee kids came around just to see the white-skinned new comers.

"Aren't you going to lay a camp?" John asked.

"I will in a little while. Do you know what Eskippakithiki means?" George said, changing the subject.

"I don't speak Shawnee, so it's pretty likely I don't know what it means," John replied with a touch of sarcasm.

"Means 'a place called Blue Licks.' 'Eskipp' means 'Blue Licks,' 'ak' means 'place' and the 'ithiki' is the word in their language meaning 'called', I guess. Anyway, this is known as the lower Blue Licks. North up the Warriors Path is the upper Blue Licks. They gather and boil salt at the upper Blue Lick, I am told. Never been there myself, though," George explained.

"A place called Blue Licks," John chuckled.

"Yes sir. Funny thing to me too. Back east they call this country out here Kentakee. I think some hunters confused the last part of this town's name and came up with Kentakee. You take the 'Ki-thi-ki from the last part of Eskippa and it would be pretty easy for some of them devils to make Kee-taa-kee sound like Ken-ta-kee. It always seemed like it to me anyway."

"Well, if nothin' else, it sure is something to ponder."

George sensed John's interest begin to wane so he bid him farewell for the evening and moved toward the north side of the village, well out of sight of John. As the day wore on, Finley unpacked his belongings and placed some of the trinkets, beads, and so forth out on a small piece of cloth to take inventory, and also to determine if he had lost anything along the trek. A couple of Shawnee men came by and, upon noticing his trinkets, stopped and began looking through them. With no regard to John, the men went through each and every item. The Shawnee spent a good deal of time handling and mulling over each item. Some even engaged in small discussions over some of the beads. When satisfied with what they saw, they would put them back and move on to the next item. One Shawnee picked up a handful of beads and walked over to Finley. He held out the beads in front of Finley and asked to trade a beaver pelt for the glass beads. Finley, not understanding a word of Shawnee, felt certain the man wanted them so he nodded in agreement with no idea what he'd get in return. The man took the beads and left. A few minutes later the man returned with a beautiful tanned beaver hide and placed it where he had taken the handful of glass beads. Before the day ended, Finley had traded nearly every bead, bauble, and trinket that he had brought along.

As John Finley lay by his campfire that evening, poking the coals with a stick, he thought about his plan to go hunting. In this village, he could get all the pelts and hides he could possibly take out of this country by simply bringing a few trade items and setting up a trading shop. This day, he reckoned, he had traded for six beaver hides, five deer hides, and one elk hide as well has some other bone tools, pretty stones and a necklace of bear teeth. All these items for just the few trinkets he had brought along for the sole purpose of trading himself out of a jam. He thought of bringing in a lot more merchandise and of all the different kinds of animal hides he could obtain, which afforded him a sound and comfortable sleep that night, an unexpected benefit of his trading.

The next morning Finley moved around the town to get his bearings. Warriors and hunters began leaving the village heading in a southeasterly direction and it looked as though they followed a pretty well defined path. Some long rifle hunters used the trail from time to time, but the Shawnee, Mingo, and Cherokee were the primary users of the trail.

Some Shawnee still used the bow and worked the fine flint into arrow points. Other warriors had Long Rifles acquired by trade or capture. What a strange combination of old Stone Age tools and modern rifles, he mused. The same path came into the village and then led itself north into the woods. In fact, paths led out in every direction from the town. Finley walked over to Mundy's campsite and found his friend getting his gear packed up, ready to head out.

John Finley worked his way back through the village in the direction of his campsite, stopping on one occasion to observe an older warrior chipping, or knapping, a piece of flint into a sharp, well-balanced, triangle shaped arrowhead. After a few moments he noticed several recently made stone tools, mostly arrowheads, lying beside the craftsman.

John could see that the fields just outside the village had beans and squash growing in one area and to the south of the site stood a rather large field of corn growing in small patches. Women kept the dirt around the young corn plants chopped and free from weeds in the same manner folks back in Pennsylvania did, though the corn appeared to be shorter. By this time John had arrived back at his camp site to find George Mundy sitting by the campfire.

"Good morning' George," John yelled.

"Mornin' to you too," George simply replied.

"You heading out today?"

"Yes, I have a ways to go today."

"Hunting the mountain game or the bison?" John inquired, trying to get information about directions and destination without asking outright.

"Neither," George curtly replied.

"Ah, I see." Of course, this brought John's curiosity up a notch. After all, if Mundy was not hunting game, then what was he doing out here in the wilds of unmapped territory among potential hostile peoples on any given day.

"Well, be safe on your journey, wherever it takes you, and perhaps we will meet again."

"I expect to be back in a few days."

"Oh, I see."

Mundy hurriedly got his pack situated and headed out of town on the northern trail. John decided to spend the day going south on the trail from the village. He figured if Mundy went north he would do well to go south, keeping out of each other's way. John followed the well-defined trail south out of the Shawnee town. The trail followed the edge of the rougher mountainous terrain to the east but stayed on the flat plain. Late in the afternoon he headed back up the trail. He knew he wouldn't get lost today. Once he heard some men coming up the trail, so he slipped off the trail behind a large boulder. Three Shawnee hunters on a return trip with all the deer meat they could carry. They passed him by, never aware he had hidden behind the rock. He did not want to take any chances his first day out. The men may not have been aware of his arrival in town and thus had a different reaction to his presence, he reasoned. He had only seen one deer and he didn't get a shot off. But he had, after all, spent more of his day exploring the countryside.

John Finley had made up his mind he would hunt for a few more days until he could get all the deer hides he could carry and then he would head north up the trail Mundy used. Finley spent the next two weeks east of the great knob hunting until he had enough. He made his way back to the town and then headed north on the trail. After a few days he found himself along the shores of the great river and he followed the river upstream. Eventually he'd make it back to civilization, he was certain.

John Finley returned in mid summer, but instead of going by way of the river, he traveled by land, following a path along the south shore. John had brought two horses from home and two other men he had hired to help him carry his much greater load of trade goods. He brought with him a generous supply of trade beads, axe heads, colored felt and flax cloth, rope and various pots and pans. Traveling was slow because he and his companions had to travel upstream on a couple of major rivers to find a good crossing place. John recognized many landmarks from his earlier raft trip and picked up the trail, confident it would take him directly south to the great Shawnee Town. Along the route south, he encountered several small parties of Shawnee headed north. They casually greeted him and were congenial. Finley by now enjoyed the benefit of being well known to the people of Eskippakithiki. His pending arrival would mean many more wonderful items, many of which these people had never seen before. Finley intended to open the first mercantile business in the Kentakee wilderness. Throughout the late summer into a rainy September of 1752, John Finley worked to get his business up and running. He built his hut from trees he had cut and set in the rich fertile soil. Just like the Shawnee houses, he covered the roof rafters with moss, tree bark and just about anything else he found. Even though the summer months were hot and muggy, business flourished. Toward the end of September, as his supplies ran low, he packed up his furs, enlisted the help of five Shawnee men, and headed north back up the trail. Finley returned at the end of October of 1752, with still more supplies. He now had arrangements made for additional supplies to come down the river trail next spring and he would trade his furs to buyers on the North shore. Finley and the people of the Shawnee town prospered.

On a cold November day, two Shawnee men came to Finley's store and wanted to trade for some cloth and yarn. They did not have any furs with them but one of the men offered Finley something unusual, and the instant he saw it, he knew his life would change forever. What was offered in trade was a silver arrow point. The projectile had been hand beaten into shape from raw silver or similar substance. Since Finley arrived in the summer of 1752, he had adapted the Shawnee language to a level he could carry on a practical conversation on most topics with the native people of the town.

"Where'd you get this?" Finley asked directly. If they did not want to share that information, they would not hesitate to say so, or simply not respond. He assumed the shiny object to be a trade item from the north, perhaps on past the great river. Nevertheless, Finley figured if he opened up a trade connection for silver, he would be east coast wealthy in no time.

"Did you trade with the Iroquois, Wyandotte for this?" Finley quickly followed.

"No," replied one of the men.

"Did you find it?"

"Trade," came the reply, with no further explanation.

"Bring me more and I will have even finer cloth, beads and tools like you've never seen before," Finley began laying his plan to get this trade store to a new level.

John was surprised by another visitor into his store on this same day, George Mundy. George had another man with him on this unexpected visit.

"Howdy John Finley," Mundy announced.

"Well, if ain't George Mundy." Finley replied.

"Yep, in person. You know I love huntin' out here in this country."

"Oh, I know that all right."

"John, this here is John Swift, a friend of mine," announced George.

"Hello Mr. Swift," replied John Finley, outstretching his hand for a shake.

John Swift was a tall man with a roughly carved and weathered face. His dark black hair and cold, penetrating stare made people feel uncomfortable at times. He dressed the same as any other frontiersman. But there was something different about this "Swift."

"Are you huntin' here in the wilderness too?"

"Ah, Mr. Swift and I go way back, we have been through many a scrape together. He and I have been planning on doing some exploring together down in this wild country and, well, old Captain John here, finally showed up today!" George explained.

"Did you say Captain John?"

"Well, yes I am, uh...well I have commanded my own ship, mainly working out of the Carolina's and Virginia and did some merchant trading down around Cuba and the Islands," Swift replied.

"I used to be a mate on Captain John's ship," added George.

"Surprises never quit coming today, do they? Well, I'll be. I don't recall you ever saying anything about being a sailor, George," John Finley replied, taken aback by this new information.

"So, how or why would you two sea dogs be so far inland? And now turned hunters?"

"No, we... ah... I'm in a bit of trouble back east and this is a safe place for me right now," John Swift stated as matter of fact with the intent of ending this aspect of the conversation.

"Oh, well, no one around here but the Shawnee and me," John replied. He sensed this topic getting just a little too sensitive and learned more than he needed to know. John mulled over and over in his head what a seaman would be being doing out here in the wilderness. The three men sat around talking until dark, when John said to George.

"I want to show you something George."

In his hand he displayed for the two men the silver arrowhead. A long time had passed since John had seen or spoken to another white man. He used this conversation piece to keep interest and conversation going.

"Where'd you get that?" George asked.

"Traded for it right here. Some Shawnee brought it in and traded it," John explained.

"You don't say. Do you have any more?"

"This is the best thing so far; I have a couple of other small things but nothing like this."

"Wouldn't want to trade would you?" George inquired.

"You can have it George; maybe the thing will bring luck to you as you wander around in the wilderness." John knew he had few friends in this wild country that could come to his aid if needed, and this silver arrowhead was a small price to pay, an investment, to maintain a friendship. Besides, John knew he was in a position to trade for more and even better silver items.

"Why, I couldn't take it without something in return," George replied. He didn't want to be obligated.

"Please, George honor me and accept this gift. I don't expect anything in return."

"Well, if you insist, okay, then." George passed the small treasure over to Swift for him to take a look at the unusual silver arrowhead. Swift expressed little interest and quickly passed the object back to George.

"We had better get some rest if we are heading out early," Swift said to George.

Both men left John's store and wandered on over to their campsite. The Shawnee town had already settled down for the evening, each family around their own hearth.

The next morning George Mundy and John Swift head off to the north. Also, a number of Shawnee stirred about. The water brigade had already started for the day and small hunting parties of two and three warriors headed out in various directions. John thought he would spend some of this day working on his planned store expansion. The store, though already a suitable bark house, was built in the same fashion as the Shawnee houses and needed another room for his expanding fur collections.

Four:
Back to Pilot Knob

The sandstone dust of the overhanging ledge began to choke Jennifer, so she stepped out to the side of the ledge to breathe the fresh mountain air. She, Will, and Ray had kept to their plan to go to Pilot Knob so Ray could see the strange rock carvings for himself. The week old discovery of man-made carvings of lines and symbols on the rock wall at the back of a rock shelter was nothing like Will or Jennifer had ever seen before. Now Ray Deevers would observe for himself how strange the symbols really were. The instant Ray viewed the rock wall he determined to his satisfaction the carvings were quite old. From his understanding of petroglyphs, Ray determined that some of the markings were "turkey tracks." Turkey tracks were thought to be used by Indians and early pioneers as direction indicators; the road signs of the pioneer days. A turkey track was simply a single line intersected by two shorter lines at approximately 45 degree angles on each side and near the end of the single straight line. It actually resembles a bird track, specifically wild turkey, thus the name. They were carved right into the sandstone rock. Will climbed around the boulders looking, and scratching the sand with a stick hoping an arrowhead would flip out. Even though, other than the strange carvings on the back of the rock shelter, no visible signs of any prehistoric occupation of the shelter appeared, Will hoped he would find something.

"Will, I believe those are turkey tracks," Ray announced pointing at the map.

"Turkey tracks. That's what I thought, too when I saw them," Will remarked.

"What I don't know is what the other markings represent. Perhaps the lines are rivers, streams, boundaries, trails...any one of those things could be the case," Ray added.

Jennifer once again began snapping off photos of nearly everything around her.

Will became interested in a small boulder situated against the back wall of the little rock shelter. Only about a third of the boulder was exposed, like a stone iceberg in a sea of dry sand. Will used his stick to scratch around its sides and dig downward.

"I wish we had brought a shovel," Will grumbled.

"I'd say those carvings have been on the wall for many years," Ray remarked.

"Why do you say that?"

"Moss. Look," Ray pointed at the rock wall.

"The carvings are all covered with a fine moss and something else growing on the rock too. They might not have been carved hundreds of years ago, but not last week either, I'll bet."

"The moss is what makes it hard to see, too. The light and the place we stood taking pictures is how we noticed it in the first place," Jennifer chimed in.

"You're right," Will agreed.

Ray had found his own spot to scratch around closer to the back wall and the strange markings. Will continued his now half-hearted excavation with the stick when he hit something not part of the boulder. With his interest intensified, Will began digging harder with his stick, then alternating his dig using his hands. The object became visible at the bottom of the small hole and Will recognized as a bone. Will thought it was some kind animal long ago dragged up beside the boulder and consumed by some other animal. When Will opened the hole wider he noticed that the bone was large and ran under the boulder. Other bones began to appear indicating he had discovered something out of the ordinary. By now Will had dug a hole two feet deep and had caught Ray and Jennifer's attention.

"Whatcha got Will?" asked Ray.

"You look like a dog trying to find a bone," said Jennifer, laughing at the hard effort Will put into digging a hole.

"As a matter of fact, I do have a bone here."

"Let's see," Laughing, Ray moved over closer to the boulder.

"Probably some varmint, but what is strange is that the boulder is right on top of most of the bone. This is a leg bone of some kind, and there other bones here. They all seem to be right under this boulder," Will added as he finally extracted the bone and lifted it up for Ray to inspect. Ray's light-hearted laughter evaporated into a serious stare at the object Will had retrieved.

"Oh shit."

"Oh shit, what, Ray?"

"A human leg bone," Ray exclaimed the instant he saw the bone.

"Human? You think so?"

"Oh yeah, it's human all right. I'd bet on it."

"What's a human leg bone doing under this rock?" Will asked.

"Probably a burial site or some poor dip wad was under the ledge when the boulder just dropped on him," Ray added.

"No way, that couldn't have happened. What are the odds of that?" questioned Will.

"It could happen, it does happen," Ray defended his previous assertion.

"So what, some guy just so happened to be right here and while standing there a boulder fell on him?" but both Will and Jennifer gave a cautious glance at the rock ceiling above them.

"Didn't you ever here of the Mammoth Cave Mummy?"

"Oh, yeah, right. What's that about one in a million odds?"

"Mammoth Cave Mummy? What are you talking about?" Jennifer asked.

"This Indian crawled down in the cave collecting some type of mineral or something, using canes as torches way back in the cave. A big boulder fell on his ass, pinning him right there until he was found in modern times all mummified." Ray knew a hearsay version of the story and thought he had even seen something on the National Geographic Channel about the mummy. He was confident, however, they were holding a human leg bone.

"If it is Indian, then maybe we'll find some artifacts, beads or arrowheads or something," Will added and started digging more.

"Could be, unless, of course, this is a modern human and well, this..."

"Oh God! What if this is a murder victim! I mean someone murdered and buried him here under the cliff!" Jennifer abruptly interrupted. Will saw that Jennifer realized the three stumbled upon a dead body.

"I'll be damned." Ray said under his breath. The three began to look around the area and pay more attention to their surroundings, thinking that perhaps they had inadvertently put themselves in danger by being here. No one knew or even commented, for that matter, as to why they felt that way, but all of a sudden a very serious and unsettling situation developed. During the afternoon a few more bones were removed, but no artifacts. As Will dug toward the end of the boulder he could not have imagined what he was about to find. He carefully scooped out handfuls of sand at time. Just as he was about to quit for the day and suggest that they head on home, he found it.

"Well, now here is something. An arrowhead I do believe," Will announced to the others as he brushed off the sand and dirt that was clinging to the arrowhead. It felt different, though. The artifact didn't have the feel of flint, but appeared metallic. The arrow point was obviously hammered into the shape of a Christmas-tree-shaped projectile about two inches long. It was a dull gray, with no signs of the flaking patterns common to arrow points made of flint or some other stone. The arrowhead was entirely symmetrical and sharpened to a fine point. Though gray and tarnished, the hammer and scratch marks from fashioning the object were easy to recognize.

"This is funny," Will commented as he carefully turned the arrowhead over and over in his hand.

"What's funny?"

"This arrowhead, has no flaking or chipping on it. I don't think it's made out of flint."

"Let me have another look." Ray reached for the arrowhead and Will handed the unusual find to him.

"I think that this might be a metal arrowhead!" Will suddenly exclaimed.

"Metal?" Ray asked.

"Yes, I'm pretty sure it's metal, at least it doesn't feel like any flaked arrowhead I've ever seen."

"Maybe it is metal. And you're right; I don't think it's flint," Ray concluded.

"Let me see it," Jennifer commanded.

"That's sure something you don't see every day," Ray noted after carefully inspecting the object.

"How about iron? I seem to recall there was a period of time when Indians used iron and steel arrowheads," Will commented. Ray bit on the projectile as if he was performing some type of analysis of the taste of the material. Ray was used to working with steel and iron in his shop and for whatever reason only known to Ray, he had studied the feel, texture, and even the taste of those metals. Unsatisfied, Ray took out his pocketknife, opened it and cut on the arrowhead as if peeling an apple. A small shiny flake popped off. The dull, gray-black surface hid the true shiny, silver color.

"There's your answer folks."

"Looks to me like silver."

"Sure looks like silver. That would be my guess, anyway." Upon further examination Will, too, was convinced that the arrowhead was indeed made out of metal. This was even more bizarre than any of them could have imagined. Will handed the arrowhead to Jennifer. Jennifer carefully studied the artifact and decided she would make a close-up photograph of the object. Will and Ray had returned to the hole and the bones, continuing their excavation until they had recovered several bones, including the skull.

"Did either of you ever hear of anyone finding a metal arrowhead, much less a silver one, in this part of the country?" Will asked.

"The only metal arrowheads I am aware of come from out west. Why would there be a silver arrowhead up here with a skeleton and a strange map carved on the wall above it? Surely, this can't be connected to the silver mine lore."

"What silver mine?" Will and Jennifer both said at the same time.

"Yeah, the lost silver mine of John Swift. You never heard of the legend?"

"Oh that, I've heard my dad or someone down at the newspaper talk about it." Jennifer answered. Will knew nothing of the story or a least couldn't recall anything at the moment.

"What about the legend?" Will asked.

"Well, they claim that in the late 1700's a man by the name of John Swift discovered a silver mine somewhere in eastern Kentucky and spent a few years mining ore and smelting silver."

"No way. There's no silver in Kentucky; it's a geological impossibility."

"No, it's true." Jennifer added.

"Anyway, supposedly, he wrote down this information in a journal along with directions to the mine, but after he became blind he couldn't find the mine anymore. I always thought it was kind of a made up thing, but I have hunted for the thing a couple of times," Ray continued.

"So, no one has ever found this supposedly lost mine?" Will inquired.

"No, not to my knowledge. The mine has never been found but clues were left. All kinds of clues, mostly general descriptions, you know rocks, creeks, and turkey tracks, stuff like that."

"Well, what if this is connected to the silver mine?" Will inquired.

"You don't find silver metal arrowheads everyday and especially not with a dead body," Ray concluded.

"What about the rock carvings on the wall? Ray, does this arrowhead change anything in your mind about what it means?"

"Well, it could be a map to the silver mine. But could just as easily be a bunch of punks' idea of a joke. I'd guess a map. How old? Don't know. Why, it could mean the Swift mine is right here."

"Yeah, right," Will responded. The three scratched around the boulder and other places in the small rock shelter the rest of the afternoon. Not finding anything else they gently placed the bones back beneath the rock as they had found them, except the silver arrowhead; Will kept that. They filled the hole with the sand Will had worked so hard to remove. On the way back home Ray thought about the carvings on the rock wall.

"There is no scale on this map, but just for the fun of it, let's say the long vertical line on the right side of the carving is a river, and the two lines on top are the Ohio River. That would make the long line the Red River, the Licking River or the Big Sandy River if the mine is in eastern Kentucky," Ray reasoned.

"Let me think on this for a few days and maybe we can get us a plan together," said Will.

"What about the human bones? I mean, shouldn't we report them to the police?" worried Jennifer.

"Well, with the arrowhead normally it would be an Indian burial site, but this arrowhead is metal," Ray quickly answered.

"I don't know. I do know we definitely have a dead body. If you are sure this is old enough to be an Indian, Ray," Will questioned Ray, concerned about the discovery.

"Most likely an Indian burial site. In fact, I'm amazed the relic hunters hadn't already dug it up," Ray responded.

"And if it's not an Indian burial site?" Jennifer questioned the current thinking of the Will and Ray.

"Since we are the only ones that know about it we have time to report it, maybe enough time to try to figure out the map. Hell, it could be old John Swift himself and we are standing near his silver mine, who knows?" Ray reasoned.

"I'm more inclined to agree with Ray. A rock is on the bones and with the arrowhead this is almost certainly an Indian burial site. Even if the arrowhead is silver, there is always a first. Besides, we didn't remove the bones from the site, only the arrowhead."

"If you guys think this is the way to go, I guess so, but this sure would make a good story in the paper and I would have the pictures."

"No! No newspaper article and no pictures. We need to keep this just between us. Agreed?" Ray shouted. Ray's serious demand bothered Will, and Jennifer's face was showing the same displeasure in Ray's tone. Because Ray insisted on keeping the discovery secret, more doubt and concern about the human bones clouded Jennifer's thoughts. Will noticed the enthusiasm of discovery had disappeared from the rock shelter. Everyone was silent, too silent for comfort.

"Tell us more about the John Swift stuff," Will prompted, just to break the uneasy silence.

"Actually, I have read a copy of the supposed journal. Once I went to the 'John Swift Silver Mine Weekend' in Jellico, Tennessee. I learned a lot about the legend. What a hoot," Ray laughed.

"You mean they celebrate a weekend about this in Tennessee?" Jennifer asked.

"Surely you're kidding," Will added laughing.

"No, no kidding. I went down to Tennessee with Louis Eversole. And as I recall we got pretty drunk one night. Before that, we went to some trading ground and saw all kinds of treasure hunters. Louis knows his stuff about John Swift silver mine tales, I can tell you that much for sure. He's been huntin' it for 20 years, I'd imagine," Ray added.

"He must not know too well if he ain't found it in 20 years," Will laughed out loud. Jennifer grinned but contained an outburst so as not to embarrass Ray.

"Me and Louis have been on a few silver mine hunts and a couple of times he was sure he had solved the legend mystery and found the mine. He told me once of old lady Timmons who had spent her family's fortune up somewhere in the Red River Gorge country. I do know where there are a couple of turkey tracks carved in the rocks, one at least was supposed to be connected to the silver mine. There are others, too, he told me, but I can't remember," Ray said.

"Well, where are they? The turkey tracks I mean?" Will asked. He thought this was getting more interesting as the day went on.

"Listen guys, let's take that drive next Saturday and see those turkey tracks. How about that?" Jennifer suggested. The three agreed. After the drive back to Frankfort, Will and Jennifer dropped Ray off at his place and then went to her apartment. They decided to stay in at her place and get a pizza delivered, watch TV, and mull over their day's adventure. Will pulled the silver arrowhead out of his pocket, went to the bathroom, where he cleaned it as best as he could. With the pizza delivered and a movie going, Will and Jennifer sat cuddled together. Will turned the silver arrowhead over and over in his hand.

"If this thing could talk I wonder what story would it tell," Will thought aloud.

"What thing?" Will held the object up for her to clearly see.

"Oh that thing. Yeah, well found with a dead person, it likely has a big story."

Five:
Swift Returns Alone

December in the wilderness was cold and wet. It rained mostly, but the daytime temperature often dipped into the mid thirties, making conditions downright unpleasant. The people of the Shawnee town tended to stay in their bark houses, except for a few hunters and the regular water brigade, though they made fewer trips to the creek on cold rainy days. Finley's store seemed to always have visitors and this pleased John. Toward the end of the month John Finley had traded for a few items made of silver; mostly flattened pieces with bead-holes punched in them, but nothing like he had hoped to trade for this year. He had spent much of the summer trying to find out from the natives who most often visited his store where the silver came from. Occasionally some of the ornaments and jewelry items the Shawnee wore included pieces of hand-beaten silver. The whole thing certainly remained a mystery and John had not made any progress on solving the case. The trading business had been good otherwise. John had practically every available space from the ground to the roof piled high with fine, tanned furs ready to take back east to the coast and sell for a premium price. Besides, his supplies ran low on the items the Shawnee wanted most, so trading had begun to slow a bit until fresh stock could be brought in. From time to time trappers on good terms with the Shawnee would stop by to pick up some items they may have lost or just wanted in order to remind them of home. John kept knives, sharpening stones, cups and other handy items. Although John had built his store just like the Shawnee houses out in the town, he had removed himself from the town and situated his store back on a little knoll right on the Warriors Path. The location seemed perfect to John. The store was made of upright posts set in the dirt in a circle about twelve feet across. The posts were set about two or three feet apart with smaller limbs and twigs filling between the uprights and the whole thing covered in tree bark held in place by mud and plant fibers. The roof comprised of smaller poles covered with bark moss and leaves. The whole thing had mud and moss daubed into the open spaces. The hut delivered much-needed weather resistance and was even warm on cold nights, despite needing weekly attention to repairs.

One morning, John observed a single man in the distance coming toward his store from the West, riding one horse and leading another. As the man rode his horse up to Finley's store John immediately recognized the man as John Swift, whom he had met before when introduced to him by his friend, George Mundy. In his mind he quickly recalled their conversation. John also took note his friend was not with Swift.

"Hello again Mr. Finley," Swift announced upon his arrival.

"And greetings to you Mister, uh, Captain Swift."

"No need to refer to me as Captain; John will do. Not much to captain out here in this country, wouldn't you say Mr. Finley?"

"No, I guess not."

John Swift got off his horse and tethered the two to a post set in the ground by Finley's store. Ample grass grew around the store for the two weary animals to pick at while Swift and Finley got reacquainted. John thought perhaps Swift wanted some supplies though he was in no way acting urgently, so he assumed there was no emergency.

"How's your trading business doing?" Swift inquired.

"I sure can't complain. This has been a gold mine for me this summer, all the furs I want and I think the only deer I killed I ate. The Shawnee practically kept me in food all summer. They love those beads and especially the cloth you know, but they really want the iron items most. They want bullets too. You know some of these Shawnee now have rifles. I don't know where they get them or the powder, but they do get them somewhere."

"The way I hear it the French are trading rifles to the Indians all up and down the frontier."

"Why do reckon they would do that?"

"Trying to get the Indians to fight the Red Coats, I suspect."

"Anyway, it's been a remarkable summer," John answered. Even with the polite conversation John Finley was wondering about Mundy and why he was not with his friend Swift.

"Where's George?" John inquired.

"Ah, well, George left me several days ago. Said something about having had enough of this country and headed back home to Pennsylvania," Swift replied in a lighthearted manner.

"Doesn't sound like old George. He loved coming out here. Least that's what he always told me, anyway."

"You know George; when he changes his mind he sails in new directions," Swift added.

"Did he leave back east or were you already out here in the wilderness?" John pressed.

"Well, we parted ways upon the river. George decided he didn't want to come back into the wilderness anymore."

"I sure thought old George had his heart set on spending his days in the open country of the wilderness. It seemed to me he couldn't wait to get down here when we came down the river together."

"I don't know about that. I'm just telling you what he told me."

"The Indians are getting pretty tough to deal with up north. Some of them are siding up with the French. Some of the others, like the Shawnee, are getting just downright mean. There is going to be trouble of this country, you can count on it," Swift said realizing he rambled on too much and decided to end this portion of the conversation.

"Hmm, well, I only knew him for a short time, certainly not as long as you two have been together."

"I can tell you, I've known George for many years and when he decides something, well, it's gonna' be his way."

What about you, no furs?" John questioned, hoping to get a little information about what Swift had been up to. Why had he come back to the Shawnee town, why didn't he have furs and what was he carrying on those pack horses that was so heavy? John wondered.

"I planned to send out some furs with George when he came by. He said he would collect my money and keep it safe for my return," Finley added. Swift sensed John Finley getting a little more distrustful. "Since I've not seen George, I made other arrangements," Finley added.

"I thought I would explore around the south part of the Warriors Path," Swift added, ignoring Finley's comments.

"That sounds like a good plan. How long are you going to be around this part of the country?" John asked, thinking he probably will not get a true answer.

"I can't say for certain, probably another week or two. That depends on the weather as well. It's been a wet fall and winter doesn't look like it is going to be very agreeable either. I thought I would scout out some places and maybe find a little better hunting next year."

"Do you think old George will come back?"

"Can't say for sure. In my opinion he won't be returning to this part of the country. What about you? Are you going to stay down here all winter?" Swift asked.

"Probably not. I suppose I will go back and load up on supplies and come back next spring. I've been hearing about Shawnee problems up north. These Shawnee treat me kindly and don't seem to be stirred up about nothin'. Things are fine with *these* Shawnee," John rambled on.

Swift studied John Finley as he rambled on, sizing him up in his mind. Now alone in his venture, and though he did not actually need another partner, he knew it was never a wise idea to work alone in the wilderness. The constant chance to get hurt, sick or encounter a band of hostile Indians loomed over frontiersmen. Swift reasoned a new partner might be the wiser choice. Swift liked John Finley and the fact he got along well with the Shawnee. Besides, Swift knew no other white men in the area.

"John, would you be interested in partnering up with me on a little venture here in this country?"

This caught John by surprise. He wondered what kind of venture Swift might have in this country requiring a partner. John paused and thought for a long time before he answered. George Mundy was Swift's partner so why did they dissolve their partnership, John thought.

"I've established a pretty good set up here, I can't ship out all the furs fast enough. Besides I got a pretty exclusive deal here with the Shawnee, no competition. They get new goods and I get furs that sell well, as you know, back east. I found two men that bring mule packs with new supplies down the river trail. I meet them and trade furs for their goods and they buy the rest of the furs from me," John answered. He knew he had not said yes or no. He stalled for time to make a decision.

"I can see you've done well for yourself,' Swift pointed around the hut at the stacks of animal furs.

"The only thing, I never got much more silver traded in, though. Just a few small items like the point I gave old George."

"Those Shawnee trade all the way up to the big lakes and down through the Cherokee country, I'm told. They may pick up an acorn or two, here and there, would be my guess," Swift explained.

"Acorn?"

"Silver piece, copper point, whatever they can trade for. I call 'em acorns," Swift grinned.

"So what about joining up with me and filling in where old George left me hanging?" Swift pressed again.

"What kind of venture?" John inquired.

"A very, very rich venture," Swift replied.

This less than specific offer left John with even more questions. He knew not to press the issue and that if Swift wanted to sell him on a partnership he would have to come up with more specifics than that. But Swift did not get more specific; he couldn't until he knew for sure that John would join him. John concluded that Swift was more or less 'feeling' out the situation.

"Well, I need to get my place closed out and get my furs out of here. Besides, trading is real good. You wouldn't believe the past few months. I kind of need a little time to think on it if you don't mind, Mr. Swift," John replied.

"Well, I'd better get going. Maybe we'll meet up in a couple of months. I am leaving in a few days, headed east. I expect to be back sometime in the early spring. Maybe I'll stop by and check on you. Think about the business partnership, will you John?"

"Oh, I will give serious consideration and maybe when you get back into this territory we can discuss further. I kind of need to see how this plays out and I am still hopeful to trade for more silver. Those Shawnee are gettin' the silver from somewhere and I sure would like to find out."

"You do that, John."

"Yes, well, be careful and good luck," John answered.

Swift was gone as suddenly as he appeared. The next supply trip John had arranged would not arrive until March. His trading business would not do as well in the winter months since his stock of items had grown short. But John still had trade items and even though some days during the month no one visited his store, most days John made several trades to his benefit, he reckoned. John also entertained hopes more of those silver items would show up this winter. He had become disappointed since not a single silver piece had shown up for a trade during the later part of the summer.

Even though he tried to get information about the origins of the silver, he could not find any Shawnee warrior that would even speak of the silver items.

As the end of 1752 came to a close, things ran quite smoothly. It ended up being a relatively mild winter, though the snows were becoming more frequent during the later part of December. By now life in the Shawnee town had slowed dramatically. Trading continued, but at a much slower pace. John knew in the spring he would need to get a fresh supply of nearly everything. John did occasionally wonder what happened to George Mundy and why he had left the wilderness. He thought a lot about Swift, too. What partnership venture had he offered, he wondered over and over.

One cold January morning the unthinkable happened to the Shawnee town. Early in the morning, just before daybreak, when most of the villagers slept, the Shawnee town came under viscous attack by the Iroquois from the north. Because of some disagreement among the Indian nations of North America, the Shawnee received an unmerciful and embarrassing defeat in the early morning attack. Finley was startled awake by the screams and crying of the mothers and babies. The rifle shots put him on full alert to events happening outside his door. Rushing to the door to peer out, John was horrified to see the Shawnee town being set afire. People ran everywhere, some being clubbed or shot by the unknown intruders. Finley noticed some of the Shawnee warriors were making a gallant defensive effort but were outnumbered. John instinctively realized it would be only a matter of seconds before the invaders would arrive at his store sitting on the hill away from the town. His situation being nearly hopeless, he knew he was likely about to die. As John grabbed his rifle, two Iroquois warriors had already reached the deer-hide door of the cabin. John lifted the already loaded long rifle and aimed at the door at the same moment the door was kicked open. He fired off the one shot hitting his mark and did the job. The other warrior thrust his spear toward John. The aim was to kill, but somehow John deflected much of the jab with the butt of his rifle. Even so, the sharp stone cut deep into John's leg. As John fell he grabbed one of the iron ax heads on the table by the door. John swung the ax head wildly at his would-be killer. Luck sided with John Finley on this day. The Indian was stunned and fell backwards. This was the time needed for John to grab the spear which only seconds ago severely wounded him and use it on its owner.

John bolted from the rear door of the cabin. Adrenaline was pushing him giving him the strength he needed to escape. Survival instinct had kicked in and the pain in his leg went unnoticed. A few yards from the cabin John turned and watched several warriors rushing his cabin and flames already consuming the roof. Only then did John feel the burning pain of his leg wound. His clothes were covered in blood.

Six:
All Is Lost

In January, 1753, John Swift, once again, chose to return to the wilderness. The good life on the coast took a great deal of money to support. A stroke of luck saw that January had been unusually warm. This made the trip easier for John Swift. He spent the fall, and the first part of the winter, in Charleston choosing a more desirable climate. However, with the weather much warmer in January and low on cash, Swift needed to replenish. He had gradually moved north up the coast until he reached Virginia. Swift headed down the Ohio River, as he had many times before, but this time he traveled by horse rather than by river raft. Traveling alone, Swift needed the extra carrying power of the horses to help him on this latest wilderness expedition. When he reached the crossing point of the Warriors Path on the Ohio, he turned South. Swift followed the familiar path southward toward the Shawnee town. After about a day and a half, Swift arrived on a low hill he had seen on previous visits to the area. The Shawnee town became visible from this vantage point. What John Swift witnessed came as a complete surprise: the town was gone! He didn't notice anyone milling about the area he knew to be the town, and any remaining dwellings were little more than barely husks of charred rubble. Swift set out on a much faster pace down to the town. As he approached, it became increasingly clear that something terrible had happened. Most of the houses had been burned to the ground. Tools and family belongings appeared in disarray scattered about. There were no people. Everything was destroyed.

John Finley's store had not escaped the destruction. The once thriving business had been utterly eradicated, and John Finley, like all the other souls of Eskippakithiki was gone; vanished. What had happened? Swift wondered. Where had everyone gone? Had they been killed, and if so, where are the bodies? Swift looked around on the ground near the Finley store to see if there remained any evidence of what had happened. A few beads and items were scattered about but most everything was either burned or gone. Swift thought hanging around out here in the open was not an especially wise plan. He carefully moved back toward the Warriors Path and decided he should get back into the woods and out of sight. He went directly east to the first big creek. This location put him well off the Warriors Path and directly east of the burned Shawnee town. Swift considered heading west toward his treasure cave, but since the Shawnee trail to the Falls headed that direction, he thought it might not be safe. As darkness approached, Swift made camp on a gravel bar along the meandering creek.

During his restless night at the campsite, Swift pondered the fate of the Shawnee town. He remembered he had not met a single Shawnee -no one in fact- as he came down the Warriors Path. This was an unsettling situation he had encountered, the full gravity of which he did not fully comprehend. He simply did not have enough information to know what had happened in the few months since he had been gone. Swift kept a small fire going but wondered if he was being watched by some unknown and yet-to-be-determined enemy. Even though he let the fire go out, Swift slept little.

Morning turned much colder. The low clouds and occasional snowflake announced the imminent arrival of a winter storm. Swift thought he ought to ride out the storm in the rock shelter camp on the mountain. Being close to the shelter and the likelihood of a blizzard arriving, this seemed like the best option for the remainder of the day. He had not been back to the shelter since he left his partner George Mundy there. He probably should check on the rock camp anyway, he thought. This would also provide the opportunity to observe and assess the Shawnee town as well as the surrounding area. Swift took great precaution when he made his trips to his precious silver, and insisted George Mundy do the same. Sometimes they would split up and come from different directions to the place that was so important to Swift and Mundy. The two of the them could retrieve in a single visit enough silver riches for both men to live rather extravagant life styles back in Charleston. They claimed, of course, that they hunted furs and hunting was so good they developed a very lucrative business. Neither man actually hunted, though. They—made a couple trips each year, wandered around killing time so as to give the appearance of hunting. In this way, friends and acquaintances on the coast never became suspicious. Luckily, however, both men were loners, so being around people on a constant basis was not necessary for either. About noon Swift finally reached the summit of the mountain. He and George had begun to call the high vantage point Pilot Knob. This high point reminded the two seamen of the perch, the pilot of boat would use to navigate intercoastal waters. This lofty mountain offered a clear and excellent view of the countryside in all directions.

The overcast sky had surrendered to scattered clouds with sunshine patches darting about over the landscape as Swift rested on the mountain. He saw the light plumes drifting upwards from his campsite near the creek below. Smoke from another campsite a little farther down the creek from the place he camped the night before caught his attention. Swift was unaware that anyone had camped nearby. He thought he might hang around before he headed out to his treasure cave. If someone saw him, tracked him, they could follow him. Swift could not allow that to happen.

After a couple hours Swift was beginning to get tired of just waiting so he thought he might return back to the creek and go check on the other campsite. He needed to know who else was in the area, especially since the Shawnee town was gone. Looking west he could see the abandoned town. While he had no particular affection for the Shawnee, as long as they were in the region few white men would venture into the area and this would mean fewer people would have the opportunity to stumble upon his secret. By mid afternoon Swift reached his previous night's campsite and he kept on walking down the lazy creek that meandered around until he came upon the site. Swift moved into the trees up from the creek. The campfire still burned and he could see a man sitting by the fire. Swift came on out into the open since he was sure it was a white man. As he got closer he recognized the man he saw.

"John? John Finley, is that you?" Swift yelled out.

"John, yes," John responded dazed and confused, not yet knowing who approached him.

"What are you doing here?" Swift asked, noticing John didn't bother to get up.

"John Swift? I'm real glad to see you." John sounded relieved, though dazed and a bit disoriented. He was obviously very happy to see a familiar face.

"What happened, John?"

"I'm hurt. Real bad I think. Oh, man, it hurts."

Swift could see that Finley was in pain. He also noticed the blood stains on his clothing. He could not tell what the extent of the injury was but he reasoned that this must have something to do with the destruction of the Shawnee town.

"Here, let me a look at your wound."

Swift carefully pulled back the flaxen cloth trousers and saw the heavy gash in the leg just above the knee. He figured the wound was at least three inches long and was deep into the leg muscle.

"Ohooo! Yeeaaww!" Finley groaned and complained.

"How did you get this?"

"Two of those Iroquois warriors came running up the hill and toward my cabin. The village was being destroyed, so I knew for sure they aimed to kill me. I shot one in the doorway. Before I could reload the other one popped through the door and jabbed at me, aiming to hit my heart, I suspect. I jumped away and he caught me in the leg with his spear. That dang stone spear blade was sharp."

"Wonder why he didn't finish you off?"

"I grabbed an ax head and whopped him up on the side of the head. I was falling away as I swung so I didn't have much control of the ax. But, enough to knock him senseless for a minute or two."

"That's when you got away?"

"Slicker than bear grease. I knew there would be more in a minute, so I took off in this direction as fast as I could. I was bleeding badly and the farther I came the weaker I got. I made it here stumbling, running, sometimes crawling by the time I got to the creek."

"John, you are lucky to have survived, you know that?"

"I know and my luck just keeps getting better. Look here, you just happen to come along."

Swift tore some strips of cloth from Finley's trousers and made some new bandages. He could see that Finley had rubbed something and placed dried leaves on the wound. The bleeding had stopped but Swift could see that the spear had cut deep into the flesh, nearly to the bone.

"It's gone, the store, the furs the whole damn town is gone, burned to the ground," Finley rambled on. It was obvious to Swift that John Finley was still in a state of shock from the ordeal.

"What about the Iroquois? What happened to the Shawnee?"

"Three days ago the whole damn Iroquois nation attacked the town, killing all they could and burning everything else. It was an awful mess."

"Why in the world would the Iroquois do that? Why would they go to the trouble of coming down here?"

"I don't know. It sure came as a surprise to those Shawnee and to me, for that matter."

"I went to the village; there is nothing left. It's all gone, John," Swift replied.

"I escaped up into the woods and kept running until I got to this creek. I followed the creek until I got here and I just couldn't go on any further. I've been here for the last few days, three I think, without any food." During his fortunate escape from the attack, John, wincing in pain with each step, managed to limp along but finally dropped from shear exhaustion to the ground to crawl to the cold, muddy creek. A pile of drift wood and debris near him made a rough shelter and managed to crawl into the pile and stayed there the first night. The natural shelter had accumulated on a shallow gravel bar in a bend in the creek. Year after year the spring rains would cause the creek to flood its banks, picking up dead limbs and debris along the stream. On this gravel bar the creek made a sharp turn, thus leaving trapped logs, sticks, and leaves which had allowed John to hole up like a wounded animal.

"I still don't understand why the Iroquois would attack the Shawnee? They speak the same language and always traded with them."

"Ah, I don't know, but before the attack some of the warriors talked about how some other warriors killed a high-ranking Iroquois chief. This might have really made them mad and this attack was a revenge attack."

"The whole town, those who survived, fled up the trail and left. I don't know if they are even back," Finley added.

"I didn't see any bodies at the village. They must have come back and collected their dead the next day," Swift remarked. "I've not seen a Shawnee or any other Indian since I've been here in these parts," Swift added.

"What about my leg? How bad do you think it is?" Finley winced as he positioned his leg so Swift could see better.

"It's a fairly deep wound and it's what I call proud flesh but I've seen worse."

"It's starting to look a little angry but I don't believe the infection has spread just yet."

"Like I said, it's bad but I've seen worse. Do you think you can walk?" Swift asked.

"I'll give it a try but lord have mercy, it hurts. I don't know. I get real tired out though." John Finley was near exhaustion. Swift knew that if John didn't get him some food the cold air would take him. Finley needed sustenance and they both needed to move away from the Warriors Path and the destroyed Shawnee town.

"Here, eat some of this," as Swift handed John a piece of jerky.

John took the jerky and ate the first food he had had in three days. Immediately the nourishment had an effect on John. He was glad that this miracle of a chance encounter with his new friend, John Swift, had happened at this time. Otherwise, John figured he would be dead in another day or two, either by starvation or by the hands of hostile Indians.

"You need to keep up your strength and we've got to get you out away from this creek." Swift knew they were much too close to the Warriors Path and it would only be a matter of time before some warriors, be it Shawnee or Iroquois, would be coming down the path. The Warriors Path was the most traveled route by the Natives in the entire region. The Great Falls of the Ohio Trail met up with the Warriors Path here near the Shawnee town. This was what made it such a great trading location for John Finley. It was just an issue that Swift always had to be aware of and deal with during his many trips back into the wilderness to retrieve more of his treasure. As long as the two men stayed around in the area of this creek they were vulnerable to the same savage attacks that had just happened to the Shawnee Town.

"We've got to get going and move to another location so you can rest up, build your strength and get out of this country. I hate to say it but your trading this year is over."

"I know. I've lost everything. There is nothing left."

Swift extinguished the small fire that John had managed to keep going from the large pile of dried drift wood beside his resting place.

"Can you stand up?"

"I'll try. You might need to help me here." John struggled but couldn't put much weight on the injured leg.

Snow flakes began to fall lightly from the overcast sky. Swift pushed John onto one of the horses and Swift climbed on the other one. As the day went on the two men slowly moved toward the mountain Swift had just come down earlier. He needed to get his friend back to the rock shelter camp. As darkness neared they had climbed a good portion of the mountain. Swift intended to get John up next to the giant cliff and under the rock overhang for shelter. The snow was coming down heavier by the hour and getting much colder. Swift wondered how John Finley had even survived the past three days cold and wet and with no food to sustain energy. Finley was indeed lucky to have survived.

By dark they reached the base of the cliff and worked their way around to a very nice rock shelter that provided plenty of overhang to keep out the snow and rain. There was plenty of dry, dead wood. Swift and Mundy had used this shelter before and had stockpiled plenty of fire wood for situations like this.

"I'll get a fire going. You need to eat some more jerky. Tomorrow I will kill us some fresh meat," Swift told John.

"Give me a day or two and I'll be okay. I just need some food to get my strength back," John said.

"I'll be back in a little while. I need to take the horses on top of the hill above us. There is a clearing with some dried grass there."

"Oh, I won't be going anywhere."

"You'll be fine and ready to go in a few days," Swift replied.

John Finley was about to get the first restful night's sleep he had in the last three days. Swift made his way to the top of the mountain and turned the horses out in the mountain-top pen he had built on a previous trip. The mountain top was unusually flat and had a good growth of buffalo grass. Only one narrow escape route from the little pasture offered added protection. Swift skillfully tied possum grape vines to small trees, forming a fence and gate system.

John Swift sat by the fire and kept it stoked and wondered if he should tell his friend his amazing secret, and if so, how he would tell him. He also knew he had to take care of John Finley's wound.

"John, we need to burn that wound."

"I know. It's the only way," John acknowledged.

Finley, gazing into the fire, noticed that John Swift had already placed his knife blade in the fire and paled in anticipation. This was going to hurt real bad so he braced himself. Swift focused intently on the knife laying on a rock with the blade extending over hot coals. This crude process had proven time and again to be an effective way to sterilize a wound. Most every hunter has undergone such ordeals.

"Now then, here we go," Swift calmly announced retrieving the red hot knife.

"Oh boy, Umm, I dread this you know," John miserably protested.

"This is only going to hurt for a couple of seconds. Here bite on this stick." Before John could get his mind off placing the small stick in his mouth Swift laid the searing hot knife squarely on the infected wound. John bit hard on the stick, grunting and screaming through his teeth. The putrid smell of burning flesh surrounded the two men.

Seven:
Follow the Turkey Track

"Ray, can you get my car fixed before 5:00 PM today?" Roger Hampton asked just before noon.

"Depends on what's wrong with it," Ray replied.

"The thing dies, sputters, and misses. Something is wrong is all I know. But I need the car for tomorrow. It's important."

"Sounds like a fuel filter is clogged, or the gasoline. Nothing usually goes wrong with those vehicles. If it's nothing major, we ought to get er' done today."

"I need it done today."

Roger Hampton, a well-to-do business man in town, had made a small fortune in the real estate business. He loved to wheel and deal in land transactions and he especially liked to buy struggling family farms and sell to developers. Saturday was a big day to show off property to prospective home buyers and he needed his car ready for hauling his potential customers around. Although Roger had two other high end cars that he could have easily used, he considered this his 'lucky' sales vehicle and he did not want to show property without it.

"I'll put the car on the machine here in a few minutes we will see what's going on," Ray offered.

Ray Deevers knew cars inside and out and people came to the shop asking exclusively for him to work on their cars. He could sense, almost supernaturally, the problems and solutions to nearly anything that had a motor. Systematically thorough, Ray seldom made mistakes in his specialized work. Ray had been tinkering and building cars since his teenager days. Even though he went to a trade school, most of what he learned came from his uncle who owned the shop where he worked. Roger, as well as everybody else in town, knew Ray Deevers' reputation as a great mechanic, though some considered Ray a little on the odd side. He could be nice as could be one minute, then the next, go into a rage. Most folks kept their distance but Roger was pushy himself.

"Just get it done Ray," Roger snapped and handed Ray the keys to his Lexus GX 460.

Roger would have normally taken his expensive vehicle to the dealer to handle but he knew he would not get anything done today and he really liked using that vehicle in his real estate business. It gave the impression that Roger Hampton was doing very well, selling and buying a lot of property for his clients. In fact, he was very successful and considered by most other realtors as the best in town. Roger was charming and friendly when he was selling property. But when he was not trying to sell something he was a different person altogether. Ray considered him to be a stuck-up, snotty bastard. But he was a customer, so like most folks in town Ray just dealt with and avoided, whenever possible, Roger Hampton.

"I'll be here at 5:00 o'clock to pick it up," Roger yelled over his shoulders slamming the door behind him.

"We'll do what we can, but I can't promise," Ray yelled as Roger slammed the door.

The day turned out to be harder than expected. Parts were late for some cars that had been in the shop for two days. One of the guys got sick and left work nearly as soon as he arrived which meant more work for Ray. When 5:00 o'clock came Ray had not gotten around to Roger Hampton's Lexus. He was just hooking up the diagnostic machine when Roger showed up.

"Oh shit Ray, the car is not ready?" Roger hatefully spoke over Ray's shoulder.

"No sir, Mr. Hampton, we have been swamped with a seal job, five brake jobs and an axle replacement. On top of that, the parts ordered for cars ahead of yours just arrived not long ago. I am only now getting to yours. I am sorry but we are simply running behind today."

"I guess you will be here all night or early in the morning to work on my car, Ray. I have important buyers at ten in the morning I have to pick up at the airport. Damn it! I can't even rent a car anywhere this time of day for tomorrow," Roger hissed sarcastically.

A couple of the mechanics working on other cars became more attentive to the conversation between Ray and Roger. It was heating up and co-workers would not hesitate to intervene if things got out of hand.

"If there's no big problem I will get it done tonight."

"You had better get it done. This can't be much of a problem."

"Well, I don't know. If it's a bad problem, and by that I mean requiring parts we don't have, then the first thing Monday we'll get it fixed," Ray offered.

"No, no Ray, you get the damn parts tonight. I don't care how," Roger snapped.

"I will not be in tomorrow; I have some personal business to attend to," Ray announced.

"The hell you say, Ray. What is so important you can't take care of business?"

"I guess you didn't hear me. I'll fix the damn thing as soon as I can. If you don't like that then take your damn car and shove it up your fat ass!"

"Hey boy, you better calm down a bit," Roger snapped back.

Roger surprised at Ray's sudden surliness, in a much calmer voice, made one last attempt.

"I'll tell you what, Ray. Get it fixed by nine in the morning, ready for me to drive to the airport, promise me, and I won't say anything to Charlie."

Charlie Wright was the owner of the shop and Ray's uncle. Roger was making a direct threat to Ray, trying to intimidate Ray into changing his mind about finishing the job Monday. Roger Hampton loved to have the upper hand in a negotiating situation. He fully intended to agitate Ray.

"I'll do what I can, Roger. Good Lord! I can't promise you a damn thing other than I won't be working on it tomorrow!" Ray bellowed out.

"Why you little shit! I am going to talk to Charlie about your pissy little attitude toward customers. We'll see what old Charlie has to say."

"You had better shut the hell up if you want me to fix your damn car."

"Okay. Okay, Ray. I just need the car. Okay?" Roger pleaded in a high pitched, child like voice.

"Okay."

"Now, what did you say you had to do tomorrow that was so important?"

"Not that its any of your damn business Roger, but some friends and me are going up in the mountains looking for rock carvings, uh well, you know Indian carvings," Ray blurted out.

Ray realized that he had said too much to Roger, who thought that was an unusual answer but nevertheless it piqued his curiosity.

"Rock carvings?" Roger spoke, puzzled. He wondered what in the world Ray was up to.

"Yeah, getting out and exploring, hunting Indian stuff, hiking mostly. I wouldn't imagine this is stuff that would be very interesting to big businessman like you, Roger. Just forget I mentioned it. But I am not going to miss the trip with my friends."

"Who is going with you?"

"Nobody you know, some friends."

"What time are you guys leaving? I might like to go with you after I finish my business deal. I enjoy that kind of stuff, especially finding land deals, stuff like that."

"I don't think you'd be interested in this trip and, uh, no Roger you can't go." Ray flatly laid it out to Roger.

"Well, just get the car fixed, Ray," Roger concluded, a little upset he didn't get his way.

No sooner had Roger stomped out the door, Ray told the other guys he was leaving. He also told them that tomorrow he was going with his friends to the mountains and to make sure the part was ordered for Rogers car. The shop was open until noon on Saturdays but with a smaller crew.

Will sat on the horn in front of Ray's house early Saturday morning. It was 7:00 in the morning and Will had already picked up Jennifer. He had filled up his Chevrolet

Silverado pickup at the nearest gasoline station. As usual, Will had packed his back pack with every conceivable kind of survival gear: fire starter kits, first aid items, duct tape, space blankets, light-sticks, fish hooks and line, about everything you would need. He never went on any kind of outing without his survival backpack, as he called it. He also had put his revolver in the glove compartment.

Jennifer had her camera equipment neatly situated in a large shoulder bag. The bag was big enough to carry both cameras with various lenses as well as her favorite tripod. Jennifer practically never went anywhere without her camera equipment. She had learned long ago that great photographs do not wait for a day when it is convenient to bring along the camera. Carrying her camera equipment had become a matter of habit to Jennifer, and part of her when she went anywhere.

"Come on Ray," Will yelled out and blew the horn again.

"Okay. Okay. Hold your horses!" Ray yelled, running out the door, looking a little ramshackle.

Ray hoped in back seat of the extended cab truck and they were ready to go.

"Anyone hungry? I sure could use some coffee."

"How about stopping downtown at the Coffeetree? I love that place," Jennifer suggested.

"How about it Ray, you OK with that?"

"Sounds just great to me, I need something to kick start me this morning. Let's go."

In five minutes they walked into the coffee shop. Finding a parking space along Broadway was easier than Will thought it would be but then again it was early.

Roger Hampton walked into the garage at about 9:30. Only one fellow puttered around working half heartily on couple of vehicles neither of which belong to Roger. "Where's Ray this morning?" Roger curtly asked loud enough for anyone in the building to hear.

"Why Mr. Hampton, Ray is off today."

"He was supposed to be here."

"I thought he told you he was going on some kind of hike or something." The fellow, encouraged by Ray's handling of the situation yesterday, felt embolden to question Roger.

"Don't get smart with me boy." Roger saw his car right where it was the day before. He left the place and got into his car and went to his downtown office. As luck or fate would have it as he drove down Broadway he caught sight of Ray along with his buddies, coming out of the coffee shop.

They headed east for the mountains. The drive took them past Lexington to the Mountain Parkway and eastward.

"Okay Ray, where are we going?" Will asked. Will was excellent with directions but needed some guidance from Ray on this one, since Ray up to this point had not been specific as to their destination.

"We need to go to the Red River Gorge. I know of a turkey track carved there. It's carved right out in the middle of Rock Bridge," Ray said.

"Oh, I know that place. I have been there before, made pictures. It's been several years, though. I'm not sure I could find my way back again though." Jennifer said.

As the three explorers headed east past Winchester they came to a place he had told them about before Ray pointed out as Eskippakithiki. In fact, the Mountain Parkway was built through the flat area that in 1752 was the largest Shawnee town in Kentucky. A short distance to the east, perhaps two miles, stood the mighty Pilot Knob. As they sped along, they encountered a flat plain that was very noticeable from the rolling landscape to the west. Pilot Knob was on the extreme eastern edge of the geological oddity known as the Cincinnati Arch. A large section of the central Kentucky land area was uplifted in ancient times. The limestone that was once deeply embedded in the earth was heaved upwards by subterranean tectonic activity. This, in turn, caused the top layers of rock to erode away much faster and exposing the limestone. The Bluegrass Region of Kentucky is a direct result of this titanic creation. The western edge, at the other end of this terrestrial upheaval, is exposed around the Falls of the Ohio. The arch extended north to Cincinnati, for which it was named, and to the south around Danville, Kentucky. Eskippakithiki is on the eastern end of this formation. This site selected for the Shawnee town was probably due to the rich, level land with few trees, plenty of grass and nearness to the Warriors Path.

"Recognize that place up there?" Ray questioned, nodding out the front window toward the skyline ahead of them.

"Pilot Knob. Been there," Jennifer quickly answered.

"Twice in one week as a matter of fact," Will added.

"You know that's amazing that the first truly level land Daniel Boone saw in Kentucky was the site of the old Shawnee Town. Funny thing," Will said.

"Looks like that's our mountain up there. Pilot Knob is the closest high mountain to the Indian village."

"I wish I knew more about the history of this area. It seems awfully important in the big scheme of things, plus the fact that we found a silver arrowhead right up there under the cliff so close to this place," Will continued.

"I am sure there are some historical records to be found on the subject. I could do a little research when we get back home," Jennifer suggested.

Finally, after what seemed like hours of driving, they reached the graveled parking lot and Rock Bridge picnic area. From the edge of the parking lot the trail led immediately over the gritty sandstone cliff, winding downward. Will, Jennifer and Ray quickly grabbed a bottle of water each and headed down the trail. The Rock Bridge trail led the three adventurers off down a short half mile walk down the crest of a ridge. The obviously well used path brought the trio to one of the most famous and most unusual rock formations in all the country. Here the creek had completely eroded through the sandstone conglomerate rock creating a 'rock bridge' across the creek. Ray had seen the carving before and immediately scrambled up the rocky outcrop and made his way out on the bridge that spanned the crystal clear waters flowing slowly under the bridge. In a matter of seconds Ray located the odd carving.

"Hey, here we go," Ray yelled.

Will and Jennifer climbed up the rocks to observe, for what they had traveled this far and spent a Saturday morning searching. Ray had seen this track before and wanted the others to see it and compare it to the one carved on the rock wall at Pilot Knob.

"This turkey track has been here for as long as anyone can remember," Ray added.

"Looks like the one on the rock wall," Jennifer remarked.

"Well, this'n here is supposed to point the direction to the John Swift silver mine, at least that is what some of the treasure hunters claim. This is Swift Creek you know," Ray explained.

"Swift Creek!" Will commented in surprise.

"Named for the John Swift's Silver Mine?" Jennifer questioned.

"Yep, sure is Swift Creek. There is a historical marker on the court house lawn in Wolf County that says as much. In fact, I do believe we are in Wolf County right now. I think Swift Creek starts up there around the town of Campton somewhere," Ray spouted out. Somehow, on this subject, Ray Deevers was a virtual encyclopedia. Ray had recalled nearly everything he had learned in his limited exposure to the Swift legend. Will was a bit embarrassed that he had never heard of the Swift legend, especially since he had studied geology. He never spent much time in eastern Kentucky where the legend is solidly established, and because his geology schooling was out of state, he really was learning about Kentucky geology in his hobby of exploring. Jennifer had seen an occasional newspaper story on the subject, and had heard folks talk about the story from time to time.

"People have spent a lot of time and effort searching these hills for those lost silver mines. A natural rock bridge crossing the creek would seem to me to figure into a good marker for finding the way to the mines, I would imagine," Ray continued.

"Which way is the turkey track pointing?" Will asked as he aligned himself with the track.

"Well, depends which direction you think it was intended to point. Most of the people I know seem to think the track points in the direction the track is headed as if it were a real bird track left by a turkey walking. The middle toe of the track looks to me to point up that ridge."

"That is a westerly direction, I think," Will noted.

"We just came from that direction," Jennifer added. She knew directions as well as Will and Ray but she was being sarcastic as they had driven two hours east just to reach this spot. Jennifer was not as impressed with the turkey track as Will and Ray were but she was fascinated with the stone bridge and had already begun to climb down in order to take some photographs. This was the only place in the region that a completely natural stone arch span across a major creek. Will and Ray sat in the middle of the bridge for a good while, flipping twigs and loose quartz pebbles into the lazy creek below.

"So, if the turkey track on the wall at Pilot Knob is carved there to point at something, do you think it was pointing west?" Ray asked.

"If we only knew for sure the rock carving was a map then the turkey tracks might mean something, but like this, we really don't have anything," Will admitted with an air of frustration.

"I, for one, do believe with some certainty that is a carving of a map on the back of that rock shelter at Pilot Knob. And if we knew what the carvings and symbols meant, we might actually be on to something," Ray concluded.

"I mean, this is one turkey track, and what do the lines mean? And those other crazy markings? " Will was totally confused by the unusual petroglyphs.

"I know someone who does know a lot about markings, carvings and the like if you guys are willing to share the rock map information with him," Ray suddenly announced.

"You talking about that fellow you mentioned the other day?"

"Louis Eversole. Louis knows a lot about this kind of stuff. I've tried to learn a little over the years but Louis has forgotten more than I'll ever know about this kind of stuff and especially Swift stuff."

"Suppose we drew out the map or just some of the map and let him look at it. Would that be useful?" Jennifer asked.

"Oh, a good idea. We could sketch out some of the map and let him take a look, see what he thinks," Will said.

"In fact he lives not too far from here," Ray added.

"Maybe we can give him a call and stop by today. How about it Ray, do you think he would mind?" Will asked.

"If he's home, Louis would love to talk about this stuff. He lives for it. He is the one that took me to Jellico, Tennessee one weekend to that Swift festival. Remember, the one I was telling you about?" Ray replied.

After the hike down, the three hopped back in the truck. Finding themselves a mite thirsty, they stopped by a little country store on the main road to get something cold to drink. Ray rummaged around in the store cooler hunting for his favorite drink, feeling the bottles to see which was the coldest.

"How about an Ale8-1?" Ray asked. Ale8-1 was a light ginger flavored, carbonated drink made locally. For many people in the area, it was a daily staple of life.

"Sure, why not, I like them and I've sure earned and burned the calories today," Jennifer replied.

"Yeah, get me one too," Will said.

"I grew up on these. Nothing like a good ol'e Ale8," Ray proudly explained as he reached for his wallet to pay for the drinks. Will and Jennifer walked toward the truck while Ray paid the elderly lady for their drinks. Grabbing his change, he headed the door out to catch up with his friends.

"Where to?" Will asked.

"To get to Louis we need to go down to Sand Gap," Ray responded.

With that they were on the road headed for Louis Eversole and an education on the mysterious Swift legend.

Eight:
Louis Tells A Story

Louis Eversole lived up a hollow in the mountains along a small clear stream. Louis and his wife, Sarah, lived with at least six dogs and therefore always aware of visitors a good two minutes before they got to the front porch. They had lived on this small mountain creek for 40 years. Louis and his wife Sarah grubbed out a small garden beside the clear mountain creek running down past their house. The house and various out buildings rested comfortably between the rocky, hemlock covered hillsides typical of a mountain homestead. Louis Wayne Eversole was considered an expert on the legend of the John Swift Silver Mine and had spent twenty years or more chasing after the dream tale. Years ago, he had found the turkey tracks, haystack rocks and three creeks but he never claimed he had found a mine or any silver. In fact, Will Morrow had with him in his pocket more silver found in this country than Louis had ever seen. Ray had convinced Will he should meet Louis and discuss the tales with him. Of course, they were not going to say anything about the map.

Louis was sitting on his front porch with Sarah enjoying the cool breeze coming down the hollow over the rippling creek. Will pulled his truck up in front of the house. Louis, although not fearful, was curious and tried to recall anyone he knew who would be driving a fine new pickup truck. With dogs and his handy rifle by the front door, Louis knew he could determine the danger level once someone showed themselves from the truck. Ray jumped out first so that Louis would know who it was.

"Howdy Louis!" Ray yelled out.

"Ray? Ray Deevers! Well, what in the world are you doing up here in God's country?" Louis questioned as he got up from the porch swing and moved toward the steps leading up to the porch. "Hush dogs!" Louis yelled. The dogs immediately quieted down but milled around sniffing the guests as each got out of the truck. The boss dog marked the truck tire, indicating the truck and visitors were now in his territory.

"Louis, this here is Will Morrow and Jennifer Morgan. And I apologize for just dropping in on you all without calling ahead," Ray introduced them.

"Nah. Ain't no problem Ray. Glad to meet you folks, come on up on the porch and sit and a spell. We don't get much company up here," Louis politely invited.

"Thanks Louis. This sure is a pretty place you have here," Ray commented.

"We like it. It's quiet anyway. Say, are you folks thirsty? Honey, why don't you bring these folks something cold to drink, maybe some of that good sweet tea you make, if you don't mind," Louis turned and glanced at Sarah.

"No, thanks Mrs. Eversole. We've had cold drinks on the way up here. We appreciate the offer though," Will answered for all three.

"Are you sure, it ain't no trouble at all," Sarah quickly followed.

"Oh, yes, Mrs. Eversole. Will is right. But we appreciate your kind offer," Jennifer quickly and politely responded.

"Well, Ray what's on your mind?" Louis point blank asked Ray while studying all three people one at a time.

"Louis, we get out, uh, the three of us get out ever now and again to rock hunt and general exploring cliffs and caves. The other day we ran upon a turkey track and some other markings. Well, here, Will you explain it to him," Ray said pointing to others.

"Got the silver mine fever, do we?" Louis jokingly remarked, eliciting a modest chuckle from everyone.

"Mr. Eversole," Will began.

"Call me Louis. There ain't no big 'I's and little 'u's around here. Louis'll be fine," Louis interrupted.

"Okay, Louis. We are interested in the John Swift Silver Mine. Ray here says you're the man, the one that knows all there is to know about the Swift Lost Silver Mine. We've been interested in the legend and all, well, we just have come up with a few questions," Will fumbled for the words.

"What do you want to know?" Louis questioned.

"Anything you might want to share about your experiences and knowledge of the legend."

"Heck, you can check on them computers internet or something and find all about John Swift," Louis responded.

"We can't find out what Louis Eversole knows on the internet; I'll guarantee that," Ray boasted. With that statement Louis was encouraged and primed to tell all. Louis had spent years following leads, tales and not many folks asked him about the story much anymore. In fact, not many people knew about the tale of the lost silver mine.

"So you think the turkey track carvings you found might have something to do with the silver mine?" Louis questioned.

"We don't know. I'll tell you one thing though, I never saw carvings like this before," Ray answered. Both Jennifer and Will gave Ray a casual, quick glance just to let him know not to talk too much. Ray got the message and became quiet. Louis paused for an uncomfortable amount of time.

"Well, let me see. I started, well, got interested you might say, in the sixties. There were some fellers from Virginia that came into this country and spent a small fortune lookin' for that silver mine. I eventually hooked up with them, as a kind of a guide you might say, to these hills. I had heard of the story all my life, mostly from my daddy, but I never was much interested until the Virginia boys came along. After taking them to various places each year (they would come every year in the fall) I learned a lot about the silver mine. They were convinced that the silver mine was somewhere down around the cliffs of Chimney Top Creek," Louis began.

"They had maps, testing equipment, and most important to me a copy of what they claimed to be the authentic journal left by John Swift himself," Louis added.

"Did the journal give exact directions to the mine?" Will asked.

"No, not directly. It was more like clues. It described rocks and creeks. The journal, I have a copy around here somewhere, Swift claimed to have written himself so that he could find the mine again. He said that he mined silver, smelted silver and made counterfeit English crowns in the wilderness south of the Ohio River and west of the big mountains from 1760 until 1769. Swift claimed he was captured by the British and put into prison for siding with the colonists on one of his trips to England," Louis continued.

"Why did he go to England?" Ray asked.

"Oh, well, John Swift said he had a very successful shipping business prior to the revolutionary war and actually owned a fleet of sailing ships, according to his journal," replied Louis. "Anyway, while in England he was thrown into prison for many years. By the time he got out, Swift was blind and couldn't find the mine. So he wrote down everything he could remember, descriptions of rocks, rock houses etc., and with others acting as his eyes tried to return to his precious mine," Louis concluded.

"Let me ask you, how did he find the mine in the first place?" Will asked the all important question.

"George Mundy. He met George Mundy when Mundy was a war prisoner in General Braddock's army. Mundy was a Frenchman that had been captured by the British and colonists. Swift says that he befriended a man by the name of George Mundy who told him he had been mining silver south of the Ohio River. Apparently, after that, Mundy took Swift to the mine along with a company of men to work in the mine. That's the way I understand how it went anyhow," Louis said.

"Braddock's army? George Mundy?" Will was getting confused.

"Well, you see, Mundy had found the mine from the Indians and had been working the silver out himself. It always seemed to me old Mundy might have bought his freedom by telling Swift of the silver mine. Anyway, Mundy led Swift and some of his associates to the mine around 1760, according to Swift's journal."

"Do you still believe the mine exists?" Jennifer interjected wanting to get to the bottom of the line of questioning.

"Yes I do," Louis said wholeheartedly. "Just because I ain't found it after searching so long, doesn't mean squat. I've not been in all the right places. Ray, do you remember going to Jellico?" Louis turned to Ray.

"Sure do, we had us a heck of time that weekend. Met some strange people though."

"Well, each of us were bitten by the Silver legend and it may seem a little strange, but I got to say I have had some good times and thought I was close once or twice," Louis said.

"Seems like if Swift sailed ships he would know how to clearly mark his trail to the mine," Will pondered.

"Well, he was a captain of his own ship and claimed to own more ships. He did write down the latitude of 38 degrees and 11 minutes in his journal. So we can only conclude Swift had the proper instrument to plot coordinates," Louis added.

"What about the longitude?" Will asked.

"Unfortunately, all the journal says is that it was near 83° longitude. I always thought Swift left it that way since all he really needed to do was get into the general area and he could find the mines," Louis responded.

"That opens up quite a big area, I guess, if the journal information is correct," Ray added.

"Where do you think the mine is located? Uh, assuming it really exists, of course," Will laid it out point blank.

"Son, if I knew, we sure as hell wouldn't be havin' this conversation, would we? Oh, I guess I've always felt it was somewhere in these cliffs around here. All the landmarks Swift mentions in his journal are here, and we are pretty close to the 38 degree latitude and there sure are plenty of places it could be buried on these mountains. I just have not been able to put it all together," Louis concluded.

"We think the carvings we found are some kind of a crude map," Will remarked.

"What kind of a map?"

"Well, in fact this map and the carvings, are on the back wall of a big sandstone rock shelter."

"How do you know it's a map?"

"Well, there's more," Ray interjected.

"Do you have a picture of it?"

"We have a drawing of it," Jennifer said as she pulled out the map.

"Let me see here, I've seen a lot of carvings and markings the past forty years," Louis responded. Louis carefully studied the hastily drawn map. He couldn't immediately tell anything from it right away, other than easily recognizing the large and small turkey track markings. The map only contained the turkey tracks and the lines. The other symbols, the eye, the x's, and the half moon with lines on it were purposefully omitted.

"How big is this thing, the carving I mean?"

"I'd say it is five feet high and probably six or eight feet across," Ray explained.

"That big, huh? And you say these markings are carved on the wall of a rock shelter?"

"Yeah, although they're covered with moss and other stuff growing on the rock. We would not have seen the thing except for the way the light happened to hit it on the day we were there."

"And these lines, Louis pointed, are carved all the way across the map?"

"They are."

"We think the map is in Kentucky somewhere but can't figure out where."

"Ray thinks this is either the Licking or Big Sandy River cause he thinks the lines at the top are the Ohio River. What do you think?" Will asked.

"Are the carvings deep?" Louis asked.

"Pretty deep. Someone spent some time carving these symbols into the rock for sure. They wanted the carvings to be there for a long time. There were no names or initials carved, either."

Louis became more interested now. Although he had seen about every kind of carved turkey track in the country he was quite certain he had never encountered anything like this. He would love to see the rock carving for himself. Perhaps it was a piece of the puzzle he had been trying to solve for the last twenty years. Louis knew equally as well that he would not get all the information and likely would not be invited to see the rock carving during this visit; it was just the way treasure hunters behaved.

"So what do you think Louis? The Licking or the Big Sandy?" Ray asked.

"If I had to guess right now I'd say neither," Louis finally announced.

"Neither?" Ray exclaimed in disbelief that Louis had just shot down his theory.

"My opinion is it's the Warriors Path," Louis added.

"Warriors Path?" Will questioned.

"Yes, the Warriors Path. You see, if these lines represents the Ohio River, and I think they do, then why wouldn't you put all the rivers in the map? Just putting one river in would virtually make the map impossible to use. Heck, a person wouldn't know if they were on the Big Sandy or the Kentucky River, or one of the other rivers, or even a big creek. Nah, I'd say it was the Warriors Path," Louis concluded.

"Where is the Warriors Path?" Jennifer excitedly asked.

"Runs along the edge of the mountains before you get to Winchester. Runs all the way from up north down through Cumberland Gap into Tennessee. It's on the early maps of Kentucky, the one John Filson made, I believe," Louis answered.

"Well, I'll be," said Ray, astonished by this new information. Ray knew about where the Warriors Path was located based on this description.

"Do turkey tracks point to something, generally? I mean do they point in a direction?" Will asked Louis for confirmation to his previous claims.

"I always heard and believe they do. A simple way to show a direction to go. The turkey foot would be pointing in the direction the 'turkey' is walking," Louis offered.

"Well, this certainly has been interesting and we very much appreciate your time and help," Will said.

"So, you folks think you are on to something?" Louis asked.

"Something, but who knows what. It's fun to chase after it, though. Good exercise and heck, we meet some interesting folks like you and learn a little history too," Will commented.

"I guess it wouldn't do any good to ask where this rock carving is located," Louis remarked.

"Let's put it this way, it's on the western edge of the mountains," Ray answered.

"Then I'm pretty sure the line on the carving is the Warriors Path. Look around the rocks, there might be more turkey tracks and other carvings. Check it out good," Louis advised.

"Mr. Eversole, may I take you and your wife's picture?" Jennifer politely requested.

"Why, I don't see why not."

After the photographs were completed and the group loaded up, they headed back home to Frankfort. Now they had all new information and an appreciation for both the famous legend and at least one searcher of the treasure.

"I noticed you never showed him the silver arrowhead," Jennifer said as they drove west on the interstate.

"No, I was afraid it would have been a bit too much," Will said.

Ray agreed. What they did know was that they needed to regroup and refigure the meaning of the map. They also knew they had found not one, but two, turkey track carvings much closer to the Warriors Path than the one they had seen on the rock bridge.

Nine:
Swift Draws a Map

The weather made a turn for the worse getting much colder. The snow had continued falling throughout the night. Now fresh snow, six or seven inches deep covered everything. John Swift had a good warm fire burning from the ample supply of dried wood he and George Mundy had gathered during their previous visits to the camp. Their rock shelter provided safety from the environmental elements not to mention the added protection from any wild animal looking for an easy meal. John Finley began to wake from his first good night's sleep in three days."

"John, I am going out to kill us something fresh to eat today. With this snow we'll need to lay in for a few days. You need to eat some food to build your strength. I shouldn't be gone long with this much snow. First, I'm going to go up and check on the horses, make sure they have enough dried grass to last 'em while I'm gone."

"That'll be good. I appreciate what you have done for me. I very likely would have died if you had not come along. I am indebted to you, Mr. Swift."

"You would have done the same for me, no doubt."

"Nevertheless, I am eternally grateful to you."

"While I'm up there, if the snow lets up, I'll take a look from the top of the cliff above us here to see if there is anything going on down at the Shawnee town. Fire a shot if you need me. I should be back by afternoon with something to eat," Swift said. And with that Swift headed out of the rock shelter and began his climb to the top of Pilot Knob. What should only take few minutes, took much longer trudging through the half foot of snow that had fallen in the night. Swift was especially interested in the situation down in the destroyed Shawnee Town of Eskippakithiki. He made his way to the high ledge and a protruding rock. The clouds had begun to break up and the snow was now limited to intense isolated squalls. This allowed for partial views of the horizon. Swift scanned the skyline for any signs of life. Shawnee town, or what was left of it, barely stood out in the white landscape. There wasn't any movement, not a single person or thing moving around out in the flat plain. He brushed the snow from the rock and sat down. Swift used his knife to carefully carve a turkey track into the rock. The soft sandstone yielded grain by grain as Swift cut back and forth on the stone. Satisfied he and Finley were alone in the immediate area for the time being, Swift turned and walked out the long ridge to find his horses standing with their hindquarters braced against the cold, westerly winds. Snow covered their backs. The horses had pawed and nosed away the snow to find the dry grasses. They were doing fine, Swift reckoned, so he moved on in search of something to kill for their next few meals.

Feeling much better after a restful night's sleep, John Finley sat by the fire and stared out into the distance at the fresh snow. What happened to the Shawnee? Where had they gone? Would they be back to rebuild their town? John thought. Then there is Swift. What was he doing there and how did he find me?

John added more wood to the fire and lay back down on his crude bed of leaves and pine needles. Finley, although exhausted from his ordeal, felt much better this morning. He could move about, more or less hobble and drag his injured leg along to move around. By mid afternoon John heard a shot in the distance toward the east. Three hours later Swift returned to the cave carrying a deer half rib cage over his shoulder.

"Got us some real food here John. This will do you good and me too," Swift simply stated as he threw down the fresh meat and began butchering it into smaller pieces. Swift cut the venison into chunks and began to sear it quickly on the hot stones around the fire to seal in the juices. If he let the meat sear in the flames, it would have cooked too fast and would be tough to chew. He learned long ago that game tasted much better if cooked slowly on flat, heated rocks placed within the fire; and moving the meat to different areas of the hot rock controlled the temperature so the meat cooked more slowly which made it more tender and easier to chew. Both men ate until they could hold no more that evening. Swift made a strong coffee from the supply of coffee tree beans he'd placed in a gourd and hung on the back wall of the shelter. Pioneers often used these beans from the coffee tree as a substitute when they ran out of their regular coffee supplies. The coffee was made by drying, roasting and pulverizing the seeds and then boiling the grounds. He and Mundy gathered the beans on previous spring trips from a large stand of coffee trees near the Big Spring. He figured they would be there for several more days until John Finley was strong enough to travel, or if he chose he could stay at the camp. Leaving John Finley here would not be the right thing to do, Swift considered. The weather could get worse and finding his way would get more difficult. This could be a problem, he thought. In any case, Swift knew he would leave when the weather improved.

John Swift liked John Finley. He admired Finley's guts to set up a trading post right there in Shawnee Town. And Finley had been nice and civil toward him even after he had been told about the "trouble" back in Virginia. Besides, it is good to have a friend in this hostile country. Swift decided he would stay, keep the food and fire going for John Finley, and deal with the questions Finley was bound to ask as he got better.

A week passed and John Finley was up and about. The weather had improved greatly with warming temperatures the snow melted away rapidly. John had his strength back thanks to the solid meals his friend provided. Although sore from his wounds, John had prevented infection, thanks partly to the dried up wild Comphrey he found on the creek bank. But it was mostly due to the cauterization from the hot blade of Swift's knife.

"I think I will be ready to head out tomorrow," Finley announced one evening.

"That so," Swift commented.

"Yes, I think I have my strength back pretty good and can travel, maybe not as fast as I like but I can get around. It would be much easier if you sold me one of those horses. I don't have anything to buy it with but I will make good on getting you payment with fair interest," Finley suggested.

"John, I wish I could but I can't sell you my horse. I need them for my business interests you see."

"Well, then, I reckon I'll walk."

"Where are you going to go now that your store is gone?" Swift asked.

"I guess I'll head north up the Warriors Path to the river, maybe just head on back east. Unless you still need a partner in that business you offered back in Shawnee Town," Finley skillfully stated.

"I don't know, if you're up to it yet." Swift remarked.

"Well, I'm not hundred percent, for sure, but I can't stay here any longer either. If you're not gonna take me in on that partner deal or sell me one of those horses I guess I'll head on out in the morning. I do want you to know I appreciate all that you have done for me. I was a goner' for sure if you had not come along."

Swift hesitated, "There are things you need to know and I can promise you things will be changed for you from now on if you join in with me. Understand, John?"

"Well, as long as I don't have to kill anyone I expect there is little that can surprise me," Finley jokingly remarked. John really didn't have a clue to what Swift was eluding to but expected he was about to find out.

John Swift had to make the call now, whether or not he should let John Finley in on his fantastic secret. That would mean once again he would have to split the riches. He reckoned there was plenty for the both of them and then some. George Mundy had become dissatisfied with his share and wanted more. That could not stand as far as he was concerned. John Finley sensed that Swift was thinking the idea over and the long silence became increasingly uncomfortable.

"Well, John, am I in or not?" John Finley asked.

"I need to tell you some things, very private things. Only George Mundy and now you, when I tell you, will know these things. I am talking about amazing things you will find hard to believe. Believe me, this is all true."

"My store, my furs, and my fortune, everything is gone! I have to start over, so I doubt that there is little I wouldn't believe right now."

"Do you remember the silver arrowhead you gave old George back in Shawnee town last summer?"

"Yes I do. I traded for a few other things with some of the Shawnee but never got those rascals to tell me where they came up with the silver. I kept watching for more to be traded but nothing else showed up."

"Well, they got the silver from me and George."

"They got the silver from you and George?"

"Yes. We would trade them silver to get them to help us on occasion. But that is not important. What is important is where the silver came from in the first place," Swift added.

"You traded silver with the Shawnee," Finley repeated to make sure he understood what he had just heard.

John Swift knew that when he continued his secret would now be shared with another. This would change their friendship forever, Swift knew that. But he needed help to get his riches out and John Finley was the only person he knew in the wilderness well respected back east. The question he had in his mind was whether or not Finley would accept him when he knew the truth; who he really was. He was about to find out.

"That's correct. It was original silver George and I acquired. The Shawnee just fashioned the silver into something more useful for their purposes."

"Where did you and George get the silver?"

"I'm coming to that point, just let me explain very clearly. It's a little more detailed than just where we got it."

"I don't understand."

"Let me tell you a little more about me and my previous business," Swift began.

John Finley sat up and listened as Swift began to explain. He couldn't figure out in his mind what direction Swift was headed in this explanation.

"John, in not too many years we will end up in an all out war with England. Back east in nearly every section of the country people are increasingly becoming upset with the King's control; unfair taxes, pointless laws and requirements. A rebellion is on the horizon. The political people increasingly talk about separation and forming our own country. I am much in favor of it myself. I have been for several years now."

"Well, it's a good reason to be out here, the way I see it," Finley remarked.

"For several years I commanded my own ship and owned a few more. One English ship, two Spanish-made ships, and one ship made in Boston. I believed in, and continue to this day believe what we did was honorable, but some might say my business was not exactly legitimate."

"What do you mean?"

"Well, the fact of the matter my associates and I spent a lot of time waging our own private war against the King. We would take into custody any English ships we came upon. Occasionally a Spanish ship also, but never a ship under a colony or French flag."

"You mean you are a pirate?" John knew quite well that boarding and taking a ship was an act of piracy. John never met any pirates since most had either been caught, hanged or had simply disappeared into some other part of the world. John Finley also knew this information changed his relationship with John Swift; that much he was sure of.

"The English called us pirates and some of the colonist too, but they didn't understand. Our efforts aimed to do as much harm to the Crown as possible. Most people had grown tired of the rules, taxation, and restrictions handed down by the King. We did our part, we thought.

"So you pirated English ships headed to the colonies."

"Sometimes we would capture ships carrying a lot of gold and silver. The Spanish ships had a lot of gold and silver and we took those only because of circumstances in and around Cuba. My associates and I made our main effort to hurt the King, when ship loads of crowns where headed for the colonies."

John being aware dealing with pirates was both risky and deadly business, felt nothing good would come from falling in with the likes. But it didn't sound all that bad hearing Swift's explanation and even seemed patriotic. If Swift was a pirate making a fuss now could present a very awkward situation, especially since Swift has risked his own life by staying behind to nurse him back to health. John Finley knew he was in a situation now.

"We worked out of Virginia mostly, and we did legitimately transport goods. Fortunately we never got caught for the ship boarding activities."

"Most of the pirates have been caught and hanged. How did you escape that?"

"Usually we sailed to and from Cuba and the islands bringing goods back and forth. An occasional trip to France and England of course, kept us unnoticed. I still own in partnership in one ship now under another captain. He and the crew are not in my former business. We have a regular trade route mostly passengers now."

"What about George?'"

"He was my first mate on the ship I commanded. I sold the Spanish ships. The English ship grounded and we scuttled her. My Boston built ship is the one I still own in partners with the current Captain. It's all above board and legal.

"Anyway, when times were good we managed to capture one English ship with a whole cargo of English Crowns headed for the colonies. We took the ship, the silver and anything else. We then scuttled the ship and marooned the crew in a place so they could be found and rescued. Me, George, and a few of the crew brought the crowns down the great river and found a safe location to hide them."

"You mean you brought silver crowns into this country and hid them?"

"George and I make a trip about once or twice a year to carry out some of the silver to live on and support our ship trading business. Crowns trade well in the colonies."

"So George and some more of the crew are in on this deal with you?"

"Just George and now he up and skip jacked on me."

"What happened to the rest of the crew? Don't they want more of the loot?"

"They received their agreed share. Some are on my ship now and some, well, some have died or moved on. These were good men, though. Don't doubt it. They felt as strongly about the terrible unfairness the King is putting on the poor people here in the Americas."

"Well, I guess. Pirates? They are a pretty rough bunch and don't most people along the coast hate pirates?" John question as he attempt to resolve the issue in his mind

Swift looked at John with a dead serious stare. Now came the time for John to balk on the deal if he was ever going too. Swift had begun to run various scenarios in his mind knowing he would choose a course of action depending on John Finley's response. Swift liked John and wanted him to be a partner. If Finley balked on the deal Swift knew he could not hesitate to silence him. Swift was prepared to do that, too.

"They do publicly, but only for fear of punishment from the King of England. Don't you see John, the colonies in America are going to break away and I believe sooner than later. If not, no one will ever acquire anything; England will keep us too poor. The fact is in private most people consider pirates heroes. After all, the money is often spent in taverns and stores along the coast."

"So there is a hidden treasure of silver crowns somewhere here in the wilderness?"

"Yes, and beyond anything you can imagine John. We made three trips over three months to get all the silver into this country. The majority of the treasure is silver crowns but there are some silver ingots and a few gold items. Most of the gold, we have already taken out. To be on the safe side I had the men carry the silver to one location. After they left, George and I, with our pack horses, moved the silver to a safer, more secure location. We spent one whole summer to get it all moved."

"Why haven't the crew who helped you come searching for your hiding place? Surely they came looking for more when they run out of their share or tell someone else."

"Some might, for sure, but my guess is they all moved on to other adventures out to sea. They weren't much for wilderness; the sea is their home."

"I understand," John acknowledged.

"So there it is except where the silver is located. Only two people in the world know the location, and you'll be the third."

"Sure sounds like a good thing to me and explains why I never saw either you or George with any furs, ever. I always wondered what you two actually did out here in this wild country. Makes sense now. And those heavy packs you carried, I guess they were full of silver."

"Of course. We carried out between us and a couple of horses enough silver to have several good months of high style living back in Virginia or wherever we decided to go. Personally, I sailed a lot. Since I have a ship, most folks thought we were doing very well in the shipping trade. Sometimes we did take a load of furs to England. The ship does manage to pay the mates and bring in a little profit. These silver crowns out here in the wilderness are much more profitable; I can tell you for certain."

"I'm in, but I must ask why would you bring me in since I did nothing to help you gain this treasure? What will George say?" John asked.

"First, let me say George is a loyal first mate. He wouldn't question my decision to bring in a third partner. Besides, George, I think, is out of the business. He most likely has found other interests and all the silver he needs from our many previous trips. I have not heard from him, something could have happened to him, injured, sick or something. I suspect we'll not be hearing much from George in the future, but if we do, he is a full partner. Trust me John, we stashed more silver stored in that well hidden cave than you and I and George will ever use in our life time."

"That much silver? And you want me to partner up with you and George?"

"Yes, it really takes two men to get out a good supply of silver. Stream crossings, food gathering and just dealing with the Shawnee is a lot for one man. You also get along real well with the Shawnee and if we get caught by a group of angry Shawnee hunters you might be an asset to me these days," Swift continued.

"Like I said, I'm in."

"I tell you what; tomorrow we'll head for the cave."

"Where is the cave, how far, in what direction?"

"Two full days ride from here. Here, let me show you. I'd planned to mark down the directions to the cave somewhere, in case I get turned around, so I can still find the cave. I can also use my ship instruments to plot the latitude and longitude, but I might not have those things with me on a trip. A good, safe directional map only we know would be good for both of us. Especially you should anything ever happen to me." Swift drew his knife and walked to the back of the dry shelter and on the flat rock wall of sandstone began carving out a crude map. He put unusual symbols and drew lines that representing known landmarks in the area. Swift carved turkey tracks and other strange markings. He carved each symbol fairly deep into the soft sandstone rock, stopping to explain to John each symbols meaning. Each symbol, Swift explained, was a location in the region. One only needed to find the location represented by a symbol to put themselves in real position to locate the cave. It was simple and crude. There was no need for details, just symbols such as lines, turkey tracks, an eye shape and several small x's. With Swift's narrative as he finished carving out each part of the map, John grasped the general location, but knew he had to visit the cave in order to understand the true hidden location.

"Well, I'll be. I'll bet I still couldn't find the cave by myself if I tried to with the map," John said laughing.

"I can't put too much information up, John. Those Shawnee and who knows who else will be up here under this cliff for one reason or another and they will probably find this map. One partner is all I need. They will not find the cave based on this map," Swift confidently asserted.

Ten:
Warriors Path Solved

Back at the Brick Yard Will moved into his routine. He usually showed up around one or two in the afternoon and got his bar station set up. Bar tending was an easy job although certainly one Will never intended to do his whole life. He planned to go back and finish school, get his degree in geology, and get a job with an oil company taking him to interesting places. The loss of his parents sidetracked such plans presently. With a healthy life insurance policy and the family farm, Will's plans had been put on hold. In the mean time he simply worked at the bar as a matter of both doing something and meeting interesting people. Jennifer went out of town for a couple days to visit one of her old school friends in Bowling Green. Jennifer didn't have any special urgent assignments from the newspaper, making this a good time to take the trip she had planned all year. Ray always back at the shop with work found himself backlogged as usual. Roger Hampton stopped by to check on his car, though he now didn't seem so urgent to pick it up. After Ray did not get the car repaired by the Saturday morning deadline, Roger thought he would make Ray and the garage wait on him.

"Ray is my car ready *now*?" Roger sarcastically remarked.

"Yes sir. Your car is ready. We had to order a new computer module."

"Well, Ray, you little shit, you caused me a lot of trouble this weekend."

"How's that, Mr. Hampton?"

"You were off farting around in the woods, chasing after some kind of Stonehenge or something, instead of being here, doing your job."

"We couldn't get the part until today so it didn't make any difference. And it wasn't Stonehenge; it was a rock carving! Your car is done and the keys are up front."

"Ray, what about the rock carving?"

"Nothing, but some rock carvings, up in the Red River Gorge, that's all." Roger Hampton smart and cunning, could read people well enough to know that Ray Deevers knew more than he was telling. Roger thought he would keep an eye on Ray and maybe even do a little detective work himself.

"Did you miss me? Jennifer asked.

"Yes I did, baby. Always do. Can I come over tonight after work?" Will asked, hoping for an invitation.

"Honey, I just walked in the door and I am tired. By the time you get off work I will be sound asleep. I am going to take a hot bath and sleep in my own bed tonight. Okay?"

"Sure, okay. I just missed you."

"I missed you, too. One thing; we went to the library and did a little research on early Kentucky history."

"What did you find?"

"A lot of good stuff. We even found a couple books about the John Swift Silver mine legend. We found one neat thing, an early map of Kentucky."

"What about the map?" Will asked.

"The map included, plain as day, the Warriors Path. Did you ever hear of John Filson?"

"Seems like I have but I don't recall the details. I suppose an early pioneer since he made an early map, right?"

"Well, yes, but he also wrote the first book ever written about Kentucky. With his book he drew this map, probably one of the first maps of Kentucky. Looking at the map the Warriors Path is as big as anything. And guess what else?"

"What?"

"The Warriors Path goes right by Pilot Knob and Indian Old Fields."

"Well, I'll be damned," Will declared.

"The Warriors Path goes right by Pilot Knob and Eskippakithiki or whatever the place is called," Jennifer exclaimed, nearly breathless from excitement.

"I made copies of the map and some important pages from some of the books. I also copied Swift's journal from one of the books I came across. Thought it might be useful."

"Wow, wonderful, baby. Let's go back to Pilot Knob this weekend, how about it?"

"Okay by me, what about Ray?"

"Sure, ol'e Ray has been this far with us on this thing, can't leave him out now."

"Good, I thought the same thing."

"Now go on and take your bath and get some rest. I'll call you tomorrow."

On Saturday morning the three met at a restaurant in downtown Frankfort and had breakfast. The three ate perhaps too much food for a hard morning walk, but the country cooking was just too good to pass up. By pure chance, and bad luck, Ray thought, Roger Hampton sat in the next booth. Of all the people, Ray thought. Roger ate breakfast here every morning. Roger considered this his favorite hangout most mornings. So, this was not unusual for Roger to be seated in a booth with coffee and a newspaper. Will chose this particular place this morning only because Jennifer often liked to meet him here.

"Where are we headed for today?" Ray inquired in a low voice. Ray now became uncomfortable talking about anything with Roger Hampton so close by.

"Pilot Knob," Will whispered back, picking up on the hint to keep talk low.

"Why are we going back again? We only found the one silver arrowhead," Ray dropped his voice now to almost an inaudible whisper.

"Warriors Path, the Warriors Path, Ray. It passes right through the area somewhere, maybe even right by the Knob."

"How do you figure that?"

"I found a map with the Warriors Path clearly marked. The trail went right through the area, crossed the Red River and everything," Jennifer explained.

"What map? I mean where did you find a map and are you sure it is the real thing?"

"It's real alright, Ray, believe us."

Roger Hampton had been pretending to read the morning paper, but became more focused on listening in on this interesting conversation in the booth next to him. Roger had heard the silver arrowhead mentioned and having had the conversation with Ray earlier, felt the three were on to something of interest to him. Not the silver arrowhead of course, but the land supposedly the treasure came from would be worth a lot of money, and someone would surely want to make a deal. Roger finished his coffee, left money on the table and got up to leave. He turned and pretended to notice Ray for the first time.

"You out rock hunting again this weekend Ray?"

"I doubt it," Ray grumbled.

"Hey, Ray, I was only making a comment. I mean I couldn't help from overhearing you talk about going up in the mountains, maps and silver arrowheads and all."

"We are going for a hike up in the Gorge country. Good fresh air and exercise after a week of hard work," Will inserted.

"Just having some fun, Roger, that's all," Jennifer added.

"I see. Well, if you find any buried treasure call me and I'll help you spend the money," Roger said laughing walking out the door.

"That son of bi...," Ray started to say.

"Hush Ray, don't be that way," Jennifer interrupted in a whisper before Ray could get it all out.

"Don't tell me not to be that way!"

"Ray, are you all right?" Jennifer asked, shocked by Ray's quick recoil to her reprimand.

"Come on, lets go," Will said. He'd had enough and was disgusted with Ray and Roger, but mostly with himself for allowing their conversation to be overheard. Will and Jennifer had no way of knowing Ray had already sparked Roger Hampton's interest by his outburst in the shop.

Will fully prepared for the outing with a cooler iced down, snacks water, and of course, Will's trusty survival backpack.

"I am not going without something to dig with this time," Will said pointing to the small utility shovel he had thrown in the back of the truck.

"Well, you did pretty well with a stick and your bare hands the last time. Do you think you might find some more silver under that rock?" Ray said jokingly.

Roger sat in his car looking through his list of appointments for the day and had not pulled out yet. The three partners laughed and joked as they drove off, so absorbed in their day's planned adventure they didn't even notice Roger Hampton's Lexus slowly pulling out behind them on the one-way street and followed them at a distance out of town. Roger followed them all the way to the mountain.

The climb up the long mountain trail seemed less strenuous this trip. Perhaps the three explorers had become accustomed to the trail or perhaps they simply better paced themselves as they were aware of the trails steep accent at the top. In either case, within an hour, the three stood under the ledge and stared intently at the giant map carved on the rock wall in the back of the shelter.

"Let's assume this line is the Warriors Path and the two lines at the top are the Ohio River, this turkey track is by the Warriors Path," Will reasoned aloud.

"But I thought Louis Eversole said turkey tracks usually indicate a direction."

"He did."

"So this one is pointing toward, uh, Lexington? Well, not the mountains anyway," Ray responded.

"So what's the plan guys?" Jennifer asked.

"Ray, is there any kind of notable thing west of here you can think of? Like a cave, river or anything noticeable two hundred years ago?" Will questioned. If turkey tracks, he thought, pointed a direction, then there must be some destination to be reached by going in that direction.

"Nothing I can think of right off the top of my head."

"Look, hold the map up like the Warriors Path shows on the Filson map, those marks there might be the Indian Old Fields--the Shawnee town," Jennifer said.

"And your point, Jennifer?" Will asked.

"Okay, if the Warriors Path goes by near here, and I think the Filson map indicates the trail does, Louis himself said it was down here somewhere. I think the Warriors Path would go right to, by, or near the Shawnee town, wouldn't it?"

"Anyway, the wall map carving has a bunch of marks here. See, look for yourself. If there is a turkey track carved here on this rock somewhere pointing west, I'll guess that is the old Shawnee village," Jennifer concluded.

"Well, we know there is turkey track here in this shelter on the wall. Heck, how about this big one right in the middle of the carving," Ray added.

"If this is some kind of map carved on the wall, these turkey tracks only represent the real thing somewhere else. I mean, what if those marks really do represent the old Shawnee town out there?"

"If that's what this means, then this rock shelter, this mountain, is part of the map. We could be standing on the spot indicated by this small turkey track. For all we know there might be a turkey track carved up on top of the cliff above us somewhere. At least that is the way it seems to me."

"You might be right," Ray agreed.

"One way to find out. Let's go," Will said.

Back up the cliff trail they scrambled one more time. Once on top of the high vantage point, they took in the view and again just as breath taking as the day a couple of weeks ago that Jennifer took her photographs. They had not considered looking for carvings up here on top. It was windy today and the breeze rustled through the thick stand of Virginia pines as they reached the summit.

"Wow, this is beautiful up here," Jennifer commented.

"Okay, look at all the exposed, bare rock and check carefully. Let's spread out. Check everything including the names carved in the rock. Some idiot may have carved right over the tracks. Up here if there is such a marking it would be pretty much worn away just like the one on Rock Bridge," Will said.

The bare rock at the most prominent point of the mountain was divided in three sections. Each person took their section and set about the task of looking at every inch of the exposed rock. This was no easy task, but the idea of the silver arrowhead Will had in his pocket and the bones of a dead human in the rock shelter down below kept them searching. They found plenty of carvings but they had been carved in the past few years by kids who made the long hike up the mountain. Will looked out over the valley below while Ray and Jennifer finished searching their section of the exposed sandstone rock creating the top of Pilot Knob.

"The Warriors Path likely came right down that way, along the edge of the hills and probably hit this creek below and went right by the Indian Old Fields north along these mountains. Nice smooth trail right on up to the Ohio River, I'd bet." Will surmised.

"In one of the books I checked out at the library this week, I found out the creek down there was named by Daniel Boone and John Finley. They called the creek Lulbegrud after the people in the book 'Gulliver's Travels,' which Boone said he and his party read on their trip during evening campfires," Jennifer said.

"No kiddin'," Ray remarked.

"Yes and according to this book, Boone and his party were attacked by some Indians which they fought off, and jokingly one of them said, 'I guess we got rid of those Lublegruds.' They decided they would call the creek and their campsite Camp Lulbegrud. The next day Boone supposedly climbed to this knob, this place we are standing and viewed for himself the beautiful levels of Kentucky."

"Boone never said whether John Finley told him about his store operation at Eskippakithiki," Jennifer continued.

"Whoa, wait a minute here, what store operation? You mean in the Indian Old Fields?" Will asked.

"Yes, according to the book I told you about, John Finley spent time in this area much earlier and actually had some kind of trading store in the Shawnee village. Boone had asked Finley to guide him to Kentucky in 1769 after his first failed attempt in 1767. "

"Well, *Gulliver's Travels* was written way back in the 1600's by none other than one Jonathon Swift! Get it? JOHN Swift!" Jennifer proudly explained. She was confident this was no coincidence.

"You've got to be kidding," Will said.

"Boone and Finley were supposed to be up here on this very rock too? You don't suppose they had something to do with the rock carving below do you?" Ray questioned.

"Well, sure is one hell of a strange coincidence when you think about it," Will said.

The three sat on the rock for a while, each pondering the events. Will decided to read *Gulliver's Travels* tonight when they got home.

"I've thought of something. The rock shelter is not directly below us here. It is farther around the ridge top. Maybe the turkey track is above the rock shelter," Will suddenly said.

"What would make you think it made any difference?" Ray asked.

"No reason, only a wild guess. It's not here at this spot and probably doesn't exist at all. But if it is on this mountain we should check directly above the rock shelter," Will concluded.

The three jumped to their feet instantly and started off around the edge of the high cliff. In a few minutes they reached the precise spot directly above the rock shelter. There was little bare rock exposed here, but enough on the edge for Ray to see it.

"Well, I'll be damned! Here we go!" Ray yelled.

Will and Jennifer rushed over to see the faint but still very visible turkey track. The track pointed west. Now they could assume the one on the wall map below represented this one on the top of the cliff. The three had a since of direction and an idea of what the map actually represented.

"Okay, guys, this track points like the map below shows." Will pulled out the drawing they had made of the rock wall map and aligned it with the turkey track.

"Let's assume the one line carved on the wall is the Warriors Path, this line here. Whether it means anything or not, the carving down below is a map of sorts because we found this marking by following the map!"

"At least this turkey track appears to be located on the map."

"Okay, now there is this turkey track and it points west. These marks here, as Jennifer has already figured out, are the Shawnee town. This turkey track points to something west beyond the Indian Old Fields, but what? Then west of that is a big turkey track pointing north. How far north? How would we ever find it? Will had more questions than answers. Neither Jennifer nor Ray could make anything completely rational out of the situation.

"Logically, with this prominent place, and if the Indian Old Fields are correct, likely a significant place is west of here. Perhaps the Lost Silver mine of John Swift! Ooooh!" Jennifer jokingly remarked.

"Will, this is going to be near impossible to sort out. I don't know. Never heard of anything west of here unless you count Lexington," Ray said.

"We need to do a little more homework, guys," Jennifer said.

The three walked back down the mountain to the public parking lot. The Nature Conservancy, owners of Pilot Knob, provided parking and the well marked trail system resulting in cars always being in the lot. The explorers never paid any attention to the other two cars in the parking lot. One of them was Roger Hampton's vehicle.

Eleven:
Swift takes Finley to the Treasure

The air warmed through the night, not comfortably warm, but enough to be noticeable at daybreak. From the protection of the rock shelter facing west toward the Shawnee town, John watched the sunlight hitting the tops of the trees in front of the protective rock ledge. John sat by the fire awake, studying the markings Swift had scratched on the wall the previous night pondering his present situation. He knew he had to make a life changing decision this morning. Swift carefully gathered his gear together for his pack occasionally glancing at John, looking for any kind of reaction. If he went with Swift he will become part of his life of pirating and who knows what. If he backed out now what would be Swift's reaction? John weighed out his situation back and forth in his mind unable to commit firmly.

"You going to get ready to go John?"

Shaken from his thought John responded with little hesitation. "Yes, I'll be ready presently." He had made his decision, for better or worse, besides, he thought things couldn't get much worse than what he had already lived through. Traveling with the man who saved him from dying and offering a fortune with no strings attached, did not sound bad at all. In fact, his misfortunes are making a turn for the better, much better, he figured.

"About how far are we from the treasure?" John inquired. Now knowing he was committed to becoming involved in this new adventure, he wanted more details and felt comfortable about asking.

"We have a good distance to go. I hope we can make the Big Springs by dark. The trip should take us two days, maybe a little more."

"Big Springs? Where is that?"

"Well, John, it's due west of the Shawnee...,well what's left of Shawnee Town, down there. I'd say about twenty miles, as the crow flies."

Swift walked over to John and began to kick the dry sand of the rock shelter into the fire. There was no need to leave anyone, especially hostile Indians, any knowledge of their recent stay at this campsite. After Swift put out the camp fire, he packed most of his gear on the horses tied to trees below the rock shelter. The horses bit and gnawed on the bark of the trees, already bored from waiting to get started off the mountain. Swift had already fed the animals the dry grasses he had stored in the shelter from the previous fall. Since the rock shelter provided a good, safe place, Swift and Mundy made a habit to gather up grasses and store in the dry rock shelter for their animals as they made trips. Out on the open savannahs the animals found grasses even in the winter but up here high on the mountain any food to sustain the beasts would have to be brought up the mountain. During some of their stay, Swift would put the animals on top of the knob. On the north side the land gently sloped and had an abundance of wild grasses. A short fence of vines and rope along one side and the sheer cliff drop-off on the other three sides made for a good corral. But in his hasty effort to get John to the dry, safety of the rock shelter, Swift did not take time to fence the horses on the top of the mountain as he routinely done. John

Finley got his gear together, which consisted of very little, since he had lost everything he owned at the Shawnee town destruction.

"About this map. Which one of these symbols represents the place we are going?" John studied the carved map. Swift pointed to the peculiar eye-shaped symbol.

"That is the Big Spring I've been talking about. This is a good place to camp, kind of protected, and a good water supply out in the flat country. The Shawnee know all about it, but not many hunters, but a few I suppose, have heard of the place."

"Is the treasure cave located there?"

"Well, there are caves for sure, but not the hiding place for the silver. No, the cave keeping my treasure safe is a much better place to remain hidden, even from those nosey Shawnee."

"Why are we going to this Big Spring? Why don't we head straight to the cave?"

"Well, for one thing we can't get to the cave today. We need a good place to stay tonight. We always, always, have to be careful approaching our treasure cave. Do you understand John?"

"Yes, of course, I understand. I didn't mean to be so pushy on the matter, I'm sorry for asking so many questions. You know what we need to do and when to do it. Pay no mind to me." John realized he might be pushing a little too much too fast. After all, he had agreed to be John Swift's new partner, replacing Swift's old buddy George Mundy. John realized he had better ease back a bit. "The Big Spring is a landmark to set your bearing to the cave, right?"

"Correct John, good. Of course, you can think like a seaman if you set your mind to it."

"How did you come across it? The springs, I mean, and well, the cave as well?"

"Shawnee told Mundy and me sometime ago about the springs. The cave, well we kept looking and found the perfect spot, we thought, and so far we've been right. Coming from the east trail we always use the springs as first night's camp on our way to the treasure cave. We need to get going, though. We are more than four hours from Shawnee Town. We might not even make Big Spring today."

Over the course of the next few hours, John Swift and John Finley headed down the mountain and out across the flat plain. The two crossed the Warriors Path near the edge of the vast plain stretching north and south from the town. The Warriors Path followed the largest creek in the area but ran closer to the edge of the flat plain, no doubt the route used for many years, and the easiest and fastest way to travel by foot. The creek was the same creek where Swift had found Finley half starved and close to death only a few days ago.

The two men approached the burned and destroyed town. They made an extra effort of vigilance not knowing the situation of possible hostiles lurking about. The Shawnee had not returned. Only a few days ago the town of Eskippakithiki had been busy and alive with activity. Children played, women ground dried meats and vegetables into a powder meal and warriors chipped flint and mended bows for their hunts. Now all the activities of a busy everyday life stood ghostly quite and still. The eerie sight gave both veteran woodsmen an uncomfortable feeling. The two figured the whole town had fled and relocated somewhere else. Those killed or injured had been removed. Swift and Finley spent a few minutes rummaging through the remains of his store site. The hut was burned and his furs gone. Only a few stones and metal items lay among the burned out rubble. Anything of value had been carted off by the invaders. The two crossed over the town and headed west. Swift would stop now and again, take out a compass and realign his direction. As the day progressed, Swift continued to stop and calculate his direction. He stayed off the major trail to the river falls from Eskippakithiki but followed in a parallel direction about a mile to the south of the trail.

The two travelers reached their destination late in the day, nearly dark, in fact. The sight of the spring was a welcome relief from the long trip. The water boiled up from beneath the earth in crystal clear pools. John had not seen anything quite like this during his time in the wilderness. The spring was located in a large depression with plenty of grasses and cover so they could build a fire hidden from view by others who happened to be in the area. Both men had concerns about the Iroquois. If they were caught by the Iroquois the situation would be bad, no doubt. The various Indian tribes all seemed to be in a upset and hostile mood. There was large amount of open grass lands around them where bison often foraged during migrations through the area. The bison were always moving through, searching for good grassland. No doubt some hunters would be following the bison. John Finley built a fire from the scattered dry limbs in the little valley while Swift cleaned the squirrel he had shot from a big Burr oak tree not long before they got to the springs. Swift found a green sapling, cut it and sharpened both ends. With one end Swift carefully skewered the squirrel onto the stick and stuck the other end into the dirt, angled over the coals. The squirrel began to cook in short order on the hastily made spit. Both men settled down by the fire after John had gathered an armload of firewood. For a long time there was little conversation.

"Tomorrow we will arrive at the forks of three streams. The cave is located on one of the streams, not far from the mouth," Swift said as they settled down and built a small fire.

"How much further?"

"Not as far as we came today, so with an early start we should make the forks by late afternoon."

"The silver head, the arrowhead, it's made from the same silver," John suddenly blurted out as if he had solved a riddle.

"Yes, the silver arrowhead. The Shawnee took the crowns we paid them and beat them into objects important to them. They liked the silver, not the crowns. The Shawnee, of course, have no use for money but they do need tools to work and hunt with."

"Oh, I see," now John understood.

"What did you get in return from the Shawnee?"

"Not killed, mostly."

"Like my trade beads and metal knives?"

"Sometimes some warriors are not happy about white men in this country killing their game; and they do consider this country and everything here for their purposes and others are intruders. So from time to time depending on the occasion, we would pass along a few crowns to the Shawnee for directions and mostly for them not to follow us."

"Ah, makes sense. Old George took the silver arrowhead from me like he'd never heard of such a thing, when all along he knew exactly where the silver came from, didn't he?"

"I reckon he, we, did. But we couldn't let anyone know of our secret treasure, not even a good feller like you, John."

"I see. I suppose that's the way I'd done it too."

"Well, now you know, John, and tomorrow you'll find out for yourself. Do you reckon that squirrel is done?" Swift tried to conclude the conversation.

"We have been heading west most of the day but the big turkey track you drew on the wall back at the camp was pointing north. Why is it pointed north?" John asked.

"You sure are full of questions John. You'll understand tomorrow. It'll all make sense then. The first time I came into this country when we hid the stuff we headed south away from the big river. A few places along the way I left some markings, turkey tracks and stuff to help us find our way back to the site. Not all of the markings indicate direction, though," Swift explained.

"This spring is due west of Shawnee town and the cliff camp," John surmised.

"Pilot Knob," Swift said.

"Pilot Knob?" John questioned.

"Yes, Mundy and I named our camp under the cliff. It's a good lookout spot, agreed?" Swift explained.

"Yes sir, it surely is a good lookout."

"Like the ship pilot's lookout." Swift added grinning.

"That reminds me, a little cave is located down the creek here and in the cave I carved a symbol with the coordinates of the treasure. Remember, I marked this spot, this spring here, on the map back at the rock shelter. I put those numbers here, so if I can at least find this spring, I can find my navigation to the cave. Ah, just part of a seaman's habits, I guess.

Both Swift and John awoke before dawn. They broke camp, chewed on some jerky, rounded up the horses and headed west out of the sink. John had begun to imagine what the treasure room would be like. As they walked along, watching the sun come up over their right shoulders, Swift motioned to stop. John froze in his tracks, watching Swift. John moved his eyes around as far as he could, scanning the horizon trying to detect what had spooked Swift.

"The Great Falls trail to Shawnee Town is up ahead," Swift whispered.

"I doubt if there will be any Shawnee traveling today," John commented.

"There might be some others, perhaps Iroquois roaming around these parts. We can't take a chance."

"This is the trail Mundy and I used to followed those Shawnee to their town," John observed.

After crossing the path Finley had come down a little more than a year ago he couldn't recognize anything at this crossing. By mid-afternoon they descended down into the gorge of a great river. John remembered crossing this river but did not recognize anything from this direction. Swift made sure they would only cross the Great Falls trail at the river crossing.

"Ahead, the three streams that come together," Swift announced and pointed.

"I see it. It sure is three streams coming together. This big one and two more on opposite sides. You don't see that too often or at least I haven't."

"That is why I used it as a landmark. I've found no other place in the region where this happens. We knew these landmarks would not be lost. Find these streams and you are almost to the cave," Swift pointed out.

When the two reached the main river they walked along the river bank down stream. The river could not be crossed easily at this point. They moved along the river bank until they came to the mouth of one of the creeks that flowed into the river. It actually was not much of a creek. It was more like a ditch slowly meandering along with various little pools of water, broken up by some dry sand bars. It looked to John as if it was a creek drying up. True to Swift's map, exactly across the river from where they stood was another stream flowing into the river. The stream across the river was much larger than this small, almost dried up stream the two were presently crossing. John presumed it to be the other prong of the giant turkey track. After they crossed the "dry" creek they continued along the same river bank for another half mile until they reached the ford in the river, the rivers' shallow crossing point.

"This is a bison crossing and the trail to Shawnee Town," Swift said.

"I do remember crossing here when George and I traveled with the Shawnee," John commented.

"This is about the only place to cross the river in either direction for several miles without getting wet unless you got a boat. Our cave is real close but hidden so no one will ever find it."

"How did you find this cave, anyway?"

"Well, that's another story altogether," Swift replied.

"I'd say it probably is, I mean, for you to come this far out to hide all those coins."

"Our first trip into this wild country, we hid coins in various places and from time to time would go back and move some of 'em, just to throw off track the mates helping in the operation. As I told you before, George and I moved the silver to a safer location so only the two of us would know the location. The whole process took us quite a while to move the stuff. I'm sure some of the old crew scouted around looking at the spots we originally hid the stuff. Those who did look were surprised or thinking' they were looking in the wrong place. Originally, we hid the stuff farther east of Pilot Knob and the cliff shelter camp."

"That's pretty clever," John replied.

"We thought so. And, as far as I know, no one ever found the silver, but we won't know that until we get to the cave."

"But how did you find this cave?" John persisted.

"Well, in those days, George and me packed up as much silver as we could carry and headed west. We traded some of the silver with Shawnee to safely pass Shawnee Town. We went way around it, but they left us alone. Well, some of the warriors followed along and would aggravate us until we traded some of those crowns for hides we didn't want. We headed west following buffalo trails until they finally merged here. We decided to hide the silver somewhere near this river. That way, we could if we wanted, float on down the river to the Ohio. It seemed like a good plan at the time but we never used the river."

"So you decided to stop here and hide the silver?"

"Well, when we came to this ford in the river, we crossed and went down the stream, like we are about to do now, to set up camp for the night. Right here at the mouth of this big creek, we noticed the steep cliff area up there. The next morning we decided to climb up in those rocks to see if we could find any caves. And low and behold, there was! The marking of the turkey track was purely accidental, but we did notice while camped, there were streams coming into the river on both sides of the river opposite each other. The rest just fell into place."

Crossing the river they came to a series of gravel bars and shallow areas in the large river. Although the water was very cold it was not frozen. The two navigated their way carefully from one gravel bar to the next trying to avoid stepping into the ice cold river, though it was very shallow and would get little more than their boots wet. They ended up wading across the few places where stones or gravel bars were simply not available to step on.

"They come down off the hill, the bison. I guess they're coming from the Great Falls crossing and this is likely the best place for them to get across the river and get to the good grasslands east of here." Swift conjectured, while pointing and gesturing. "I'd imagine they've been crossing here for hundreds of years," he continued. He had crossed here many times along with his friend George Mundy to replenish their wealth. The men never witnessed the bison crossing, although the evidence of their recent use of the ford was always visible.

Once across the river, the two new partners headed back up the river on the opposite bank. They reached the third stream of the three. Swift stopped and looked around as if to get his bearings.

"We need to go up this stream a piece and we'll be close," Swift announced.

In a few minutes of working their way through thickets of black willows and passing many large sycamore trees, Swift halted the trek. He tied up the horse he led; John Finley did the same.

"We can camp here tonight. We are out of sight of the river and the buffalo crossing. Our fire should not be visible from here," Swift recommended.

"How far to the cave?" John asked.

"It's up there. Right up there," Swift announced pointing up to the ledges high above them.

John looked up at the steep hillside with a rocky face visible in spaces that small shrubs and overgrowth could not grow.

"The cave has a good hidden entrance. There is no trail except for varmints and the ledges are pretty narrow so we need to be careful," Swift noted. "I'll start a fire if you want to get some firewood. You'll find a lot of driftwood down there on the bank," Swift continued.

With nothing more to be said, John began his search for firewood. As darkness settled into the river valley the two travelers made sure the horses were tied so they could munch the lush grasses and weeds growing on the river bank.

"In the morning we'll hook us up a long run line for each of the horses since they can't get up the cliff. We can move them closer to the base of the cliff, out of sight of almost anyone," Swift remarked.

"Sounds like a good idea," John agreed. The two settled down for a restless sleep.

Swift set out climbing up the hill, first along one ledge, pulling up to another as the first one would get smaller and smaller until it simply run out. Eventually they reached a ledge with a large limestone boulder the size of a small cabin that had fallen away from the main cliff and rested on the ledge. It looked as if the boulder completely blocked the ledge. But as he watched Swift approach the boulder and disappear behind the rock, he realized how well hidden this cave must be. When John arrived at the spot he saw Swift disappear he carefully climbed behind and around the boulder. The ledge continued on about another five feet and abruptly ended, in a shear drop off.

"Where are you?" John yelled out.

"Here, down here," Swift yelled.

He heard a faint, muffled sound and searched around for a moment. He couldn't tell where the sound was coming from. A footprint in the dry dust by a small dark hole in the rock wall behind the boulder gave the secret entrance away. It was a small opening, barely noticeable and just big enough for a person of average size to slide through. As he leaned closer to the opening he heard clearly Swift moving around down in the dark hole. John dropped his pack and slid head first into the small opening. Swift had already lit one of the torches he and George had made last time they visited the cave. John continued to slide downward into the sinking entrance nearly twenty feet before the opening began to get bigger. He could see Swift plainly now, about fifteen feet from him, standing up holding the torch. Swift lit another torch and propped it up with a pile of rocks against the wall of the cave. The cave, once inside, was surprisingly large. It appeared to be about fifteen feet high and maybe twenty feet wide in the immediate area. The walls jagged in places and the floor had a number of rocks that had fallen from the roof of the cave in the past. There was no stream or sign of water and the cave was very dry. As John stood up and walked toward Swift he could see that Swift was studying the ground intently.

"Nobody has been here except a few varmints. The entrance didn't look like it had been tampered with either," Swift said.

"Look. You see there, John? We covered the cave here from wall to wall with fine dry dirt behind us after we hauled out our last load here to the entrance. We would know if anybody had found our cave," Swift proudly pointed out.

"Where's the silver?" John asked.

"Get yourself a torch John and light 'er up. You're going to want as much light as you can get in a minute."

"So you and old Mundy even thought to have torches ready right here by the cave entrance."

"We tried to take care of as many little details as possible to save time. The less time we had to be here loading up, the better off. While our horses are tied up down there and this entrance is open, there is always the chance of someone happening along and discovers our secret."

"Hold on. A little farther down this passage, John, You'll see," Swift proudly stated. Though Swift had been here many times, he could barely control the excitement building. Not only did he have the pleasure of visiting the treasure cave again, but the pleasure of showing it off to John. He knew the situation was fine and he knew his treasure still had to be in its safe location.

The two walked a short distance to a passage shooting off to the right. Swift moved down the small passageway until it suddenly opened up into a much larger chamber. In the large room John could see kegs and boxes stacked against the wall around the room. Stopping by one of the kegs that had the top removed John could see the shining silver. Suddenly, John Finley became aware that the room was practically filled with silver, so much that he could hardly comprehend what he was seeing.

Twelve:
In the Sink Cave

The map puzzled Will. The strange symbols certainly meant something. Will had proven his ability to solve some of the map by predicting the symbol of the turkey track on top of Pilot Knob. The turkey track pointed west toward the next symbol, an oblong circle, resembling the shape of an eye. Ray, and Will himself, had never seen anything like it before, nor had they even heard of such a rock symbol. After leaving work, late as usual, the phone was ringing when Will came in the door.

"Hey," Jennifer said.

"Hey babe," Will replied.

"Anything happen tonight?"

"Nah. Seemed like the same old crowd to me, even down a bit. I was ready to leave by 11:30 but the boss decided the time for a major cleanup had to be tonight and I'm tired."

"Well, want to hear something interesting?" Jennifer teased.

"Sure," Will answered as he walked through the house taking off his coat and shoes, headed for something cold to drink.

"Well, today I had to go shoot some photos in Lexington. While on the shoot I overheard some people talking about some event or something going on this weekend at a place called McConnell Springs. It sounded like an interesting place and a good place to be photographed. So, on the way home, I decided to stop by and see these place for myself. McConnell

Springs is a pretty big deal as a historic place," Jennifer explained.

"It sounds familiar but I can't recall having ever been to the place. What about McConnell Springs?"

"Well, if you follow the general direction of the turkey track west you will eventually come pretty close to McConnell Springs."

"You asked what important land mark might be out that way. McConnell Springs is directly west of the Indian Old Fields and Pilot Knob, and your turkey track that points west," Jennifer continued.

"McConnell Springs, why so important anyway?" Will asked.

"It's probably the main reason Lexington was settled because of the abundant supply of water that a town could build around, at least in the early days," Jennifer replied.

"Why would that be an important location on this map?" Will questioned.

"It most likely does not have anything to do with the map. But it sure is the only significant land mark I can find directly west of the Old Fields. At least during pioneer days and assuming the map is old. I am going to check and see if I can find anything else about McConnell Springs. That is the only historic thing I could find. See you tomorrow?"

"Sure thing. I should be over about nine," Will replied.

"Okay. Good night."

"Good night."

"Here boy! Come on Toby!" Will yelled out the back door. The big dog came running up from somewhere behind the house where he had been barking seriously at some night critter. Toby spent his evenings in such pursuits, waiting on his master and friend to return home. Will gave Toby his food and fresh water on the back porch, petted him a little and went in the house to shower. Nights at the Brick Yard could be tiresome and Will wondered sometimes why he would even do this kind of job.

Business was good as usual at Wright's Garage. People waited in the parking lot nearly an hour before the garage was opened by Charlie Wright, Ray's uncle. Ray was running late this morning but most days, he was on time. He was a good mechanic and as a result he never had a shortage of vehicles to be repaired. People often asked specifically for Ray to work on their car. His reputation for fixing about anything on any make of an automobile became common knowledge throughout the county. Ray often worked late into the evening hours until he was completely exhausted. He was not the business type and never really learned that part of the operation. Instead Ray had learned everything about mechanics. Everyone else had gone home for the evening and Ray was finishing a tune-up when Roger Hampton showed up.

"Hello Ray. I came by to pay up for the work you finally assed around and got done," Roger smartly said as he walked in the shop door.

"What are you doing out here so early? What time is it anyway?"

"I want to get my car. It doesn't matter the time."

"Well, I guess you're welcome, Roger," Ray replied, not stopping doing what he was doing and not even looking in Roger's direction.

"How much do I owe you Ray?" Roger asked.

"The front office is closed Roger. Why don't you come by later and settle up," Ray replied.

"I don't want to come back again later, let me settle up now."

"Roger, I don't know what the bill is, you know that. I just turn in the parts costs and my labor time. They figure up the charges up front. I can't take your money here." Ray felt the agitation begin to build up. Roger Hampton was simply an irritation when he was around and Ray wished he'd never taken on Roger's car repair job.

"If this ain't something! First, you couldn't get the car out on time, now I can't even pay for it. Hell of an operation you got here, Ray."

"Roger just come back tomorrow and pay the bill, okay? Here are the keys, go ahead and take the damn car. You can come back and pay them tomorrow."

Roger watched for a minute like he was interested in Ray's work. He wasn't interested, though. In fact, he didn't know much about cars at all.

"Did you and your pals find your secret treasure the other day?" Roger asked.

"What are you talking about?"

"You know damn well what I'm talking about, Ray."

"You mean the buried treasure? Hell yes, so much silver to pack out I am taking a break here working on this damn car just to get some rest. What's it to you anyway?" Ray disliked Roger Hampton and this made him more upset. He had not told Will and Jennifer about the comment he had made to Roger before. He let them assume Roger accidentally figured it out on his own the other morning at the restaurant.

He should have told them, he thought. He felt bad about keeping this secret and he thought Roger could be trouble.

"I was just wondering if you found that treasure. And you say the find is silver?" Roger pressed.

"It was nothing. We were just out hiking and enjoying the outdoors," Ray tried to recover. He was not very good at being secretive. Ray was not a good card player either and certainly not a good liar. He stopped what he was doing and began to clean up his work area, hoping Roger would take the hint and leave.

"Say Ray, I know about the John Swift Silver Mine. Is that what you goofs are looking for?"

"What if it is?"

"Hey, don't be so hostile Ray. Hell, I know a lot about that fool's tale. I've studied the subject before. There is no such thing you dumb ass!" Roger laughingly said.

"That's what you know. We might know something different." Ray knew he shouldn't have said that.

"Tell Charlie I'll be back to pay sometime later this week. I have too much to do tomorrow to chase around paying bills. Besides I might just go silver mine hunting later this week. How about it Ray?" Roger taunted.

"Yeah. Yeah, whatever," Ray grumbled.

Roger finally left and Ray finished the shop clean up and returned to his work. Ray knew he should have told Will and Jennifer about his slip-of-the-tongue incident. This was a decision Ray pondered and required attention before he met Will this evening. The three explorers met often to consider their next move.

"So tell me more about this McConnell Springs," Will said.

"Well, as I said before, the spring is located in Lexington, and named in 1775, when used as a campsite. It has been important in the history of Lexington over the early years," Jennifer explained.

"What connection does it have with Pilot Knob?"

"None. But it's the only historic place I could find west of Eskippakithiki, the direction the turkey track is pointing."

"You know, the map could be just a directional map or some hunters messing around while camping under the cliff. It may not have anything to do with a treasure map, Swift's silver or anything."

"Ah, but what if it is something important? What if it is a map to someone's personal treasure, maybe not even connected to pioneers or John Swift? And don't forget there was a dead person buried up there with a silver arrowhead," Jennifer encouraged.

Jennifer sensed Will was becoming increasingly frustrated with the riddle the three had taken on.

"And besides, I cannot figure how we could ever get any further. The only thing we know from this stupid map is that there is one hell of a big ass turkey track. That's all we know. Not even where to begin looking for it and not anything else," Will said, getting frustrated with the whole thing.

"On the other hand, what if the symbol before the turkey track is McConnell Springs and there is another marking or sign there?" Jennifer gave a positive spin.

"You mean like another turkey track?"

"No, I mean a symbol like the one on the map. It looks like an eye-shape to me. What if that is somewhere around

McConnell Springs? If we found that, then we only have two symbols left. The one, if you look at it, is lined up with the big turkey tracks. They're all in a straight westerly direction from the first one at Pilot Knob and where the wall map is carved," Jennifer replied.

"Maybe we should concentrate on the symbol the farthest from Pilot Knob?"

"You mean the one that is near the Ohio River, if the line represents the Ohio River?"

"Louisville, hmm. That's interesting," Will replied.

"Let's say you are right about the Ohio River thing, wouldn't that put that marking, whatever it is, somewhere around Louisville?"

"Let's see here, just a minute," Will said while shuffling for his Kentucky highway map, another item he always kept in his pack. Will hurriedly found the location of Pilot Knob and plotted a line roughly due west with his index finger.

"Louisville is due west. I never thought of that. But why would that be on a map carved on a rock cliff in the mountains of eastern Kentucky?"

"So if that is where the last symbol is located, it may be the treasure or the treasure may be at the rock shelter back at Pilot Knob. What we need to do is find this eye-shaped symbol. We need to think in pioneer terms. Forget about Lexington and Louisville, neither one existed in the days of John Swift," Jennifer surmised.

"I guess it wouldn't hurt to take a trip down to McConnell Springs and take a look around," Will concluded.

"Good. I think you're right. We should," Jennifer said.

By the time the weekend arrived, Will, Jennifer and Ray couldn't stand it any longer. Will called Ray at the shop on

Saturday morning. He figured Ray would already be working trying to get caught up from the week's backlog, something Ray never seem to accomplish. He answered the phone since he was the only person in the shop this early in the morning.

"Ray, what are you doing boy?" Will asked.

"What I do every Saturday. Tear up cars!" Ray laughed.

"You want to take a short trip today with me and Jennifer?"

"You know I do. I've been thinking about the map," Ray started.

"Save it, Ray. Me and Jennifer will swing by the shop around noon and pick you up. That okay?" Will interrupted.

"I'll be ready. Heck, it's 10:30 now. I had better get cleaned up a little bit," Ray answered.

After picking up Jennifer, Will stopped by the BP station and filled the cooler with ice and some snacks, then the pair drove to the shop to pick up Ray. They followed Old Frankfort Pike out of town to Lexington. They found the park with little problem, practically driving directly to the parking area. A few visitors milled about the parking lot going to and from the fairly new visitor's center. After the three got out of the truck, Jennifer loaded up her camera bag and headed straight toward the visitor center. Will grabbed his pack and locked the truck. Ray walked with Will, following Jennifer.

"Ray, where you aware of this place?" Will asked.

"No. I don't think I've ever heard of this place. What makes you guys think this has anything to do with the map and Pilot Knob anyway?"

"Ask Jennifer."

By this time Jennifer had collected a copy of every available brochure and map the center's information desk had available and ready to hit the trail. Will and Ray, after a brief look inside the building, simply turned and left with Jennifer as she led the way down the wide trail.

"According to this map we should be coming to the Blue Hole," Jennifer offered a guided tour.

"What exactly are we supposed to be looking for here, anyway, Jennifer?" Ray asked.

"I don't know, maybe nothing. Two things though, Ray."

"What two things?" Ray asked, clearly confused now.

"Okay. I've already told Will according to what I read, this spring was a famous historic landmark back in pioneer days, apparently well known to many of the earliest settlers in the state. And, it is in perfect line with the Indian Old Fields and Pilot Knob," Jennifer explained.

"And this means what?"

"Yeah, go ahead and tell him your point," Will added.

"Will, do you have the map with you?"

Will pulled out the worn roughly drawn map and held it out before them.

"It's nearly worn out; I still have the picture Jen made somewhere here in my pack," Will noted and began to search his bag.

"Now take a good look at the map. There is another symbol; this one here in the shape of an eye somewhere west of the first two symbols." Jennifer pointed to the map.

"So you think the next map symbol is here at McConnell Springs?" Ray asked.

"It could be, I guess, but good lord, where?" Will surmised.

"Well, we predicted the turkey track on top of Pilot Knob. It was on the map and sure enough on the rock," Ray added.

"Maybe there are some caves around here," Will suggested.

"I would guess several caves are in this area. That could be the problem," Jennifer noted while focusing her camera on the deep, emerald water billowing up from the earth.

"We can walk the trail and look for caves. Heck, maybe this valley is in the funny shape of an eye. Perhaps we might find a big carving on the side of a rock ledge."

"This most likely has nothing to do with anything, but I am glad we came. I was not aware at all of a historic place like this in Lexington," Will answered.

"This is like looking for a needle in a haystack. No, I take that back, it's more like looking for, well hell, I don't know what it's like looking for," said Ray.

"Ha, ha, Ray," Jennifer sarcastically remarked.

"No, wait. Think about it. The only thing we need to find here is a cave," Will said.

"You're assuming, of course, that the turkey track pointed to this spot. It could be pointing to a rock in Frankfort or--- Ray froze, holding his breath with his thought.

"Or what Ray?" Will asked.

"Guys, I have an idea about the other symbol."

"Let's see that map again."

"If this is the Warriors Path and this line represents the Ohio River, this might be the falls of the Ohio at Louisville. So this symbol most likely represents something around the river."

"Not bad. Not a bad thought, Ray, but exactly what it represents could be anything."

"What if it represented the town or even a fossil? Those are pretty big and well known fossil beds in the river at that place you know," Ray concluded.

"Let me see that photograph of the carving?" Will asked Jennifer.

As soon as he saw it, Will recognized something that he had not even bothered to notice before.

"It is a strange marking, could represent a fossil, I guess. Jennifer has already figured out that the turkey track and the eye-symbol are in line with Lexington and Louisville. So it is very possible this symbol does represent the Falls, but why?"

"Because it is the easiest place for anybody to cross the Ohio River. The Falls of the Ohio is really what started the city of Louisville. In some of those histories we've been reading, the Falls was mentioned as a point where pioneers would cross the river."

"To the Falls of the Ohio, if my guess is right," Ray chimed in.

"So, what does that mean?" Jennifer asked.

"Not a clue. But it must mean something or the creator of this rock carving wouldn't have gone to so much trouble putting the symbols in a row. What we do know, if Ray is right, is that between our turkey track, the one we found, and the Falls of the Ohio are three other markings. One appears to be a large turkey track, the "X's" and the other is an eye shape. That is what we know. We have assumed that the "X's" represent the Indian village."

"Jennifer, did you happen to bring the copy of the Swift Journal? The one you copied on your trip," Will asked.

"Yeah, it's back at the truck. I'll go get it," Jennifer said.

"Give me the keys. I'll go back and get it. You two enjoy yourselves. You've let me tag along on every trip so I'll go and get the journal," Ray nobly offered.

"I don't mind going."

"No, no, it'll just take me a few minutes. I'll be right back."

"Thanks Ray."

Ray headed back up the trail toward the parking lot. By now considerably more cars filled the parking lot as more visitors began to arrive at the springs. When he arrived at the truck and unlocked the door he began rifling through the glove compartment. Ray noticed Will had put his gun in the glove compartment. He wondered if the gun was loaded, but didn't check. He knew Will had a permit to carry the weapon. After sorting through some of the papers he found the photo copy of the journal and was just about to retrieve it when he was startled by a voice from behind.

"Hello Ray," Roger Hampton calmly spoke.

Ray recognized the voice and it grated on him. He felt sick to his stomach as he turned around to face Roger.

"What are you doing here, Roger?" Ray immediately asked. "Did you follow us here?"

"This is a public park I reckon, Ray. I've wanted to come down and see this park. Where are your little buddies, Ray? I see you are in Will Morrow's truck."

"Yeah, they're here, if it's any business of yours."

Ray turned back to the business of the glove box and retrieved the copy of the journal, grabbing up with it the .38 caliber Smith and Wesson. He stuffed the gun, wrapped in the journal, into his pocket. He had no idea why he did this other than the fact he felt threatened by Roger.

"Perhaps you guys found something here at McConnell Springs that fits with the map on the cliff at Pilot Knob?" Roger asked.

"You asshole! You've been following us! I wish I had kept my mouth shut about this," Ray fumbled out the words.

"Do you and your little explorer friends think you have found your buried treasure here at McConnell Springs?"

"Roger, why don't you go to hell," Ray slammed the truck door and walked away pushing the key lock remote over his shoulder.

"That's no way to treat one of your good customers. I was just having a chat."

Ray headed toward the visitor center, hoping if Roger followed he would loose him. Ray didn't want Roger to show up in the presence of Will and Jennifer. If that happened they would be mad and probably he would never get invited on one of these trips again. Ray thought about the mess he had made by opening his big mouth. Now Roger Hampton was sniffing around like a dog trying to pick up a trail. Ray thought he had to do something.

Inside the center Ray pretended to be interested in something down a hallway and he went in the first door he reached, the office of volunteers.

"May I help you?" asked a young female volunteer sitting at a desk.

"I was just interested in some more information," Ray stumbled for words.

"Most of our printed information; maps, etc. are located out there in the brochure rack. But I would be happy to sign you up for our volunteer cleanup day next Saturday," the young volunteer courteously replied.

"Thank you very much. You've been very helpful, but I think I will pass on the volunteer thing right now. Maybe later."

Quietly slipping out the door, Roger Hampton was nowhere to be seen. Ray went out a side door to the building, avoiding the front entrance and parking lot heading back down the trail to find Will and Jennifer. He had hoped to be able give the slip to snoopy Roger.

Thirteen:
Finley Leads Boone to Pilot Knob

For the next few years John Finley would meet up with John Swift and make a trip to the treasure cave once a year. The trips had almost become routine. Usually, Swift would send a message, by letter, to John alerting him on the next planned trip. John would usually make the trip, but on occasion didn't make the trip. The two always met at the rock shelter cave at Pilot Knob because the location was easy to reach by using the Warriors Path. The Great Falls had become much too busy and crowded to be considered a good meeting place. Some people had put up crude buildings and a regular ferry had been established by one of the old raft captains. The Falls of the Ohio had become the place to cross the mighty river. Probably the most significant reason the two chose the eastern route was because they used horses on every trip. The horses made trips much easier and faster along the trails leading to the east. The trails became the most practical way to remove their precious cargo from the wilderness. They limited the trips to only one a year, in the spring. John Finley had moved back to Pennsylvania but did not spend much time at home. With his bountiful source of money he moved around a lot, pretending to be a horse trader.

John Finley never got over the fact his trading post and fur business had been destroyed by Indians. When the Indians struck up an alliance with the French and claimed the area where the two rivers joined, John enlisted as a scout in the army. John didn't care much for the British in the colonies, but he even cared less for the French. John, like many of the pioneers moving in and out of the western wilderness, were threatened by the new alliances between the French and Indians. The whole matter didn't sit well with John. General Edward Braddock's army was comprised of British regulars and an assortment of local militiamen. The locals provided support for the British regular troops, and though times seemed in complete turmoil in the colonies, the main focus remained on the French and their Indian allies struggling for control of the wilderness. The northern Indian alliances with the French proved to be difficult for the colonies and everyone was eager to put an end to the Indian and French hostilities. John Finley's unequalled knowledge of the western frontier became significant to the military. Braddock was advancing a rather large army of skilled soldiers northward toward the confluence of the Allegheny and Monongahela Rivers. The two rivers joined and formed the mighty Ohio River. At the juncture, the French had established a fortification with the intent of protecting their interests to the west. General Braddock had no intention of allowing such a situation to stand. It truly was a peculiar time in the colonies. People had become upset with British control, yet they feared the French using the Indians to claim all the western lands.

A young pioneer named Daniel Boone also enlisted as a wagon driver in Braddock's army. Boone, a rough cut sort of fellow, had hunting skills that were practically unequaled. Though a short, stocky man, he was extremely strong. Boone was equally comfortable working with horses and any animals for that matter. His team driving skills combined with his outright contempt for the French traders moving in and around the wilderness territories brought him to the service of the British. Daniel Boone arrived from

Pennsylvania and eager to get out and explore the world. A wagon driver carrying support supplies was considered a good job for a young man. Daniel Boone met John Finley and like most folks became very interested in the stories that Finley told of the wilds in the west. Many evenings were spent around Finley's campfire, John commanding the attention of the others with stories of Shawnee Town.

"Can I ask you something, John?" Boone questioned. Daniel Boone being a curious person by nature and always interested in learning something of the wilderness he had heard so much about.

"Why yes," John replied.

"How far have you been back in this country?"

"I've been as far as the Great Falls of the Ohio and then all over the territory south of the falls."

"I have heard of it but I have never talked to anyone who has been south of there. They call it Kentakee, I believe. What's it like there?" Boone inquired.

John thought for a moment. He thought about what was at stake if he gave too much information. "A beautiful, level plain with game beyond anything you can think of. To the east are some rugged mountains and Indians. There are plenty of Indians still wandering about.. Dangerous too, and they're getting madder by the day I suspect."

"Let 'em get madder. They're still going to get their asses whipped," one of the men boasted. The others laughed in agreement.

"You boys need not fool yourself into thinking these Frenchy's and Indians ain't tough. They are tough and my guess just a looking for a fight. This is their homeland, the way they see it, and I guess they will defend it pretty hard,"

Finley corrected the braggart. The men quieted, intent on listening to all the information John had to offer since none of the young lads had every fought in any kind of battle.

"Someday I want to explore that country, do some huntin' and maybe even settle down in the wilds," Boone thought aloud.

"Daniel, I don't think wondering around out in that wilderness would be a good thing to try right yet; too many Shawnee in the area and they ain't happy right now."

"I suppose you're right. But someday this will be behind us and I intend to see for myself."

"To tell you the truth I'd rather be there too. I've seen this country we are in now and the pay is not that good. I can make more by hunting and trading with the Indians, at least I used to before the soldiers here made them mad as hornets," John whispered. He didn't want to be overheard making such a comment against the soldiers.

In a few days the mighty army moving northward would be attacked by the enemy and soundly defeated. The troops, wagons, Boone and the rest retreated from the dire circumstances. The British fighting tactics had been met with surprise and gorilla warfare. After the bitter defeat at the hands of the French and Indians and Braddock's death, both Boone and Finley left. Boone headed south. Finley visited Philadelphia for a few days and then headed back into the wilderness over the mountains.

Finley figured his partner, John Swift, would be there around the last part of April or early May since that was the usual time Swift made his trip. Finley knew Swift would most likely have sent word to John's homestead, but more often than not, John was not there to receive any message. The two would try to meet up at either the mountain or Big Springs. The one who arrived first would spend time hunting and exploring the area until the other partner arrived, at which point they would make the trip to their treasure cave. Swift caught a raft ride down the river. He sometimes would go over land, riding and leading a horse or mule, but lately he had become accustomed to Finley bringing the pack animals.

John Swift had been living in style and continuing his one-ship operation out of North Carolina. He lived on one of the many islands on the outer banks and spent much of his time fishing and impressing the ladies at the local taverns. It was common knowledge Swift owned ships and had a thriving business. He did not sail much these days. Sometimes he would go on the short runs down to Cuba and back, which took no more than a month. He especially liked making such trips during the winter, but he had to be back by spring time.

Swift had long ago given up pirating as a vocation. Piracy was frowned upon now by all the people. Pirates, for whatever reason, were no longer looked upon as folk heroes against the British. Even so, colonist had increasingly become discontented with their treatment at the hands of the King.

After the brief military career Boone headed back to North Carolina, married and settled down. Boone lived on a small farm and eked out a living for his family. Boone loved to go on long hunting trips into the mountains to the west. He dreamed of going through the mountains to the Kentakee land. Boone often thought of the stories told by his military buddy, John Finley, about being in the wilds, away from neighbors, tax collectors and just about everyone else. Boone made his mind up to go and find the those mystical lands himself, so in 1767, Boone with a few other of his friends and neighbors headed for the wilderness in the west. His trip immediately became marred by Indian attacks and aimlessly wondering in the rough mountains regions. He found no fine grasslands and lush canebrakes as John Finley had described to him. Boone finally gave up this effort and returned home. Daniel Boone, though he still thought of his promised land beyond the mountains, didn't have much incentive to venture back that way. That changed on a June day in 1768. John Finley was passing through Boone's home country on a so-called horse trading trip. After inquiring about Boone's whereabouts Finley traced Boone to his farm on the Yadkin valley. John decided to stop by and pay his old friend a visit. John rode his horse, leading two other horses up beside the small cabin. He could see Daniel working under a little shed behind the cabin and rode around to the back. The midday heat had driven Daniel to work on sharpening his cutting blades. Daniel had hoed the garden early and thought he would tend to the animals and corn crop later in the day.

"Hello Daniel," John yelled out his arrival as he passed the cabin and moved toward the shed. Daniel, though he tried, could not place the stranger.

"Daniel Boone, this is John Finley."

"John Finley! What in the world?"

"How in the world have you been, Daniel?"

"Oh, gettin' by. What are you doing in this part of the country? I figured by now you had done joined back up with the Indians somewhere."

"No, no," John laughed. "I do travel a lot. I am in the horse tradin' business these days." John got off his horse and led all the horses over to a small clump of trees and tied them up.

"All right to tie them here?" John looked at Daniel for his approval.

"Yes, anywhere. They'll be fine. Need to water them?"

"No, they're fine. I let them get a drink down by your creek just before I come up here." John made his way over to Daniel and sat down on the gentle sloping bank above the shed. Trees made shade beyond the small rectangular shed, which consisted of nothing more than four upright posts with some pole rafters and shakes to make a roof. The shed was great place to work on tools, milk the cow and a host of other chores on rainy and hot sunny days.

"Horse tradin' you say? Well, those are some fine looking horses."

"Daniel, did you ever make it out west into the wilderness country?"

"Awe, I made a try at it last year, south, over the mountains. Had a lot of trouble and just gave up on the whole thing when the other fellers with me got scared of them wild Shawnee."

"So you never found the good cane lands where buffalo and game are real plentiful?"

"Lord no. The whole darn trip was a mess. Got lost in the thickets, hills and Indians everywhere. I sure begin to wonder if I could ever find those flat cane lands in the west."

"Oh it's there all right; you can believe me on that, Daniel Boone."

"I didn't say I doubted you, John. I just doubt if I could ever find them. I'm sure they're somewhere out in the wild country . Comin' up from the south might be just too hard a way to travel," Boone concluded.

"If you ever decide to go again, send word and I'll lead you to those fine lands. I ain't doing much of nothin' these days, just knocking around waiting on the war surely coming."

"Things are getting in a mess, that's for sure."

"Just send word to my place in Pennsylvania and we'll meet up and I'll guarantee you'll see some of the finest land you ever will."

"Good enough, I'll remember the offer. Aren't you pretty far from home to be horse tradin'?" Boone asked.

"I have traveled all over the place for a deal to be made. I buy them and take them to other places. I promised these fine Pennsylvania horses to a man not too far from here. I thought I might as well look you up while I'm down in these parts."

"So you do pretty well at horse trading, do you?"

"I've been horse trading for awhile now and it's pretty good money." John was not much for lying. He knew in order to keep his cover story about the horses, he needed to be moving on to make the southern route passes and get to the meeting place on time.

"You are going to stay with us tonight, at least."

"No Daniel, I can't. I promised to have these horses where they are supposed to be before dark. I need to get going."

"Why, you just got here. Stay awhile," Daniel insisted. John Finley again politely refused. It was good, John thought, to see his old military buddy, Daniel Boone, again. Just as fast and quietly has he arrived, John moved out again leaving Daniel to wonder what the visit was all about. John himself, wondered why he took the time to stop only to quickly leave. He figured Boone would understand.

In the spring of 1769, Daniel Boone made ready to make one more attempt to find the fine canes and flat, rich lands of Kentakee, though people by now were calling it Kentuckee. Boone had been contracted by Richard Henderson, an acquaintance he respected highly, to scout out a good trail into the western country and find lands suitable for settlement. So on this cool and fresh spring morning of 1769, Daniel Boone and a group of men set out for Kentucky. Boone had held John Finley to his promise and Finley was with Boone on this trip as his guide. Just as he offered, Boone sent word to John and he agreed to show Boone the level lands he had seen so many times. This time John led Daniel Boone and other men the route through the mountains, the southern route commonly referred to as Cumberland Gap. John Finley preferred going to the treasure cave by the northern route, following the mighty river to the intersection of the Warriors Path. Except for a couple dangerous stream crossings, the route was fairly easy nowadays. Traveling from the south meant more mountains and rough terrain and meant a much longer route for John to reach the old Shawnee town. Once the party reached Cumberland Gap, John picked up the Warriors Path and knew to stay on the path northward until they would reach the old Shawnee town.

The going at first prodded along slow after passing the Cumberland Gap into the wild regions. The party wondered along small streams in the same area Thomas Walker had ventured years before and eventually reached the

Cumberland River at the place the river carved through the pine covered mountain yet to be named. John Finley knew the Warriors Path passed through the area and though just a trail, the path had been traveled so many times over the years the trail was easily noticeable. Once the party reach the gap in the mountains, locating the path became an easy task. At last they picked up the Warriors Path and headed north.

"This looks about the kind of territory we reached before," Boone observed.

"Lots of thickets and swamp lands down around this area, looks to me like. No wonder you got lost!" Finley replied.

"I wasn't lost. Never been lost. I was bewildered for nearly a week once, but not lost." Boone replied.

"Oh yes, bewildered. Been that way myself," Finley replied.

"But I sure am glad you came along, John. Sure rests my mind from worrying about getting these good men lost again."

John Finley knew the Warriors Path would take him exactly to Eskippakithiki where seventeen years ago he had operated his store, if only for a season. For nearly fifteen of those years he and John Swift had made at least one trip a year to Swift's silver treasure cave. Once he reached the old Shawnee town, he figured he could point Boone in the right direction and Boone would have found the treasure he sought, the level lands west of the mountains.

"Once I get you to the level lands, I will plan to head north and leave you there if that's all right," John asked Boone.

"I suppose you would be closer going home to Pennsylvania than coming back. Are you not going to hunt any with us on this trip?"

"No hunting for me. My hunting days are few and far between. Horse trading is better and easier."

"I see. But if the buffalo and deer are plentiful?"

"I'll leave the huntin' this trip to you and the rest of these boys here. You'll do well, I would imagine."

"We head north now, but we will have to be careful. We could run across Indian hunting parties. Cherokee are down in this area but they are friendly and we'll have no problem with them. But farther north we will be in Shawnee country."

"We'll handle them if we run into them, we have met them before, and though my loss was nearly unbearable, I do not fear them," Boone replied. The reminder of the loss of his son, James, in his first trip two years ago was almost too much for him to bear.

"Come on boys, pick up the pace, we need to make camp soon, so let's find us a good place," Boone growled.

Fourteen:
Roger Causes Problems

Ray found Will and Jennifer at the "boils." Here the water bubbles up from beneath the earth as if heated by some mysterious force. The crystal pool of water offered a continuous supply of fresh water. Nearby a larger pool of water named the Blue Hole, offered much more depth resulting in the deep blue color. Will and Jennifer sat on the bank of the stream formed from the springs. Across the stream was a rather large outcrop of limestone containing many small, cave-like openings. The two enjoyed the sunny afternoon, but Will was preoccupied with the possibility of a cave or markings, something supporting their struggling effort to follow the map to its conclusion. Jennifer had shot dozens of photographs of the springs from several angles and began searching for something else to become prey of her camera lens. Ray returned quietly and slowly to the spring's area to find Will and Jennifer. Ray had retrieved the journal as he promised. Though the two had hardly missed Ray, Will felt he had a pranksters duty to harass Ray a little.

"Where've you been, son? We didn't mean for you to go to Frankfort and eat lunch!" Will jokingly remarked as Ray walked up.

"Stopped by the visitor center and asked 'em about caves," Ray quickly responded. He was very proud of himself for the quick thinking on his feet.

"Caves? What did you find out?"

"Well, the people up in the Center mentioned caves. They didn't sound too sure about caves right here in the park but sure seems logical to me." Ray replied.

"I agree with Ray, we should look around those outcrops further down the creek," Jennifer added.

Ray had no further reply but instead handed the copy of Swift's journal to Jennifer. Ray searched the landscape for Roger Hampton. Only a couple other walkers came down the trail to take a look at the boils. Ray was in a spot, he figured. If Roger Hampton shows up here, hell will pay, Ray thought as he glanced around every direction.

"Well?" Will questioned looking all the time at Ray.

"Well, what?"

"Well, what! What in hell did we just talk about, you dumb shit!"

"Oh, the caves!"

"Oh the caves. God Ray, get your head out of your ass."

"Leave him alone Will," Jennifer interrupted.

"The lady in the office said there is a cave called Preston's Cave about a half mile from here down that direction," Ray pointed.

The three sat by the boils watching the water bubble up from somewhere in the earth beneath them. They had a photograph of the strange rock wall carving but had no clue what direction to go from their present situation. Will glanced through the Swift journal, paying attention to the many described landmarks and markings Swift had supposedly left in order to find the mines.

"I guess we're done here. We have found nothing and the map means nothing. If you guys are ready I am kind of ready to go back home," Ray announced, surprising everyone.

"What's your hurry, Ray? May as well enjoy the beautiful day and give Jennifer time to take some pictures." Jennifer had wandered on down the trail a bit further to the Blue Hole and was busy trying to get a water level shot of the bubbling water. Will kept a watchful eye on her in the distance.

"We have got to figure out more about this giant turkey track. We just don't have enough information about the history and stuff to know what the hell we are even doing, anyway," Ray said obviously frustrated by the whole adventure now.

"It's sure not like you to want to quit so quickly," Will commented.

"Awe, I've got crap piled up on me back at the shop, too. I need to get back to work," Ray justified.

Will yelled at Jennifer and motioned for her to come on. Jennifer finished up her photos and returned. The three headed back up the trail to the truck.

"I think we need to study up on this Swift thing and perhaps some of pioneers who first explored this country. Maybe we can understand this little better," Will said as they reached the car. Will noticed a piece of paper on his windshield under the wiper. Some sort of flyer the "Friends of McConnell Springs" put there, he imagined, grabbing the paper and throwing it into the seat beside him, not giving it anymore thought. Jennifer climbed in and slid to the middle followed by Ray taking the "shotgun" seat position. The discussion ended on the day's adventure as they headed home. Will and Jennifer dropped Ray off at his shop where he had left his car and headed to Jennifer's house. The couple spent the evening pouring over the materials Jennifer had copied from her library visit.

"I'm going online and check for anything about the John Swift silver mine," Jennifer announced.

"Oh yes, good, good," Will absent mindedly replied. Will was occupied with a book on the history of Kentucky. Jennifer had purchased at a bookstore while on her visit. He especially was interested in Daniel Boone's trips to Kentucky. As Will read through the book written by John Filson called *The Discovery, Settlement and Present State of Kentucke* it occurred to Will, most likely, Daniel Boone and others were in the area of Pilot Knob. Interestingly, Boone had attempted to make the trip to find the level farm land of Kentucky. Apparently, Boone was attempting to come from North Carolina through the mountains and had to return from his first trip disappointed. Later Boone managed to find his old friend John Finley, one book claimed, and enlisted Finley to lead him and others to the level lands of Kentucky. The more Will read the more interesting the Kentucky discovery story became. Deep into reading Will was interrupted by Jennifer.

"There are no less than a thousand Google hits on the 'Legend of John Swift Lost Silver Mine.' The first one I opened even has what it claims to be an exact copy of the oldest known journal of John Swift," Jennifer announced.

"Can you print a copy?"

"Sure can."

Together the two read over the few pages of so-called journal hoping to find something related to their discovery. The journal written as a running narrative, claimed to be written down by Swift himself. Haystack rocks, cliffs and unusual rocks described country just like Eastern Kentucky. Swift claimed to have made several trips to the mines along with several fellow miners and actually operated mining and smelting operations in the wilderness. The last thing Swift wrote in his journal addressed to anyone who ever read the journal. "Don't ever stop looking where three streams come together; it is near the richest mine I've ever seen."

Will went back to reading one of the histories of Kentucky. One particularly interesting concerned the unusual disappearance of James Harrod, founder of Harrodsburg, the first permanent town or settlement in Kentucky. That information alone surprised Will because he had always thought Daniel Boone established Fort Boonesborough first. Boone, Will learned, first came into the wilderness exploring and hunting but only established Fort Boonesborough as a hire for the Loyal Land Company of Virginia. Boone led settlers to the place, no doubt purchasing their rights from the company. Seemed like real estate work to Will. James Harrod had done the same thing but went further west away from the rough area near the Warriors Path and built Harrodsburg. But the most interesting thing, quite strangely, it seemed to Will, James Harrod disappeared while searching for silver mines near the three forks of the Kentucky River.

"Jennifer, do you suppose James Harrod had seen a copy of Swifts Journal? Because it says right here James Harrod disappeared, never to be found again, searching for silver mines near the three forks of the Kentucky River. Didn't that journal thing we read say the mine is near where three streams come together?" Will posed the question.

"Yes, I think so," Jennifer replied.

Will wondered if perhaps their rock wall map had nothing to do whatsoever with hidden treasure, much less the John Swift Silver mines.

"Honey, I'm tired, dirty and I'm going to take a bath. Do you mind?" Jennifer asked.

"No, of course not, I'm going home anyway. Give me a kiss and I'm out of here."

"Can I take some of these books and copies with me to read tonight?" Will asked as he gently leaned over and kissed Jennifer goodnight.

"Sure, take them all. Maybe you can find some more clues."

The phone rang at about 10:00 PM. Ray had fallen asleep on the couch and the ring startled him.

"Hello."

"Hello, Ray. Where did you go today?" He all too easily recognized the voice of Roger Hampton.

"What the hell, Roger! Are you following us these days? Don't have any land deals you can screw people out of?" Ray sarcastically remarked.

"Now listen to me, Ray. I think I have an idea what you guys are up to, going up to Pilot Knob and finding a map carved on the wall and running all over the country side trying to figure the map out," Roger informed Ray.

"How do you know about the map on the wall? Who told you? You followed us to Pilot Knob, you asshole!"

"Well, let's just say I found the rock carving myself. I don't believe you saw me when you were digging around up there, did you?"

Ray sensed this was bad, very bad news. He had caused every bit of this mess that Friday night at his shop when he said too much to this creep, Ray thought, What should he do? What could he do?

"Listen Roger, uh, me and, uh we, Will Morrow, his girlfriend and me are just out having some fun, goofing off, nothing more. Why, Will and me grew up together, hunted together and everything," Ray tried to explain, trying to figure out what to say next.

"Yeah, I'll bet you and your ole buddy Will share everything, huh, Ray. Look Ray, here's the deal. I understand what you farts are up to. You think you're on to something, a treasure or whatever. If by some, God-knows, once in million chances, you dim wits have actually found something, then I'm getting in on the deal. It's that simple Ray, ole buddy," Roger sarcastically laid out the situation to Ray.

"Damn you Roger, you asshole. We're good friends. Besides, 'bout the only time we three are ever together is just to go hiking and exploring the country side on some pretty weekends."

"Don't call me an asshole you little prick."

"And I don't reckon what we do is any of your business, for that matter."

"Let me explain things for you Ray, so you can understand your situation better now."

"What are you talking about?"

"Did you 'explorers' find anything over at McConnell Springs? I know you were following clues to the map. I have my own copy of the rock map now Ray. I drew it just like on the wall. I'm certain you guys think the map has something to do west of that Pilot Knob place or else you wouldn't spend your time snooping around McConnell Springs. There are no big hiking trails over there, the kind of long hikes you and your buddies are supposed to take," Roger honed in on Ray.

If Ray had been aggravated by Roger Hampton before, he now became downright fearful. Roger Hampton knew practically everything. Ray realized he had to tell Will and Jennifer soon or the whole thing would blow up. Ray felt like being on a road in dense fog and could hardly see anything. He really could not think of a response to Roger's remark. Finally, Ray fumbled out the only thing he could think of.

"Look, Roger. Just leave us alone. This amounts to nothing. This is a game we are playing. That's all," Ray answered.

"Okay, then Ray, so the dead body under the rock in the shelter at Pilot Knob, right under the rock wall map, that's part of the game too, Ray?"

"You found a body?" Ray tried to act surprised.

"Don't try and con me Ray, because you can't. You damn well know there is a skeleton there under a big rock and I haven't seen any police reports telling of a dead body. You three innocent little turds haven't bothered to report anything, have you Ray?" Roger lowered the boom.

"Roger, we need to talk, but can we do this another time?" Ray asked.

"Sure, but you need to accept the fact Ray, you guys have a silent partner now," Roger hung up the phone on Ray. Ray now wide awake, couldn't decide if he should call Will right then and explain this whole mess. Ray thought and decided he wouldn't bother them tonight, and besides, he needed to think how best to tell Will about Roger Hampton. Maybe he would stop by and visit Will at the Brickyard and just tell him the whole mess.

He hopped into his old Ford pickup truck and headed for downtown.

On a weeknight the bar was not very busy. Ray found a chair at the bar and, without the slightest signal or request; Will drew off a tall Bud draft for his friend.

"There you go buddy."

"Aww man, thanks. I need that."

"Figured as much or you wouldn't be in here tonight. You usually don't come in on Wednesdays." Ray preferred Thursday nights to stop by the Brick Yard. He was a creature of habit and Will understood many of those habits. A Wednesday night variation was unusual and Will was curious.

"So, why are you in here tonight, Ray?"

Ray shifted a bit in his seat, trying to think of the best way to approach his friend on this difficult subject. Ray knew this was not going to be easy and would probably tick Will off. It might even cause Will to lose interest in the whole thing.

"You remember Roger Hampton the other morning?"

"Yep. I do remember. He's an ass, you know."

"Oh, I know all right. You should have to deal with him on his car."

"I'll bet he is a real jerk, probably can't ever please him, right?"

"Well, uh, true, for sure, but......"

"Hold on a minute Ray." Will moved to the other side of the bar to get an order from one of the two waitresses working the tables tonight. A party of ladies ordered some fruity drinks requiring a blender, putting Will to work. He returned to his friend for a brief moment. Another patron sitting at the bar indicated to Will his desire for another round. Ray thought this is not going to be a good place to discuss this issue and decided to finish his beer and head home.

"Got to get going."

"What's your hurry, bud?"

"Six comes awfully early in the morning, but a late night owl like you wouldn't have any idea of such things, would ya?"

"Well, old Kearney Brown, you remember old Kearney, anyway old Kearney used to say: Some people are born into greatness, others achieve greatness and some have greatness thrust upon them," Will laughed.

"Yeah, well I guess it's my cross to bare. See ya." With that Ray headed for the door.

Fifteen:
Camp Lulbegrud

"I'd say this is a good a spot as any to camp. Plenty of water and protected from the wind," Finley pointed out to the group as they moved northward along the creek bank. It was mid afternoon; a bit early, Daniel thought.

"A little early in the day to stop, John," Boone remarked. Each day before the party would push as far as possible before dark. Camps were hastily made, amounting to not much more than building a fire and finding a position to sleep around the fire. In mid summer the wilderness became hot and humid, typical of the region. A campfire for cooking and entertainment rather than warmth still remained the heart of the camp.

"Daniel, I hope we make this our permanent base camp."

"How close are we to those level lands?"

"They're just west of us, I reckon. Not more than a mile or two. You'll see tomorrow. This'll make a good camp spot. Plenty of fresh water and look at the drift firewood piled up. We won't even have to hunt for fire wood. There's plenty all around us here."

"This'll do good, yep, real good," Boone replied to John and then turned to the others just catching up. "Boys, here's where we are going to stay for the next few days. We'll make this our main camp. Is this agreeable to everyone?" The others all nodded in agreement. With several hard days of travel in the wilderness, everyone was ready and anxious to set up a base camp to begin their sincere hunt.

Though no one except John Finley realized the expedition had ended up near the level, good hunting lands. Everyone accepted John Finley's expertise on the area. Finley had been here before and knew exactly their present location. After four days on the Warriors Path with little encounter with any Shawnee, John Finley felt this would be a safe spot. They had veered off eastward from the Warriors Path. Tomorrow he and Boone would go to the top of Pilot Knob and Boone would observe at last the beautiful levels for himself. Finley also felt a little uncomfortably near his former store site and the destroyed Shawnee town. He had recognized various landmarks all day as the party had made its way northward. The bend in the creek, the wide shoals and ample drift fire wood provided an excellent campsite. He also recognized the spot where he nearly died years before. Little had changed over the years except the trees and the growth along the creek bank seemed to be much denser.

"Tomorrow, Daniel, you'll see the levels of the place the Shawnee and Delaware call Kentakee."

"Tomorrow, you say. That'll be good, John."

"You'll see for yourself, your trips to this country have not been wasted."

"Looks to me we just didn't come far enough north in '67."

"No, I suspect you didn't, Daniel."

"We wondered around in a lot of hazelnut and iron wood thickets, I sure do recall. Just didn't come far enough north. We tried to head west and then north, but, well, it didn't work out."

"Well, Daniel Boone, it has worked out for you now. You'll see tomorrow."

The party set about to establish a camp. A hot fire was going in no time from the dry dead wood strewn about on the banks of the lazy creek. John had not told Boone about the attack nor had he told him about his store. The men settled in by the fire and had their evening meal from squirrels they had killed earlier in the day on their trek. The discussions always ended up the same; a review of the days events and sights, questions and thoughts about Indians, and their hopes to kill a lot of game tomorrow.

"How far does this Warriors Path go?" Boone asked.

"As far as I know, the trail goes way up into the north country." John had long ago learned from the Shawnee the Warriors Path did indeed go all the way to the big lakes. But being careful with his secret, John's had the natural instinct not provide too much information. John both liked and respected Boone. He felt Boone to be a fair and honest man, something he'd learned when they spent time in Braddock's army. On the other hand, John had an amazing secret and treasure to visit.

"You know John, this is a good camp site for us to work out of; the place is well protected and has a good water supply."

"I thought the same thing. We are practically camping on the Warriors Path, though. Leaves us a good chance to get visitors in the form of Shawnee anytime out of nowhere. Need to remember and be on guard." The other men sat quietly and listened concerned about the situation.

"I'm not afraid of any Shawnee. If they come around our camp they'll get a licking," Boone boasted. This brought laughter and a calming affect on the men.

Watches were chosen, as someone would have to stay awake with the fire all night. A rotation had been established early in the trip. The fire tinder and guard duty would be done by two or three men each pulling a three to four hour shift.

The next morning at daybreak all the men were up and activity moved into full swing, cooking and packing up to go on the hunt. John Finley and Daniel Boone prepared to go up the mountain for Boone to see for himself he had indeed reached the rich flat lands of Kentucky.

"Listen to me, all of you," Boone commanded. As the leader of the expedition his job to keep the company of men operating as a smooth and efficient organization took priority. A pep talk and some advice at the beginning of the serious hunt was in order, Boone figured. With every single man in the party focused on his every word, Boone laid out some instructions. "Most important men, be careful and mindful of your location. If you get lost you'll be on your own. Let's set a time of two nights. Any man not back to this camp by dark by the third night we will consider lost or worse. Agreeable?" Everyone more or less agreed in a grunt and head nodding gesture.

"The first person back to camp gets a fire going and something cooking, or if anyone decides to stay in a day, they would see to that chore," Boone added.

"Remember we are after furs. The more we take back the better our fortunes will be, boys, agreed?" All the men acknowledged with a resounding affirmation.

"And one final thing, men. I have been indeed fortunate to have traveled into this wild country in the company of such fine men as you. I intend to explore and hunt around these parts and be at this camp as much as possible at the end of every day. I wish you each success in your endeavors. Today, me and John are going to the top of that mountain to take a look at the countryside."

John Finley led out and Daniel Boone followed him although they were separated by several yards as they headed upland from the creek. John Finley had been this way several times so the trail seemed familiar. The two hunters moved quickly and quietly along the little flat creek flowing from the direction of the mountain. In about three hours they reached the base of the big mountain and began the gradual uphill climb stopping once by a clear branch flowing over the shale rocks that occasionally had a conglomerate stone that had eroded down from the big sandstone cap rock on the mountain above. From this point the climb became long and steep but the two men were in excellent health. And both men wore good leather boots, though Finley's appeared of a much high quality craftsmanship. Having practically and an endless supply of finances, Finley, occasionally, purchased nicer items for himself.

"Base of the cliff," John said as they reached the massive capstone of the mountain. John led the way along the base of the steep, exposed sandstone cliff until he came to a slight gap in the rock. Though the climb became steep it was not particularly dangerous, Boone noted as the two moved up the mountain. It was already a hot day, typically the same everyday in this part of the world. Deep woods birds sang beautiful melodies amid the massive canopy created by the huge chestnut trees growing all over the slopes, even up next to the cliff.

"These sure would make some good cabins back home." Boone commented as he pointed to one of the large trees.

"I suspect so Daniel, but I'd leave up to you to figure out how to get 'em back there." John responded and laughed. So did Boone.

"When we get on top you'll see for yourself Daniel. You'll see." Fifteen minutes later the two reached top of the knob. Daniel Boone stood motionless facing west. He viewed what he would later tell his writer friend, John Filson, "I saw with pleasure the beautiful levels of Kentucky."

"What a sight, and true, level as far as the eye can see. Grass land and cane breaks. No mountains or big valleys. It is beautiful," Boone exclaimed.

"Well, Daniel that is what you wanted. There it is."

"They call this place Pilot Knob. Sure is a good place to see the countryside from. The Warriors Path we came up runs on north in that direction eventually up past the upper Blue Licks and to the big river," John explained.

In the distance Boone witnessed for the first time vast open grasslands dotted with an occasional Burr Oak tree. Looking to the north Boone detected the faint outline of the Warriors Path as it faded into the distance almost in a straight line. Looking east, the land became rugged and mountainous. And looking south from the direction Boone and his party had traveled the days before, he marveled at the edge of the mountains meeting the levels of Kentucky. He had reached the fine level land called Kentakee. It was an enjoyable time and Boone didn't want to leave his lofty view of the land he had dreamed of all the years past. His friend, John Finley, had brought him to this spot and he was grateful.

John Finley left Boone to himself to take in the spectacular views. After many days of being in dense forest with high humidity the clear view seemed like coming to the surface of a pond for a breath of air.

"I'm going to head on back down the hill, Daniel,"

"Yeah, I'll catch up with you in a bit, just let me enjoy this view and figure out where I am."

John headed back down the mountain toward their creek camp. Boone would find his way back to the camp following the trail they came up. John made sure not to take Boone to the rock shelter where he had spent days recovering from his leg wound. He wanted to visit the shelter but with the map on the wall he didn't want Boone to follow him. John was a little concerned that Boone might choose another return route down the mountain and accidentally discover the rock shelter. So, John decided to wait at the base of the cliff and after a short time yelled out to Boone.

By late afternoon most everyone had arrived back in camp. Some had brought back fresh killed meat and skinned out hides. Others just wandered back in tired and hungry from their day's explorations. The hunter's kept busy about the tasks of cleaning and butchering the deer carcasses into small pieces ready to dry into jerky over the continually maintained fire. It was summer and most of the time fresh meat was handy anytime. Since so much meat was killed on this first outing, the group thought it would be better to preserve the jerky and hunt for food less in the days ahead since they might end up being in the wilderness all winter. John Finley knew his fortune lay west of his camp. He also knew the campsite he had chosen along the Warriors Path was just a short distance from where his burned out store was located just a few years ago. He wondered if the village had completely overgrown or any evidence of Shawnee Town's existence was left. He got his answer at the evening meal by the campfire.

"There must have been a pretty big Indian village just west of here about maybe a mile," William Cooley remarked. Cooley was one of the five other men that Boone had recruited along with John Finley for this grand expedition. Cooley had a reputation as a great woodsmen and hunter, the reason Boone asked him along.

"Is that so?" Boone questioned.

"Oh yes, signs everywhere and as flat as slate rock out there. It must have been a big camp. Looks like the whole place was abandoned, burnt down several years ago, I'd say. I found a lot of stuff scattered about, stone axes, logs, things like that," Cooley added. John wondered if he should tell the group his knowledge about the place. What harm could that be? None he thought. Before he could begin his explanation Boone struck deep.

"John, did you know about this place?"

"I did, Daniel."

"What do you know about it?" Boone questioned.

"Eskippakithiki. That was what it was called. A Shawnee town."

"How long has it been abandoned and what happened to the Shawnee?"

"The place burned to the ground in 1753, by the Iroquois. I operated a store of sorts in the village. It burned to the ground too and I barely escaped. In fact, I was hurt, hit in the leg by a spear and ended up here somewhere in this very creek for a couple of days before a hunter came by and helped me." The men listened with great intent wanting to hear more of the story.

"John, how come you never told me before. You actually lived out there and was friendly with them Shawnee?" Boone questioned.

"I guess I've done a lot of things I never told about and yes sir, I did live in Eskippakithiki for a short time. And I did quite well trading with the Shawnee. I made friends with them through a French hunter I met on the Ohio River my very first trip into the wilderness. He brought me to the Shawnee town. We called it Lower Blue Licks, the Shawnee called it Eskippakithiki." John explained.

"Eskip-a-kee-ta-kee. Is that right?" Cooley asked.

"Pretty close. Close enough. That's how we call it K-taw-kee now. Comes from the place right out there. Anyway, doesn't matter, the place is not there anymore."

"You traded and lived among the Shawnee?" Boone asked.

"I did trade for almost a year and I did quite well too. And, Daniel, I am sorry I didn't tell you about this place. I should have, I know. Truthfully, the place never crossed my mind once we got on the trail," John tried to explain. John hoped that Boone would accept this explanation and drop the whole subject.

"I suppose so, but I got to tell you John, I am surprised at you on this one. Tell us how you made friends and the Shawnee didn't outright kill you," Boone questioned. John Finley had deceived Boone and it was obvious. Boone pretended he really was not concerned about the matter in front of the other men. The entire hunting party stood standing around listening to the conversation. Boone didn't want any distrust to develop in the group while out in this remote wild region. John Finley knew he needed to make sure this amounted to his only mistake. Both men were great woodsmen and even greater strategists.

"It was the Frenchman George Mundy. He helped me get accepted by the Shawnee. After awhile, they came to treat me with common courtesy and traded with me. I did well in the trading business in fact," John told the group of men.

"Who burned the village? What happened to the Shawnee?" Cooley asked.

"I don't know for sure, the only two I saw was the one I shot and the other I hammered with an ax head. They weren't Mingos, Cherokee or Shawnee. Must have been Indians from up north, Iroquois I always thought," John further explained. Daniel Boone had become quiet. He had talked enough about the subject he figured. The other men now had been captivated and concerned.

"Boys, I wouldn't worry about them now, this all happened years ago. The whole countryside has changed. I doubt you'll see any Indians at all except maybe a few Shawnee out doing the same thing we're doing," Boone finally piped in.

All the hunters enjoyed a hearty evening meal of cooked venison. As the evening progressed each man, except those who choose to be up with the fire and on night watch, drifted off to sleep. Boone had a hard time sleeping. The surprise information John had given them this evening troubled Boone. It just seemed unlikely John would forget about his store while he knew exactly how to get to the mountain knob. As a matter of fact, Finley never mentioned his store and the Indian town when they served together with General

Braddock. The whole thing just seemed odd to Boone and as he thought about this day's event over and over in his mind, sleep was elusive.

Sixteen:
An Amazing Day

Will had arrived at the Brick Yard at about three in the afternoon. Although a bit later than his usual time, the difference went unnoticed. He immediately began his task of stocking the bar preparing for the happy hour crowd soon to arrive. By 5:30, the local watering hole moved into operation for the evening. This became nonstop work for Will and the other bartenders until the place closed. Not a big crowd would be expected since it was just Tuesday but busy enough. Sundays and Mondays marked Will's normal days off but sometimes he would take an extra day now and then if another bartender would cover for him. He often did the same for the others. The other bartender tonight was Fred Irwin. Fred or Freddy, as he was most often called by patrons, was a hard worker and Will liked to work shifts with him more than any others because of Freddy's personality. Freddy loved to ponder various subject matters and through his years of working at the bar, he had become well attuned to a variety of subjects. Freddy was interesting to be around and seemed to always be aware of information about most subjects though he never claimed to be knowledgeable on any.

"Did you see in the paper about that secret tunnel into Canada?" Freddy asked Will as he drew a draft for one of the waitresses.

"No, I don't remember seeing anything about a tunnel."

"Pretty amazing, smugglers and I guess illegals built a tunnel hundreds of feet long crossing right under the border."

"No kidding. Where?"

"Somewhere up on the border in Washington State and Canada. The whole thing is kind of funny actually, the country is all up and worried about the Mexican border, and the Canadians have done built a damn tunnel right into the country."

"I didn't think a problem existed getting in and out this country anyway from Canada, you know at the regular border crossings."

"Well, if one wanted to avoid identification or planned on smuggling drugs, I'd say the border check point not to be the best selection. Anyway, someone figured they needed a way in and out of the country handy. But heck, the border is over a thousand miles long and most of country is wilderness. A person could just hike across the border anyway."

"I guess you're right. The terrorists will find their way into this country somehow, for sure."

"Let's hope not."

Ray Deevers stopped by on his way home from his shop. He usually stopped by on Thursday's to see his friend Will and discuss their next random adventure. But occasionally Ray broke the habit after a hard day of work at the shop. About one cold beer and on occasion two was the limit for Ray. He had already showered and changed into street clothes from his shop uniform at the shop.

"What's up bud?" Ray asked as he saddled a bar chair.

"Same old same old."

"Try this out for size." Will said while setting a large cold draft in front of Ray.

"Oh, yeah. I can sure use this."

"Not too busy tonight. What's been happening with you bud?"

"Same old stuff. People tear 'em up, bring 'em in and we fix 'em."

Will had moved down the bar a bit to make a mixed drink for one of the waitresses. Ray studied the crowd for a brief moment then watched the television situated on the wall behind the bar. The evening news rumbled on but no one in the bar paid much attention. Ray soon lost interest as well. Will moved along the bar to the general area of Ray.

"Thought anymore about the map?"

"Not really. I don't know what else we can do. We're kind of stuck. Jennifer has a bunch of books and found some pretty interesting stuff on the internet but that is about all we have."

"Will, about Saturday. I mean down at McConnell Springs."

"Yeah, well, we never solved anything there for sure. Hold on a minute." Will moved down the bar to a new customer to take her order. Ray sipped on his draft and mulled over in his head how his approach to the miserable problem with Roger Hampton. Freddy moved into Will's position at the bar stocking ice in the ice bin.

"Hello Ray."

"Hey Freddy."

"Will says you guys have been doing a lot of hiking and what not up in the mountains."

"Yeah, we've climbed some rocks, seen some pretty countryside. Keeps the weight down," Ray responded patting both his hands on his stomach.

"Did you know they opened a new park in Frankfort, on Owenton Road? Some kind of wetlands park or something like that. Brand new, just opened this past week. They've got some good hiking trails there I hear." Freddy Irwin was always a source of new information about what was going on in and around Frankfort. Will often picked up bits of information as bartender. On this night alone, Will had already learned about a tunnel between the United States and Canada though the information was of little use to Will. Now Ray was learning from Freddy about a new park in town.

"No, I hadn't heard about a new park in town," Ray replied not all interested. But of course, Ray thought, Freddy would know all about the goings on around town.

"Yeah. It's been in the paper and all. It's a wetlands park. Maybe you hiking types should check it out."

"Wetlands park? What is that anyway?"

"You know, it's like a swamp area."

"Well." Ray simply acknowledged as if to say he really was not interested. Freddy left the bar area with his empty ice container. Will had taken care of three other customers and finally made his way back down to the bar where Ray sat perched on his bar stool.

"Say, did you know a new park opened out on the Owenton Road?" Ray asked.

"No, I hadn't heard."

"They did, it is some kind of nature park according to Freddy. I hadn't heard either until Freddy just mentioned it. Some kind of a swamp something or other. Who in the hell ever heard of a swamp in Frankfort!"

"No, can't say I have ever heard of anything about a swamp, Ray."

"But, what about our treasure huntin'? I mean when are we going again?" Ray leaned forward on the bar and whispered to Will. Ray still had not come up with a way to break the Roger Hampton news to Will. He finished his beer and listened to Freddy Irwin rattle on about the swamp place in Frankfort. Ray had become less inclined to get into the matter this evening though solving the map question still appealed to him. Bringing up the Roger Hampton issue would only complicate the situation and besides, Ray figured, Roger would probably forget about the matter anyway. If they couldn't solve the map, Roger Hampton couldn't either. Ray felt a little more comfortable about his situation, at least tonight. Will moved back and forth around the bar area working efficiently and being friendly with the customers until he made his way back to Ray.

"When are we going back out and work on that map problem?" Ray asked.

"How about Saturday morning. I need to be back here in the bar by three. But if we got an early start we might head out somewhere. Not sure where, but maybe retrace our path or something."

"Man another trip sure sounds like the right idea. Well, I do need to get on home. I'm pretty tired," Ray concluded finishing off his beer and leaving the money under his glass.

The next morning Will ran some errands around town and happened to be near the place Freddy told Ray about last night. Will was not sure what they were talking about other than a swamp park or something, but the park supposedly just opened. So he thought he would drive out the road to find the so called, by Ray anyway, 'the new swamp park'. Sure enough around the very first curve he discovered a newly constructed pull off on the side of the road and figured this must be the new park Ray was talking about. Curiosity got the best of Will so he pulled into the parking lot. Two other cars occupied spaces in the lot. A freshly constructed trail led from parking lot and headed though a small thicket of trees. With only one trail, Will figured this to be the correct route and headed out. In a few minutes he found himself over a marshy area. Cattails and black willow trees filled in the marshy area in abundance. Tree identification markers had been dispersed along side the trail with professionally written explanations of the surrounding environment. Will realized these were nature trails and primarily devoted to this wetland habitat. Ahead of him he noticed a young girl in a nicely pressed and professional looking uniform speaking to a small group of seven people. The guide explained some of the finer points of the marsh environment. He was definitely not interested in taking a guided tour and stopped short of encountering the group and pretended he had found something of interest.

"These are completely natural wetlands and have like been here for thousands of years." The young guide explained to the group. One member of the group asked what caused the marshes which allowed the opportunity for the young guide to explain the situation in greater detail. Will listened as the guide explained how these particular wetlands formed.

"This part of Frankfort all the way from down at the distillery back through Holmes Street down by the plaza tower is what geologist refer to as an oxbow," She began the well prepared explanation to the puzzled looking tourists.

"An oxbow is actually an old river channel; a place the river flowed at one time. You see, thousands of years ago the Kentucky River used to flow this way, right where you are now standing. At some point the river found a short cut that, likely by a flood The water rushed on over the low ridge between the area of the Plaza Tower and the back of the distillery. This area is roughly where the old lock and dam is now. When the river eroded the thin slice of land in this area it quit flowing down through this particular area," the guide carefully explained.

The explanation caught Will's attention. He had long wondered why no visible creek existed along Holmes Street. He had just assumed the creek had been channeled underground as the area developed. It never occurred to him and he really never paid attention to this side of the road as he and countless others rushed in and out on Wilkinson Boulevard. Just then another question from one of the tourists. Will listened intently and moved a little closer to the group.

One of the kids on the tour asked, "Why is it called an oxbow?"

"Well, an oxbow is the curved part of an oxen yoke. It's the harness made out of wood that early pioneers used on oxen to pull plows, wagons, or whatever." Will thought the guide was pretty good at explaining, much better than he could have done.

"This valley curves around from one part of the river and back to the river again, forming a large curve. They always form this way and therefore are always curved. Geologists started calling these phenomena an oxbow and that is what we have here along Holmes Street and part of Wilkerson Street, an ancient oxbow." The guide began walking farther down the board walk and the group followed closely behind.

When the guide reached the observation deck at the end of the new boardwalk the guide concluded her remarks.

"As the river continues to erode downward today, the river bottom level has dropped below the old river bed level in the oxbow. No doubt a lake existed in the oxbow for many years, perhaps hundreds of years. Today the wetlands and marsh environment is still a reminder geologic processes never stop and relentlessly continue to carve out valleys and carry away the soil to the seas," The young and knowledgeable guide explained. The dialogue of questions and answers continued between the group of tourists and guide.

After a few minutes of looking around Will headed back out the board walk ahead of the tour hopping into his truck and headed for home. All the way home Will found himself confounded by the fact that he had never recognized the Holmes Street area as an oxbow.

When Will arrived at home he went about the business feeding the animals. He had planned to mow the yard sometime today, before he had to be back at work this afternoon. Jennifer and Ray were waiting to hear from him on the time this Saturday they could make their next trip and where they would go. Will pondered his discovery as well as thinking about places he and his treasure hunting partners might go this weekend. He dipped out equal amounts of mixed feed grains to the two horses that had stood patiently for the last four hours waiting on him to feed them. Will sometimes took Jennifer for a horseback ride around the farm trails but mostly he just fed them everyday and made sure they stayed put in the pasture.

By afternoon, Will was back at the Brick Yard doing his usual stocking and preparation for the evening. He knew he wasn't getting rich and was more or less getting by in this job, but he didn't have any debts either, other than his truck payment and feeding the few farm animals he enjoyed keeping around. Still the job at the Brick Yard was fun. Will met most of his friends here nearly everyday and he always felt something better would come along. About 8:00 PM Jennifer stopped by the Brick Yard to both say hello and check on Will. Usually, she would stop by a couple of times a week mainly because Will was never home since he worked most nights.

"Hey bartender," Jennifer commented as she perched on a stool at the bar.

"What'll it be ma'm?"

"Um, let's see. I believe I'll have some Jamaican rum and Coke."

"Good choice, though not very original."

"Not trying to be original. Just get me the rum bartender."

Will continued to make drinks and chat with Jennifer when he could. Business began to pick up for the evening though it seemed to Will to be slower than usual. The noise level had increased significantly and it was getting harder for the two to carry on a conversation.

"What time do you get off work tonight?" Jennifer asked

"I should be finished by midnight. I don't have to close tonight since I stocked and opened today."

"Good, are you going to come over afterwards?"

"Will you still be up?

"Sure, I get to sleep late tomorrow."

"Well, actually, I thought we would make a trip back over to McConnell Springs. You know we never really got a good look at the place last time. Ray got in such big hurry to leave, well, I just didn't feel we checked out the place very good."

"Ah, I wish I could and want to but I just can't tomorrow. I have to be down at the Old Capital by noon to shoot some pictures of some sort of history event for the paper."

"That's okay. We can go later, it was just a thought. Maybe Ray and me will get out and scout around a little tomorrow."

"That's an idea, where has Ray been lately anyway?"

"You know Ray. He is overworked down at that shop. It seems to me he never gets caught up."

"I need to go. Stop by, okay?" Jennifer said all in one breath and was gone out the door leaving half her drink unfinished.

Seventeen:
Boone Meets Swift

After a few days at the campsite on the creek the camp had become a storehouse of deer hides. Each day the men would head out in different directions with at least one remaining behind to guard their precious fur collection. Each man took turns staying in camp for the day and would have a meal roasting on the fire for those hunters returning. Hunting proved to be the best any of the men figured they had ever encountered before. The accumulation of deer hides from east of the camp, buffalo hides from the west, and scores of other small animals spoke volumes of the wonderful land Boone and his company of men had reached. Sometimes the hunters would not all return during evening. They had traveled too far on the day's hunt and had killed too much to complete their slaughter; darkness would overtake them. Daniel Boone being most often susceptible to this because he tried to explore as much of the countryside as possible.

Boone noticed as well, John Finley did not travel far at all from the campsite. John did not seem interested in nor did he collect many furs. The group could gather as much food as they need each day so there seemed to always be an ample supply of food in camp. Finley most often headed out north east toward the big mountain. Boone and the others assumed John headed into the mountain valleys to hunt deer and elk. Most everyone stayed busy with their own bounty and paid little attention to anyone showing up empty handed at the camp. John most often brought back to camp some squirrels or an occasional deer. One day, everyone except the designated camp guard, had left the camp. Boone had not returned the night before but no one thought anything of his absence. John headed out toward the knob he had taken Boone to the first day they arrived.

John spent the morning at a casual pace. He hadn't planned on doing much today, only to make his way up to the knob and visit the rock shelter he had stayed in when he healed from his injury. The same rock shelter John Swift first scratched on the wall the map to the treasure they had visited and taken from over the years. Now much later in the year than when the two met at the rock shelter, John figured for whatever reason Swift was running late. John felt certain Swift would be along unless something happened to him. If Swift had not planned on returning he would have sent word, John reasoned.

When John reached the base of the big cliff he followed the cliff line north until at last he reached the rock shelter. As he pushed through the bushes he saw a man sitting by a small fire. Not quite sure what to do, he crouched behind a thicket of vines next to the cliff and strained to see who was there. The man had not seen John coming and was unaware of his presence. The man stood up and Finley recognized John Swift. John began to make a commotion like he was climbing up the hill unaware of anyone. This would give notice to Swift of his arrival. He saw the stranger look his way and grab for his rifle.

"John Swift, is that you John Swift?" John yelled out. There was no answer. Perhaps it wasn't and John wondered what he should do. He knew that he was committed to the situation.

"This is Finley, John Finley. I'm John Finley."

"John?" Swift questioned.

"Yes, John Finley." The two shook hands.

"I figured you might have given up and went on without me," John commented.

"I could ask you the same, John," Swift responded.

"I wasn't sure if you would skip this year's trip."

"Did you come last year?" Swift asked.

"Well, yes I did. By myself of course. I camped here for about three weeks, wondering if you would show up and, well, I figured you weren't coming so I went on to the cave." The two men, old friends with an amazing treasure, stood by the smoldering fire and talked for a long time. The map, still visible, carved into the sandstone rock wall of the rock shelter behind them, provided an interesting backdrop.

"Have you been to the cave already?" Swift asked

"No, I haven't. I am here with a hunting party. Camped down on the creek by the old Shawnee town. Maybe you ran into some of them." Finley respond.

"No, I haven't seen anyone. I came down the Warriors Path."

"There are seven of us altogether."

"You may as well come with me; the two of us can get a lot more out than I can by myself."

"I can't just up and leave the group; they'll think something is wrong."

"Sure you can! Tell them you are going to head home. They'll understand. They can find their way back the way they came."

"I don't know about that."

"You surely didn't tell them about our secret cave, did you John?"

"You know I wouldn't. A friend of mine asked me to help him find the levels of Kentucky and since I was doing nothing else, I did so. At that moment the worst possible situation in John Finley's life happened. The two were so intent in their conversation they never noticed the skilled hunter surprising them.

"John," came a voice from around the ledge.

"Daniel? What are you doing here?" John felt awkward asking. Swift said nothing. Daniel walked on into the dry rock shelter over to the two men and introduced himself.

"I'm Daniel Boone, pleased to meet you," Boone said looking Swift straight in the eye and offering his hand for a hand shake. Swift hesitated for a moment, and offered his hand.

"Ah, this here is John Swift. He's an old friend of mine," John said.

"Imagine that, me stumbling upon my old friend camped up here under the same cliff I brought you to a few days ago," John nervously added. Perhaps the added detail, a lie, would be believable enough to throw Boone off his actual discovery of the rendezvous John had made with Swift. Boone didn't believe a word though. For the past three hours he had been tracking John all the way up to this spot. When Boone had nearly reached camp earlier in the day he spotted John leaving. John never saw Boone and was completely unaware of being followed by his old friend. Being curious of nature, he decided to follow him and realized he was heading for Pilot Knob. The tension notched up high for a moment and all three men felt awkward. Boone had intruded into the two men's discussion while at the same time the situation seemed suspicious.

"I hear you and John here are part of a big hunting party," Swift remarked.

"Oh yes, rightly so. We have done pretty well the last few weeks too. If you've been around long I reckon you heard all the shots. You huntin' this area?" Boone questioned as he looked about the rock shelter for furs or signs of hunting. There appeared to be nothing, not one fur. Something didn't seem right but Boone couldn't quite figure out the situation. Boone wondered how John knew Swift to be up here camping under this cliff and even more of concern, why hadn't John mentioned this rock shelter on their first trip.

"Yes. This is a favorite spot of mine. I arrived here yesterday and have not been out hunting yet. I was not aware of others being in the area. I can move on to another area," Swift remarked watching Boone look over the camp. He surmised Boone was wondering about the absence of furs.

"No need. Game is so plentiful a hundred men could kill in these grounds."

"I suspect you're right."

"How are you fellows acquainted with each other?" Boone asked. Boone figured he may as well get to the bottom of this mysterious meeting John Finley had not bothered to mention at all during the entire trip.

"Swift was the hunting partner with the Frenchman I told you about the other night. Mundy introduced me to Swift here and we hunted a bit together but more often he would stop by my trading store down there in Eskippakithiki," John explained. The trading store was the only thing he could quickly think of in this situation. At least it seemed to John to be the best way to work his way out of this mess. He also began to feel like it wasn't anyone's business who he was friends with anyway.

"I see. I guess if you traded with o'le John here, you got burnt a few times, aye Mr. Swift?" Boone jokingly remarked. Up until now Boone thought highly of John Finley, so much that he trusted John to be his guide into this Kentucky wilderness. At this moment Boone felt that a joke might ease the tension. It was obvious that Boone had caught John Finley completely off guard in this meeting place.

"I think John got some real good trades out of me, for certain," Swift answered.

"Well, there then. John you ready to head back to camp? It'll be dark before you know it. Mr. Swift, you are welcome to join us in camp, why don't you come along with us?" Boone asked.

As Boone turned to look at Swifts reaction to his offer his eye caught the unusual markings on the cliff wall behind John Finley.

"Well look at that, did you boys notice those markings?" Boone asked. Boone knew they must have seen the strange carving and figured Swift may have made it. If he saw it surely they had seen it. The carving still appeared to be freshly carved on the rock wall at the back of the rock shelter. Protected from rain and ice, the dry shelter wall had changed little since Swift carved the rough map.

"Yes, we can't figure them out, must be some kind of Shawnee writing from that village down there," John Finley quickly replied. Swift said nothing but continued to watch Boone carefully. Finley was a quick thinker and just as quickly as Boone noticed the obvious carving, Finley came up with an explanation that seemed to satisfy him. Boone studied the carvings carefully.

"Can't say I've ever seen any carvings like these. I know turkey tracks and such, but some of these. I never..."

"Shawnee must have come up here all the time. Heck, this is the best lookout post in the area. Most likely the work of them Shawnee."

"Did you know this was here, John?" Boone asked John Finley point blank. Again Boone was somewhat mystified that John Finley brought him all this distance to the top of this very pinnacle and never mentioned the rock shelter or the unusual carvings. Boone had a hunch that something did not seem quite right here.

"I did know it was here, but never thought to show it to you on our trip up here the other day."

"I see," Boone replied. "Mr. Swift you're more than welcome to come down and visit or stay at our camp."

"I appreciate the invite and I believe I will walk down with you and meet the other men. At least let them know I'm in the area too," Swift replied.

"Good. That's settled then," Boone concluded.

It only took Swift with the help of Finley, a few minutes to dust the fire out and put things in order.

"I have two horses up on top," Swift remarked while pointing his finger straight up indicating on top of the cliff above them. "You men go on ahead, I'll go get them and catch up with you later."

"We can wait on you," Boone replied.

"No, no need, I'll catch you since I'll be on horse back. No, you two go on ahead."

Swift figured this would be much less suspicious if he just went on along. He could head out from the creek camp at daylight and be away from this group. He was a little put out with John Finley for bringing this bunch of hunters into the territory and when the opportunity arose he intended to tell John as much. This makes things much more complicated he thought, to have others running around and slipping upon them unawares. This did not sit well with John Swift.

About an hour before dark the three arrived at the creek camp. No one had any game or furs with them. John Finley wondered if Boone had followed him or if he had just by the queerest of luck happened upon him almost the same time as he happened upon John Swift. This bothered John Finley. During the evening the men sat around the big fire swapping hunting stories and tales of discoveries they had made in the past two days. But the most fascinating discovery to the other men became the simple fact that John Finley met his old friend John Swift out in the wilderness.

"Up on the mountain we found a rock carving on the wall in a rock house," Boone told everyone.

"What kind of carving?" Cooley asked.

"Other than the turkey tracks, I never saw any such carvings before," Boone confessed.

"They're some kind of Shawnee signs," John added. He hoped to throw Boone and the rest off the idea of anymore interest in the carvings.

"Well, I admit I know little about Shawnee carvings and markings, but I sure never seen anything like these," Boone added. Swift said nothing but wished he had not drawn the map for Finley or at least had not spent so much effort carving the map so deep into the soft sandstone. This could end up being trouble, Swift thought.

The next morning, before dawn Swift got up early, packed and slipped quietly out of the camp. He headed north and picked up the Warriors Path until well out of the camp and turned westward toward the treasure. John Finley left shortly afterwards and headed west toward the old destroyed Shawnee town. John and Swift would meet up at their next land mark as soon as each could. That had always been the understood plan for such unpredictable events such as this one. Swift would have to add another day to his trip to the big springs. What neither of the two men noticed was that Boone slipped out of camp following John. Boone decided he would track John Finley just to see what his old friend was up to. If he hunted, then Boone could go on about his hunt, with no harm done. Boone was suspicious of the behavior of both John and Swift. Boone being naturally curious thought perhaps the two simply had a special hunting place that Finley had not told him about. Added to this mystery was the observation neither Finley nor Swift were much for hunting. At least it didn't appear they had an inclination to hunt the valuable furs. If they were going to better hunting grounds he would find out too.

John Finley passed through the old Shawnee town and stayed on a path due west. Boone stayed behind at least a mile but followed John's trail. John stopped and built a fire near a big burr oak tree and settled down for the evening. Boone saw the little campfire in the distance and made camp also, but without a fire. A fire would easily alert John that someone else had made camp. This could spook John into turning back to the creek camp. A little before sunset the next day, Boone caught up with John at a large spring out in the flat lands. Boone settled into a small rolling rise to the south of the springs. John stacked some of the loose limestone rocks and built a fire alongside the giant pool of crystal blue water "boiling" up from out of the earth. There were other springs and creeks along the Indian and buffalo trails, but none compared to this giant spring in size. The pure water just appeared from beneath the earth at this spot. John built a quick cooking spit by lashing together some tough, green hickory saplings. On his westward trek, John had managed to jump a pheasant for supper. The pheasant would cook nicely and be a welcome meal for both he and Swift, should he arrive tonight. Otherwise, John Finley would eat grand and sleep on a full stomach. He plucked the feathers, gutted and cleaned the bird and then washed it in the spring water boiling up from the ground.

Early in the evening another man arrived at the campsite riding a horse and leading a mule and was greeted by John. Boone saw it was John Swift. Boone carefully kept himself concealed although he really had no fear of the two men, at least not John Finley. The springs were situated down in a small valley, sort of a boxed in canyon although the depth was nothing like canyons in the mountains to the east. Boone dared not enter the camp. Instead he backtracked about a half mile well out of sight and built his own campfire for the night.

Well before dawn, Boone had moved back to the spot he had found suitable to observe the entire spring canyon area. The two men still slept, the campfire long ago in the night had consumed its fuel supply and only smoldering coals emitted the wood charred smell that filled the small valley canyon. Boone settled down and nodded off now and then, just waiting on daybreak. By morning light John and Swift had renewed the fire but made no effort to head out indicating to Boone these men had no intentions of hunting anything this morning. Boone could see the two men converse a lot around the newly stoked campfire.

"Did anyone follow you?" Swift asked.

"No, of course not. I figured it would take you an extra day since you had to go up the Warriors Path away from the camp," John replied.

"I suppose you are aware this is not a good situation we have."

"You mean Daniel Boone and the others."

"John, why did you lead these men into this country? Lord, don't you know how something like this makes things complicated. Surely you do."

"Don't worry. Boone suspects nothing."

"Yes, well, maybe. But I can guarantee it won't be long before one of his men will stumble upon us with loaded down pack animals. Then what do we do? Damn, John, you should have at least thought about the consequences of bringing them into this territory."

"This will be all right. I never planned to come down this far west. I planned to leave them and so be done with the whole matter. Besides, they would have come into this wilderness sooner or later. Boone was dead set on finding the good lands and I had rather know his whereabouts than be surprised one day when he just showed up."

Although Boone saw the two men in a rather serious discussion, he could not hear what they were saying. Boone wondered what the two men were up to and why they met out here at this big spring. Something didn't seem quite right about the entire situation, Boone thought. One thing for sure; he aimed to find out what was going on.

Eighteen:
Map Solved

The summer passed with little interest in the rock carvings. The activities of everyday life filled their days. For all intent and purposes, they had abandoned their once exciting treasure hunt since they had hit a dead end. With no new leads the would be treasure hunters arrived at the same place every treasure hunter before them had, out of clues and no grand discovery. With the passage of time, their overall interest and excitement had somewhat dimmed. What they did have was the discovered rock map. They felt sure they alone had made the discovery, since no previous treasure hunter had ever mentioned a rock carved map or anything remotely similar. Ray stayed too busy as usual, always days behind in repairs. Jennifer had spent a lot of the summer following a couple of the paper's most active reporters around the region. Will Morrow had read everything he found about the history of early Kentucky and now had become pretty familiar with the famous John Swift Silver Mine Legend. One beautiful Saturday afternoon in early fall Ray was driving the river road, shortcutting to pick up Highway 421. It was one of those beautiful days when some of the trees had already changed to their spectacular color and the skies were deep blue. He enjoyed the very warm weather as he crossed the Benson Creek Bridge when he noticed Will's pickup truck parked on the side of the road. He slowed down to make sure he had recognized Will's truck. Ray pulled off to the side of the road and backed up to the truck. Ray gazed up and down the road each direction on the chance Will may have had a breakdown and started walking for help. Seeing no one he turned his attention to the river and found Will standing on the pedestrian bridge. The small park area provided access to Benson Creek just before the creek emptied into the Kentucky River. Ray figured Will might be doing a little fishing so he thought he would go down and check on his buddy and find out if he had caught anything. Will was leaning up against the rails on the old abandoned steel bridge starring at the river. He had no fishing pole. Ray wondered for a moment what was going on with Will.

"Hey bud!" Ray yelled as he approached.

"Hello Ray."

"What are you doin' man? I thought you might be fishin' or something."

"Naw. Thought about it but, I guess I'm too lazy today. Besides, I'm on my way to work."

"Never too lazy to fish, man. I've caught a lot of fish right here where this creek empties into the river."

"It was such a pretty day. When I drove by here looking down at the creek, something suddenly occurred to me."

"You got that right. It is a pretty day for sure. Now, what occurred to you?" Ray questioned.

"What are you doing out running around? You're busy on Saturdays or at least you have been all summer."

"Ah, I decided to take the afternoon off. Tired, I reckon. Now, what was it you said a minute ago about something occurring to you?" Ray asked, trying to sift through the small talk to figure out what Will pondered.

Will's eyes stayed fixed on the water glancing up and down the river intently focused on something. Ray watched his good friend, not quite sure what to make of the situation. This was unusual, it seemed to Ray. Suddenly Will made an announcement that took Ray by surprise.

"Ray, I think I've figured out the giant turkey track."

"You figured out the turkey track? What are you talking about Will?"

"The turkey track, on the map, the big one, the big turkey track, I think might have figured it out."

"Go on."

"I've done some reading on Kentucky history, the silver mine legend and other stuff on the subject over the summer. One thing I read about was James Harrod who was a pretty interesting fellow."

"James Harrod?" Ray responded if more confused about Will than when he first drove up.

"James Harrod was famous because he built the first town here in Kentucky, Harrodsburg. Only then it was a fort."

"I know about James Harrod. So, what about him?"

"James Harrod was a friend of Daniel Boone."

"Yes, I understand."

"James Harrod searched for the lost silver mine after he built the fort. At least that's what the historic records say," Will explained.

"Now I don't recall anything about Harrod. Is that so?"

"Just listen to me a minute Ray. James Harrod, according to history, disappeared while searching for the lost Swift silver mine. He told his wife goodbye and went searching for the silver."

"I sure don't remember studying that in history when we were in school. So maybe there really is a silver mine?"

"I don't know since we're talking about a legend anyway. James Harrod believed such a mine existed. But the really interesting part is that Harrod told his wife where he was going to hunt for the silver, where he believed the mine to be located."

"And where was that?"

"Well, Harrod told his wife and friends just before he left he was going to the three forks of the Kentucky River to search for the mines. Harrod never returned and presumed to have been murdered by one of his enemies or renegade Indians."

"That's fine and dandy Will, but I don't get the connection."

"OK, maps of the Kentucky River show the three forks of the river are at Beattyville, up in the mountains."

"Now Ray, I want you to look across the river there. See? Over there, where the hotel and plaza tower are." Ray looked across the river at the hotel, the levee and many structures were all that Ray could see.

"Okay, I'm looking, so what?"

"On around see Holmes Street and if you follow the valley on around you come right back to the river down by the distillery."

"I know Holmes Street," Ray snapped.

"Holmes Street sits in a valley that runs from across the river opposite us here all the way around back to the river way down by the distillery."

"I know what you're talking about; I've noticed it's a valley but there is no creek or stream. I figured the water all must be underground, like over at McConnell Springs."

"I don't think that's the case here Ray. Well, the water is underground now, but just from the street runoff. What we are looking at it is called an oxbow."

"Oxbow?"

"Remember the new little park they've opened down there on the Owenton Road? Anyway, I went down there the other day and the tour guide was telling people how Holmes Street is located in the old original Kentucky River bed."

"River bed? What the hell?"

"The way I understand, the Kentucky River, at one time flowed through what is now Holmes Street. You need to imagine a bit, now stay with me here. For some reason, probably a flood, the river made the short cut here leaving the part that went out and around behind Fort Hill, so to speak. Probably for many years, maybe even centuries the valley was a small lake and may even have appeared in pioneer times as a drying stream bed of a creek flowing into the river right over there where the hotel is now."

"I'm with you, but what's your point?"

"Even today there are wetlands, a swamp on the other side behind the state office buildings along Wilkerson Street. A wetlands, I would imagine, would be left over from a lake, pond or something. At least there would have been a lot of water always in the area, I suspect."

"I still don't understand how this all has to do with anything, Will."

"Look behind you Ray. What do you see?"

"Benson Creek?" Ray answered in a hesitant question fashion.

"Bingo. Benson Creek."

"I don't follow you, Will. I don't get your point. Explain it to me in a simple way." Ray struggled to follow Will Morrow's explanation of the oxbow phenomena. Even though Will could easily understand the effect and had noticed dozens of such geologic oddities over the years it was harder to explain than he figured.

"Ray, over across the river once was a stream, at one time that was the way this river, the Kentucky, flowed. I'm talking thousands of years ago. Follow this valley around Fort Hill and you'll see the valley comes right back to the river down at the distillery."

"Okay. I get you. It's the old river channel."

"Right. Now, try to imagine yourself up in a airplane, helicopter or something a thousand feet above us right now and without hotels, houses or anything except the remains of a stream or lake in Holmes Street, even the wetlands from the other end extending all the way around to where the hotel sits over there. The river is still here and Benson Creek is still about where it is now. You're looking straight down on the whole thing. What do you see, Ray?"

"Ah, I see three valleys coming together."

"Right, but what do the three streams look like?"

"Umm. I get it. A turkey track."

"Exactly."

"A giant turkey track as a matter of fact, exactly like the one on the map.

"Hells bells, Will you can't be serious."

"Oh, I'm serious. I think this is the key. James Harrod searched for the silver where the three streams come together."

"That rock map turkey track surely did not mean these three streams coming together. How did you come to that conclusion anyway, Will?"

"Three reasons Ray. First, John Swift said in his journal, at least in many of the copies of his journal, the richest treasures where located at the place three streams came together. This must have been an important landmark to him. Secondly, James Harrod thought the same thing because he was hunting for the silver mine where three streams came together when he disappeared which, by-the-way is historically accurate. And finally..."

"Horses ass. You just now said Harrod searched for silver mines where the three forks of the Kentucky River come together," Ray interrupted.

"And finally, this lines up perfectly with the rock wall map at Pilot Knob. Look, see for yourself." Will continued his theory, pulling out of his shirt pocket the now tattered drawn map. Ray examined it carefully once again, even though all three now full-blown-treasure-hunters had memorized the map.

"Damn, the symbols on the map line up but there is nothing on the map indicating these are the three streams," Ray acknowledged.

"That's true."

"And we don't know what this eye-thing-symbol is either. We do know Pilot Knob is the starting point and most likely the Ohio River down at Louisville is the other end of the line.

So the other symbols would likely indicate something as well."

"I see, go on."

"Here, we have three creeks coming together. At least it would have appeared that way possibly in pioneer times. Benson Valley one prong, The Kentucky River the center fork and Holmes Street oxbow the other prong, almost opposite of Benson Valley. The three drawn out as they intersect form a turkey track! A giant turkey track! We just need to find that other symbol and make sure there are no other turkey tracks, or streams coming together between here and Pilot Knob."

"Maybe you're onto something, but the idea still sounds far fetched to me. I guess we need to get out there on every road and cow path between here and there and make sure there are no other possibilities."

"Ray, if there is a treasure and our other clues are right…then buddy, we are close to solving the map, right now. Hell, James Harrod could have been here on this part of the Kentucky River hunting for the silver instead of up there at the headwaters where everyone assumed he was. Neither we, nor no one else, knew what Harrod knew. He never told anyone anything other than he was going looking for the silver. He could have easily misled everyone on that matter. Or this could be the three forks of the Kentucky River to the people of Ft. Harrod those days."

"That could be so, but you're stretching it pretty far, Will. And so what, if that does solve the map. Where is the treasure or whatever the map leads to?"

"The map. Think of the map, Ray. Use your head for a minute. If everything lines up on the map right, this three streams thing here is right in line with the falls and Pilot

Knob. The problem is that this might be a turkey track, there might be something the way the track points. I don't know. My guess is that the eye symbol will either lead you here or this leads you there or I..."

"Okay Will. Don't melt down on me here," Ray interrupted, sensing Will was getting caught up into a loop of problem/solution/problem scenario. Ray was impressed that Will had found this possible solution to the map.

"The treasure might be around here somewhere, Ray. We could be looking at them right now and not even know it," Will concluded.

"The mine? You actually think there is a silver mine around here?"

"I don't know, but I do believe if we can find the eye shape, whether it's a carving or like these streams a big land mark, I believe we will have solved the map. Maybe just a map is all the thing is anyway. It could be something pioneers used to find their way across the wilderness back in pioneer days. It could be kids farting around in the rock shelter forty years ago. It could be anything."

"Tell you what, let's go get something to eat, call Jennifer to meet us somewhere downtown and we can fill her in on this theory you've come up with."

They sat and picked at their food, except Ray. Will explained everything to Jennifer the same as he had with Ray, but with a little more focus and fine tuning. He sincerely believed the three forks of the Kentucky River James Harrod spoke about were down river from Fort Harrod rather than up river in eastern Kentucky. Not to mention these three forks were much closer to Fort Harrod.

"The bottom line is we can work through this map puzzle if we can find the eye carving. This is the key here. Each symbol leads to the next. But only if you know for certain about the turkey track at Pilot Knob. That is kind of like the base marker, it seems to me," Will said.

"Base marker? What do you mean?" Jennifer asked.

"Look, we don't know what this symbol represents. Ray says it's a fossil. We don't know if these three lines represent a turkey track or three streams. We sure as hell don't know what this eye symbol is or where it is for that matter. But we do know that the turkey track on top of Pilot Knob matches the one on the rock wall map and those other markings must represent the Shawnee village. And if we accept that base marker then the other symbols or locations line up in a straight line on the map and if the map is, well if it is a map, then these streams here fall exactly where they should on the map," Will explained. Ray ate his food and listened intently as Will explained his theory about the three streams.

"So why are you so sure the three marks on the map represent the three streams here in Frankfort?" Ray asked. Will realized he had not completely convinced his two fellow explorers his turkey track stream theory was acceptable.

"Look, I don't know for sure. But if we accept the large lines on the wall map represent the Ohio River, and I think we agreed on that, even Louis Eversole agreed. We also agreed that the single line by Pilot Knob represents the Warriors Path, then the three streams theory seems to fit."

"You do have a point, Will."

"And don't forget that James Harrod, historically, searched for the treasure near the three forks of the Kentucky River. It's just that every treasure hunter, including your old buddy Louis, concluded the mines are in the mountains of southeastern Kentucky."

"You do make a good point, Will. It does fit together," Jennifer remarked. Will sensed he had convinced his two partners by the way they acted. Mostly because they quit challenging him with questions. It was time to drive his argument on home, Will thought.

"Not to mention that I have studied maps and there are only two locations that three streams come together on the Kentucky River and really only one that looks exactly like a turkey track." There it was, laid out and understood by all three. Everyone was finally on the same page realizing what Will discovered.

"So all we have to do is find an eye carving?"

"Exactly."

"McConnell Springs. I still say that the symbol or something must be there or somewhere in that area. I say we go back," Jennifer concluded. Jennifer had been the only one of the group that was actually convinced that McConnell Springs meant something.

"Even if it did, that still wouldn't help us. We might just have another symbol. Think about it. If you were drawing a map to a hidden treasure you only have to draw it so you could understand it and when you get to the general area you probably could find it. So the symbols could be for large landmarks that get you in the general area."

"Swift was supposed to be a sea captain, you said. Looks like he would have left pretty accurate maps and stuff," Ray said.

"Not for finding his secret silver mine," Will concluded.

"Let's go back to McConnell Springs one more time, okay?" Jennifer said.

"Did you say McConnell Springs? One of my favorite spots to visit in the fall of the year, huh Ray?" Roger Hampton interrupted as he walked by their table and winked at Ray. Stunned, Jennifer starred at Ray.

"What's he talking about, Ray? He creeps me out," Jennifer bent closer to the table and whispered emphatically at Ray. Roger Hampton had just dropped a bombshell and Ray knew he had made a terrible mistake by not telling Will at the bar the other night.

"Guys, there is something I need to tell you. I should have before, but, well you need to know this," Ray confessed.

Nineteen:
The Interrogator

A few days later, John Finley arrived back at the creek camp late in the evening tired and exhausted. John had made the trip and managed to return to camp with a substantial load of silver in his pack, though not noticeable. The silver coins John had gathered at the cave would not be enough to sustain him for a whole year. He couldn't bring so much back to the camp the men would get suspicious. He felt awkward enough to come back without any game kill, though John tried to find something to show for his efforts. He had convinced Swift it would be in their best interest if he returned to the camp and separated from the hunters in a normal manner. Swift, though he disliked the idea of John bringing the hunters into this particular area, agreed with John this seemed to be the best idea and would create the least amount of suspicion. Swift himself, had the advantage of having the pack horse loaded with an ample supply of treasure. Most all the other men had already arrived at camp with their days hunt. Boone waited on Finley and he had plenty questions for him.

John found the spot he previously claimed as his own at the camp and placed his heavy pack and rifle carefully. After cleaning up around his site and generally preparing his leaf and buffalo grass bedding he had collected on the first day at the creek camp, John walked toward the main camp and cooking fire. Boone and the others had already begun to eat the evening meal which consisted of, what else but venison steaks trolled over the fire. This preferred method of cooking, some called trolling as it took little preparation or equipment. The meat was simply cut into chunks and laid on the burning logs. When the log heated and burned, it cooked the meat and added the smoke flavor from the fire. Occasionally, the wood would burn some of the chunks of meat and they would fall into the hot embers. Each man had the responsibility for cooking his own meal and used sticks to quickly retrieve their cooked meal. The only seasoning the men had was the pouch of salt Boone brought along and the supply already ran low. If the trip lasted long enough, boiling down the rich salt laden waters of one of the mineral springs in the area would be added as another task to be done.

"How was huntin'?" Boone asked. Boone, as well as some of the other men, had already noticed John Finley had arrived without any hides or meat as well. The men glanced at each other in serious momentary eye contact, and unspoken body language as if to say, 'what's wrong with this picture?' No one said a word but their looks to each other spoke volumes. They all understood Daniel Boone was in charge and sure he had noticed the situation. They had confidence he would get to the bottom of the new mystery.

"Didn't find much. I didn't do any good at all."

"Uh huh. Where'd you hunt?" Boone pressed.

"Ah mainly I wandered around west of here."

"Some of the other boys had real good luck out that direction; can't understand why your luck changed."

"Well luck has a way you know Daniel." John hadn't exactly lied, but Boone knew John was being deceitful because he had followed him. Boone aimed to get to the bottom of why Finley had not outright told him of his meeting with Swift. Boone could have followed the two as they continued westward but choose to return to camp the next day. This is a strange circumstance, Boone thought, so he pressed on with his line of questions.

"What about the Swift fellow, did you run across him anywhere?"

John became a little irritated with all the questions about his business. He also began to feel Boone had something more straightforward he wanted to know.

"What's the problem Daniel? Is something worrying you about Mr. Swift? He is a good fellow and a good friend of mine. No need to worry yourself, Daniel." John intended to put the matter to rest. The least said meant the least problems.

"I reckon nothin' is worrying me. I'm a bit curious about Mr. Swift. That's all John."

For the next few days the hunters piled in as many deer hides and animal pelts as they could possibly manage to get out of the wilderness. Boone's party had brought pack horses enough to carry an extensive amount of furs. John Finley made more of an effort to add a few deer hides to the hunting party collection in order to keep down any suspicion.

"We are going to break camp and head back home in a couple of days, John. We, the others, and I agreed on the matter while you were gone the other day. Is that all right with you?" Boone asked.

"Why sure, Daniel. I'm ready to go anytime."

'Well, one thing for sure John, you ain't going pay for all your time out here with those pitiful few deer hides you collected."

"No, I realize my bad fortunes. But I don't need much. I just come to help you fellers find the good hunting lands. I reckon I did alright, didn't I?

"You did. You did indeed John Finley and I will forever be grateful to you for your help." Now did not seem an appropriate time to out rightly challenge John Finley's misinformation. Boone had caught him in a lie and he aimed to find out Finley's reason to lie and perhaps the reason for the rendezvous with Swift at the big spring. He needed to wait on the right time to catch John away from the other men. It was a sensitive situation and Boone was a good and discreet leader.

Boone later in the evening caught John off away from the others and pressed him about his trip west.

"John, the matter about Swift. I need to tell you something that might upset you," Boone softly spoke.

"Awe, Daniel, you ain't bringing Swift up again are you? I thought we had been through all this earlier. What's really bothering you Daniel, go on, get it off your chest." John had enough of Boone's questions and figured since they would be parting company shortly, he could afford to be a little more bold with Daniel Boone.

He was surprised by the quick and terse comeback from John. It also irritated Boone, being aware John had not been truthful before and not being truthful now.

"Well, let's see, here's how it is John. You have not been exactly telling me the truth, now have you?"

"Why do you say I've not been truthful? And what do you mean by that, Daniel?"

"You know what I mean."

"No, no, I don't know what you mean, so please enlighten me," John sarcastically remarked.

"Then let me do that," Boone fired back.

"So the other day when you went west hunting, I ended up going the same way too and I caught up with you and Swift down there at a big spring."

"That so. I didn't see you,"

"Yes, you didn't see me. But I saw you two."

"I saw you two at a distance and as I was tracking something at the time I kept on going. I guess I should have stopped but I didn't," Boone added.

John realized Boone was onto him and Swift. He could feel the panic swelling up in his gut as he wondered if Boone had actually followed him and Swift to the cave. Now he needed to find out how much Boone did know about his contact with John Swift and their business. He was caught and needed a quick explanation to get out of this uncomfortable mess.

"I did meet up with Swift out by the springs. We both are familiar with the place and when we hunt this area we like to camp at those springs. Plenty of water and a good sheltered place. Lots of game comes there to drink so hunting is good."

"Well, here's the thing, John, this sure is strange to me, and the other men for that matter, you and this John Swift go out hunting but don't bring anything back. The men have been talking about your hunting over the past days."

"Sometimes people ain't lucky hunting. I guess I had some of those days."

"John, do you ever raise any cattle back home?

"Well, yes, now and again."

"I reckon you know all about bullshit. And what you are trying to feed me is nothing more than plain ole bullshit!"

"Did you tell them about seeing Swift and me at the springs?"

"No, John I haven't. At first I figured this is none of my business and surely not any of theirs. Now, with you not being exactly truthful and trustworthy, I have second thoughts."

"But this is hostile country and we are here to hunt and collect furs. You or Swift don't seem to be interested in the hunting business. Now Swift ain't part of our party so what he does ain't my business. You on the other hand, ought to level with me. That's all I got to say, got it off my mind anyway," Boone concluded.

"Daniel, you and I have been friends for many years now. John Swift has been a friend of mine even longer. I consider both of you good trusted friends. I hope each of you consider me the same way."

"I agree, but you came into the hostile country as a part of my group. The situation is odd when you go off and wonder westward with Swift after you met him up on the mountain. It's strange, very strange. And the men are upset by it too."

John now became aware his friendship with Daniel was getting stretched to nearly the snapping point. He needed to relieve the tension and settle the situation.

"Do you want me to head on out? I'd planned on heading north anyway when you headed back home."

"No, you don't have to leave the group, John."

"Well, Daniel, I will be glad to go ahead and slip out of camp tonight if you think it's the right thing to do."

"No, leaving is not necessary. But I must tell you John, I can never trust you again. Based on your explanation to me here." Boone had backed John Finley into a corner. If he was ever going to keep his friendship with Boone he had to do something now. John knew Boone well enough to know

Boone would never have anything to do with him again under these circumstances. So John played the only card he had, so to speak, knowing this could be the biggest mistake he would ever make. He had no other quick way out of his current predicament. After all the time the two had spent together during their military days, John sure hated to ruin a good friendship.

"Daniel, if I tell you something, can you keep it to yourself?" John asked.

"If you ask me to, I believe I can."

"If Swift found out I told you this, I would imagine he would kill me. You and I are friends and I ain't going to tell you everything, but it will make sense why hunting doesn't interest me or Swift."

"This will stay between us."

"All right then, come over here and let me show you something," John motioned to Boone. Boone quickly eyed the others around the camp. Some were already asleep; others sat by the fire chatting and telling stories. One even had a book reading it to the others who showed interest. No one paid attention to anyone else by this time of the evening. Most of the men, exhausted from the day's hunt, simply fell off to sleep. Boone slowly got up from his seat and walked over to John Finley's location.

"What?" Boone questioned. John opened up his pack sack and held it toward Boone. Boone became speechless momentarily truly surprised by the contents.

"Those are silver coins. Looks like crowns," Boone whispered, not believing his eyes. The entire pack John had was full of coins. Other than a little tarnished from time, the coins looked to be new. Boone was bewildered for the moment.

"Yes, indeed silver crowns, in fact," John answered. Boone, known for his direct to the point tactics, wasted no time in his investigation.

"What are you doing carrying so much silver around this countryside and where did you get those new coins?"

"Well, Daniel, it's a long story, but let's say Mr. John Swift and I have access to a silver mine."

"A silver mine? What are you talking about, John?"

"Swift has been mining and smelting silver for several years in this countryside."

"I never heard of any silver mines in this country."

"Well, you learn something every day. Maybe a Shawnee mine or something, anyway, Swift found it."

"But these are silver crowns."

"Not real crowns, Swift and some of his partners made them from the silver ore."

"So these are not real but counterfeit?"

"Yes, well, Swift hates the King and what he is doing to the colonies. Sooner or later we're going to have to fight the British. Swift figures, and I have to agree with him, circulating these coins certainly doesn't help the King any." Boone retrieved one of the coins from the pack and examined thoroughly. If truly counterfeit, these coins appeared to be excellent copies of the real crowns.

"This is illegal at best and treason at worst, I suppose you are aware," Boone flatly stated.

"Well, maybe so but this is mine and Swift's business. The fact of the silver mine does not have anything to do with it.

Most of the silver is smelted into ingots. I am helping Swift get some of these crowns out of this country."

"So you are helping Swift in this treason?"

"It's more complicated, Daniel. We don't, well, a lot of people back east don't consider anything we do against the King as treason. The whole thing is going to blow up soon. Daniel we are going to either fight for our way of life or be slaves to the King."

"So this is the business you two were up to down at the big springs; you were on your way to the mine."

"Yes sir, Daniel. We have our meeting places and we usually meet at one or two places about once a year, usually about this time of year or a little earlier. We pretty much always go to the mine and haul out what we can both carry with our horses."

"What about the counterfeiting? I mean do you help do the counterfeiting?" Boone asked.

"No. No. Swift and his other partners did all the coin striking long before I came along. We are just taking out the struck coins, I don't even know nor have met the men who actually make the coins. Swift keeps me out of that end of the operation."

"How come Swift took you in on this deal?"

"Swift lost all his partners and we made friends when I had my store over here at Shawnee town in '52. I reckon Swift felt better having someone the Shawnee trusted."

"John, I can't tell you how much you've surprised me with this. And you say the mine is near here?" Boone casually questioned.

"I didn't say where the mine is but maybe one of these days I'll take you myself."

"John, does the map carved on the wall in the shelter up on the mountain have anything to do with the silver mine?"

"It does."

"I figured so."

"Swift drew the map for me back several years ago when I first come in as a partner. The map marks spots we can go to meet, and to the mine. The mine is not marked on the map but the way Swift figured it, he only had to find some of these key landmarks and he would be able to find his mines."

"Mines? You said mines. He has more than one mine?"

"Yes, he has access to more mines," John answered knowing this not to be the truth he figured this small embellishment wouldn't make any difference. "Daniel, can I count on you to keep this between us or are you going to tell the others?" John asked.

Daniel Boone had a situation on his hands. If the other men were aware that John was party to treason they would kill him right here in the wilderness. John was too good a friend to allow this to happen, Boone reasoned. He figured he would let John Finley by on this and let him go his own way. The men already had become suspicious of John because he never hunted much. Boone thought this was really something he never would have imagined. He had never heard of silver mines in the wilderness. He had to admit to himself he surely would like to visit one of the mines. Boone also reckoned the mine was west of their camp.

"I'll tell you John, this treason thing don't seem right to me. But you're my friend and I guess your business is none of my concern. My concern is for these men and a safe return home to their families. I only hope you don't get hanged for it, and they will hang you if you ever get caught passing off one of those counterfeits."

"Don't worry about me Daniel. Besides, I might take you to the mines one of these days."

"And you say they are around here?" Boone had to try one more time, hoping to confuse John and he would slip up.

"I didn't say, but I will say this; they are not around the spring."

The next day the party broke camp for the final time and headed south leaving the now familiar hunting territory behind. Finley packed up and said farewell to his old friend Boone and headed north. Boone had a difficult time explaining to the other hunters why Finley choose not to return with them to North Carolina.

The trip back home turned out to be much slower than the trip to the hunting grounds. The horses were heavy with pelts and hides of every kind of animal. When the party neared Cumberland Gap, Boone's hunting party met with James Harrod and his scouting party headed west into the great buffalo prairies. This was a chance meeting that Boone didn't care for, but his men knew members of Harrod's group and were extremely glad to see other hunters, not only to just see other humans, but to show off and brag about their good hunting fortunes.

"Daniel, looks like you boys faired well. Where'd ya' hunt?" James Harrod questioned.

"We were up the Warriors Path; the land is level and beautiful west of the trail. I would imagine it's the same west of here."

"We did well, found a burned out Shawnee town, met a man named John Swift and Finley headed north and"...Cooley rattled on, glad to be able to talk and brag on his adventures. Boone quickly interrupted, knowing that Cooley was about to invite more questions.

"Ah, Finley went north up the Warriors Path, headed for Pennsylvania, I reckon. Ah, John Finely, a friend of mine from my army days, was our guide to the good hunting lands," Boone Interrupted.

"Cooley, you and the others go on ahead, I'll catch up with you in a bit. Don't slow down for me. I'll catch up," Boone added.

"I guess the boys are getting anxious to get home now. Looks like you boys will make some good money with those furs. What's Cooley talkin' about Swift and a Shawnee town?" Harrod asked.

"Awe, nothing much. He is mixed up; o'le Cooley gets everything mixed up. We did come across a Shawnee town abandoned a few years back. Nothin' much left now, but the place does sit right on the edge of the flat lands," Boone offered.

"He said you met a man named Swift?" Harrod questioned.

"Nah, like I said he's mixed up," Boone scrambled for an answer. James Harrod was noted for being a no nonsense fellow and interested in anything going on out here in the wilderness. Boone felt like he had to come up with some sort of answer quickly and the first thing he could think of was the book that the boys had read around the campfire during the evenings.

"Did you ever read *Gulliver's Travels*?" Boone asked.

"The book? I have heard mention of if, but never read it," Harrod replied.

"Well, at night in camp we have been reading a chapter or two to entertain the long evenings, well, uh, anyway a fellow by the name of Swift from Ireland wrote the thing. I think Cooley is mixing up the story and what really happened. He is like those Lulbegruds in the book," Boone said.

"Lulbegruds?" Harrod was confused.

"Never mind, just a funny thought. The people in the book lived in a land called Lulbegrud or something that sounds similar. I think we stayed at that camp too long for old Cooley. Yep, Camp Lulbegrud," Boone laughed out.

James Harrod now totally confused began to think the whole bunch went mad while out in the wilderness. "Okay. Whatever you say. Reckon we had better get going. We are heading due west when we get through this rough area."

"Good luck, and good hunting." Boone replied and off he went tracking after his men.

Twenty:
Back to McConnell Springs

"Do you mean to tell us Roger Hampton is aware we are looking for the silver mine treasure?" Will asked, upset at Ray Deevers for telling their secret. Will and Jennifer decided this, of course, was not good news. Will's serious and intent stare showed his disappointment in his friend Ray. Ray remained quite, looking down, avoiding eye contact with either of his two friends. He struggled to come up with words to explain his situation.

"I never intended to get that snoopy bastard involved in are search. He followed us to McConnell Springs the other day. I think he's following me every time I cross town," Ray speculated.

"Damn, Ray. This is not good. How much does he know about the cave and the map? Awe, shit, Ray, has he seen the rock wall map? Tell me he didn't see the map Ray."

"I think he even followed us to Pilot Knob," Ray added.

"Well, great Ray. That is just great. I suppose he has found the bones under the rock shelter," Jennifer exclaimed. Up until this point the whole matter, though serious, didn't seem that important to Jennifer. Then Ray dropped the bomb shell.

"He has been to the shelter and he has seen the rock shelter wall map," Ray admitted. Conversation between the group of friends came to a halt. Will and Jennifer had been taken by surprise and this statement stunned them. Ray felt terrible for letting Roger figure out their quest. But he felt even worse because he had kept this knowledge from his friends.

"How long has Roger known about this, Ray? I mean I don't even understand how the subject even came up," Jennifer asked.

"For awhile now. Uh, since he had his car in the shop back in the summer. I didn't think he would or even try to figure out anything we were doing. He made me mad one day about staying over and working on his car, the same day, I think, we were going to Rock Bridge."

"Damn it Ray! You've messed up everything now."

"Shhh Will, people will hear you. Please, calm down," Jennifer said in a soothing voice. She saw that Will had become upset even more knowing Ray started the whole mess by talking too much. If she could get Will to calm down maybe people around wouldn't pay attention to their conversation.

"Well, hell, they may as well listen."

"From now on we watch this character and make sure he or one of his hired buddies don't follow us," Jennifer concluded.

"Look guys, if you want to do this without me from now on, I do understand. I sure wouldn't want me along." He needed to make some sort of peace offering. The only thing he figured was for him to bow out and not participate in the search anymore.

"Shut up Ray. We are partners in this, so forget such nonsense. From now on we need to keep our eye on Roger and you keep your trap shut. Do you understand?"

"Let me ask you something Ray, and think about this. Does Roger know about the buried skeleton ? Did he mention anything about those bones?" Will continued.

"Nope," Ray replied, knowing he hadn't told the truth. He feared this would cause Jennifer to report the find to the police. This would of course, in Ray's mind, effectively end their treasure hunt.

Another beautiful weekend rolled around and the three took off to McConnell Springs for a second visit. They watched for Roger to make sure they had not been followed. This time they walked past the visitor's center on down the trail to the Blue Hole, the first encounter of the water coming up from the ground. None of the three seemed sure why they had come back, other than Will felt like they had left too soon before and never really gotten to check the whole area out. The air was cooler now and the weeds had stopped growing from the frosts that came early to the region.

"Okay, the rock ledges down the creek? We need to check all down the creek, even up on the banks above the rock outcrops. There could be sink holes up there," Will explained.

"What are we looking for Will?" Jennifer questioned.

"Any cave opening, anything remotely like a cave opening."

"We didn't see any cave openings before."

"We didn't search very good either. Remember Ray up and wanted to leave," Will noted. Ray made no comment but shifted his eyes away and down to indicate to his buddies his shame for what he had done.

"I think I remember a small cave entrance now that I think about it," Jennifer said.

"You do?"

"Yep. When I was taking pictures down at the boils, you pass by, I believe, a cave entrance. Some place I sure don't want to go in though," Jennifer answered.

"Let's go," Ray said.

In a couple of minutes the three stood in front of the dark entrance just off the trail just as Jennifer described. The small opening was notched out of the limestone rock, hardly even noticeable. No stream ran into the small break in the rock, though the entrance remained wet from dripping water from the land above.

"So now what?" Jennifer asked.

"Well, we need to check and see if this leads to a cave," Will said. It was a long shot, for sure, but the three had all along, banked on the long shots.

"No way boys am I going in a small, cramped space like this. What makes you think anything worth finding is in such a place anyway?"

"No, I'm not going. I'll wait here. What if something happens? Someone needs to stay out here."

"Not a bad idea," Will agreed. "I don't know if anything is in there or that the funny marking on the map represents these springs. But we've got to eliminate this location in order to continue with our map solution," Will explained. Will believed he had the three streams figured out and it seemed to him the eye shaped marking would be the source of the treasure or map resolution. The eye shape on the map could represent the springs, just like Will believed the large turkey track represented the three streams.

"I don't know about this, Will. We don't have the right equipment or know how to go exploring caves," said Ray

"No Ray, it's my idea. I'll go. Give me the light."

Ray handed Will the light they had brought with them. Will knew this would be muddy and possibly dangerous. He also knew this was the longest shot he had taken in a great while. They had come this far because of the incredible luck they had experienced. After inching his way forward to the point he was squeezing between the rock walls he thought he had made a bad judgment. When darkness prevailed over the light from outside, he switched on his flashlight. Ahead, Will could see that the break continued on and actually got a bit wider. He moved forward until he could see that the limestone walls on each side came together. He noticed a small opening to his right, very small but dark. Will leaned over and pointed his light into the small hole and could see that it opened up into another cavern area. Without hesitation, Will slid head-first into the small dark opening. He heard water dripping back in the darkness and could see that the narrow passageway went at least another 30 feet ahead but did not appear to get any larger. Will inched his way along in a duck walk through the passage so narrow it rubbed both his sides.

"You okay in there?" Jennifer yelled back into the darkness. There was no answer because Will was already out of hearing range. "Do you think he is alright?" Jennifer worriedly asked Ray.

"Sure, he's fine. He's out of hearing range and that means this is a cave that goes back a ways. This is good."

Reaching the end of the thirty foot crawl, the passage sharply turned right nearly 90 degrees and descended a few feet. Squeezing through the turn was tricky but making that maneuver put Will in a larger area, perhaps a small room.

The chamber was large enough for Will to stand up. This is promising, he thought. Ray and Jennifer sat by the entrance of the cave. They no longer could hear Will or see his light.

"What if something happens to him, Ray? What if he gets stuck or lost?"

"Nothing is going to happen to him, Jennifer. Will can handle himself all right." Ray wouldn't admit it but he was already getting a little uncomfortable himself, though he did not want Jennifer to realize his concern. Just as Ray began to form contingent plans in his mind such as going in the cave himself or calling for help, Will suddenly appeared at the entrance.

"You had us worried."

"Worried?" Will questioned, confused. In his mind he was not gone all that long, but to the two waiting it seemed like hours.

"You're not going to believe it," Will exclaimed so excitedly that he could hardly catch his breath.

"Believe what, Will? What did you find?"

"You guys need to come look for yourself. I'm not going to tell you until you see for yourself. Unbelievable."

"No way am I going in there. No way," Jennifer flatly stated.

"You can do this. The first part is a little snug but the passageway turns and opens up into a small room. The ground is only wet right here at the entrance. The cave gets dry a bit further and you can stand up. A room is back there as well as a clue, I think. I believe this is what we need," Will told the other two.

"This is our only light," Ray said.

"This is no problem, really. Follow me and we can crawl

to the right spot. Come on."

"No, I'm not going. I'll wait here. What if something happens? Someone needs to stay out here."

"Not a bad idea," Will agreed. He led the way as he and Ray crawled through the tiny passage way and reached the small room. Standing up in the room, shining the light around Will held the light on one spot on the wall overhead.

"What is that?" Ray asked as he grabbed the flashlight out of Will's hand.

"What does it look like Ray? Remind you of anything?"

"Well, I'll be, the eye shaped symbol?"

"That it is my friend! Right over your head here in this cave!" Will excitedly announced.

"Oh boy, the eye shape carving, like on the map in the rock shelter. It's right here where it's supposed to be, McConnell Springs!"

Carved into the smooth limestone ceiling of the small cave the puzzling eye shaped carving clearly resembled, though larger, the marking on the wall of the rock shelter at Pilot Knob. The carving measured approximately two feet from end to end and perhaps a foot from top to bottom. The marking had been carved into the limestone and the lines were blackened with fire soot though no sign of a recent campfire was evident.

"Don't you think the lines were blackened by charcoal or something?"

"Most definitely," Ray agreed as he rubbed his hands over the rock carving.

"Do you suppose there is some kind of treasure hid in here somewhere?"

"This could be the treasure, I can't think of any other reason to put the symbol in here, though." For the next few minutes the two explored the small opening until satisfied no other passageways existed large enough for a human to crawl through.

Other footprints left behind provided clear evidence of other spelunkers exploring the passageway in years past. Small animal tracks indented in the soft dirt left the tell-tell signs of not so long ago inhabitants. Will returned to the eye-shaped carving and studied the shape. He rubbed the carving with his hand, tracing the grooved lines with his fingertips. As Will rubbed his hands over the cold stone surface, though he could not see them, he could feel more carvings.

"Ray bring the light closer." For the next minute Will rubbed the carved markings he could feel but not see. He traced with his fingertips the faint lines he felt carved inside the eye shape.

"What is it Will?"

"I'm not sure, I think more carvings are on this ceiling than just the eye shape."

Will found a piece of charcoal left by previous explorers. He rubbed the charcoal ever so lightly over the rock inside the eye shaped carving. This was his crude effort to darken the higher surfaces leaving the indentions the natural limestone color. Being essentially the same idea as tombstone tracings, the idea worked. Ray directed the light on the ceiling of the cave as well continued to rub the charcoal ever so lightly back and forth on the cold stone surface. Before them on the wall inside the eye shape marking faintly recognizable appeared the numbers: 38.11.84.50.

"It's numbers," Ray exclaimed

"Yes, it's numbers," Will agreed.

"It's is a bunch of numbers."

"38·11·84·50, that is what it looks like to me."

"Well, there is a dot between every two numbers."

"Yes, I see that."

"What do they mean, Will?" Ray asked, bewildered at their discovery.

"I don't know but I'll bet they mean something. Do you have anything to write with?"

"Now, why would I have something to write with? I never carry a pen or pencil," Ray responded. Will rolled up one shirt sleeve and with his finger, began rubbing the smoke blacking on his arm roughly writing down the numbers they had discovered. When Will ran out of blacking he simply rubbed on the eye shaped carving to get a little more. The entire length of his arm contained the numbers.

"Let's go."

Outside the cave Will and Ray found Jennifer waiting, guarding the cave entrance.

"What's on your arm, Will?"

"Numbers. We found the eye shaped symbol in this small cave."

"You can't be serious?"

"He is serious; it's down there and has a bunch of numbers carved inside the eye. Honest to God, Jennifer, it's an eye shape carved into the limestone like on the map in the rock shelter. Except this one has a bunch of numbers. Will wrote 'em down there on his arm."

"Did you find anything else, I mean, any sign of treasure or anything?" Jennifer got right to the point of the matter.

"We didn't find anything, but we didn't have anything to dig in the dirt with either."

"What are the numbers?"

"That's what I'd like to know, but one thing is for sure, we do know the map on the cliff is real and the symbols are out here across the state. Do you have any paper and something to write with?" Will asked Jennifer.

"Sure," Jennifer rummaged through her camera bag and found an old model release form. Will wrote the numbers down from his arm in the order they saw them in the cave: 38.11.84.50. He drew the eye shape around the numbers just as he had seen it in the cave.

"There were no numbers in the eye symbol on the rock wall carving."

"No, there wasn't. That might mean these numbers are important and whoever carved the rock map didn't want them to be found unless they found this symbol here."

"That could be so. I can't imagine..."

"What if these numbers are map coordinates?"

"Map coordinates? Oh my, what if they are?" Jennifer asked.

"You know, latitude and longitude coordinates. They would mark the exact spot of whatever the map leads to," Will explained.

"That could be true," Ray chimed in on the theory.

"They do look like map coordinates, at least the degrees and minutes would fit," Jennifer noted.

"Yes, and imagine even if this is some kind of hoax, we may have figured the deal out. We can find it now, whatever IT is," Will concluded.

"Well, wonder why no one has found this before?"

"Oh, no doubt many people have seen this but without the rock wall map back at Pilot Knob it would mean nothing. My guess is most people who would have been back to this point, kids mainly, would have not thought much about it. We, on the other hand, have been following these different markings and know the numbers have to be related to the overall map. Whoever carved out the rock wall map, decided they would put the information they needed here," Will said.

"Well, if those are coordinates, let's go find 'em and solve this thing."

"We need to look at a good map of the state just to see if the numbers by chance happen to be map coordinates," Will remarked.

As they walked back to the truck each of them scanned the parking lot just to make sure Roger Hampton had not somehow found out they were here and followed them. The coast was clear and once at the truck Will retrieved, from underneath the seat on the drivers side, a booklet of maps of the entire state. On the back of the book was a key to the maps that were contained in the book. All three stared intently at the back of the booklet.

"Now, what are those numbers?" Ray asked. Will held up his arm and began calling the numbers out.

"Three, eight, one, uh, I think it's a one, and another one. The next number is eight, four, five and the last number is zero." Ray quickly looked along the edges of the map looking for numbers.

"There's an 84 degree. What is that latitude?" Ray was unsure which was which.

"The numbers across the top are longitude. Latitude numbers are on the side of the page," Will explained. Will had to learn and become proficient with map reading in his geology courses.

"I see a 38 degree number there on the side," Jennifer noted.

"That would be the 38 degree latitude. Let's see now the numbers are 38.11. That matches and there is the 84 degree. These numbers in the cave are latitude and longitude numbers. I'd bet on it," Will concluded.

"You know that means there is a specific location this marking leads too, Jennifer added.

"This means we may have nearly solved this thing. We find those exact coordinates then we find whatever is hidden there."

"What about the other numbers Will? They don't show up on your map here," Ray noted. In fact, the general key map on the back of the book of topographical maps only showed general coordinates. The numbers on the cave wall actually detailed the location in degrees and minutes of latitude and longitude. Will took his right index finger and pointed it to the number 84 at the top of the map and his left index finger on the 38 number on the side of the map and brought both hands in straight lines until his fingers met on the map.

"Here is generally where we want to go."

Ray examined the map closer.

"This is near Frankfort," Ray pointed out.

"You're kidding, right?" Jennifer questioned.

"No I'm not. Look."

"The three streams. I'll be damn. The three streams are right there. Right at Frankfort, big as anything."

"What three streams?"

"You know, what I was telling you about the oxbow. That is one of the streams and it was across from Benson Creek, remember Ray?"

"Oh, yeah, I do remember you coming up with a wild haired idea, but to think this is what the rock wall map means, I don't know," Ray replied clearly not convinced of Will's theory.

"Well, anyway, I am guessing the other numbers are the minutes of the coordinates."

"So what do we do now?"

"What we need is a good GPS system," Will suggested.

"Wait a minute, I think I have a GPS app on my phone," Jennifer realized. She had recently upgraded her phone to one of the smart phones. Included in this particular package was a global positioning system or GPS system. Within a few minutes the three headed west while Jennifer worked with her cell phone to get the satellite map program running.

Twenty-one:
James Harrod

James Harrod shared his thoughts about what Daniel Boone said during their brief encounter along the trail. Mostly the tale of Boone's adventure amounted to nothing more than idle discussion around their campfires. Harrod and his fellow hunters stayed busy exploring the lands directly west of their entry into the wilderness. But during the evening the Boone mystery remained on everyone's mind. When Harrod repeated Boone's account of the bizarre naming of the creek camp site some questioned the story altogether.

"Nah, I know for a fact, a man by the name of Swift visited their camp," declared John Logan.

"Boone claimed Cooley got everything all mixed up. They called their site along that creek after some book," Harrod responded.

"Maybe so, but Cooley told me differently. Cooley told me a man, a friend to John Finley, showed up one day. He introduced him as John Swift. Said he was a strange character, claimed to be a hunter but they never once saw him with any game kills. I never had a reason to doubt o'le Cooley's word," Logan added.

"Why would Boone say there was no such person?"

"Don't know, but Cooley sure talked about a real person. He disappeared one day and no one ever saw him again. He and John Finley knew each other and some of the men thought them two must have been up to something according to Cooley." This was a puzzle to James. He wondered why his friend Daniel Boone had not been honest with him.

Making a mental note to himself, he'd ask Daniel the next time he met him.

Harrod and his men headed on to the place they soon would establish a fort west of the Warriors Path, good crop land and excellent hunting.

It would be several months later while back in North Carolina that James Harrod decided to pay his old friend a visit. Harrod hoped to find out about the lands west of where he planned to build his fort. Harrod also had not forgotten the previous incident and intended to inquire why his old friend deceived him. Perhaps Boone could have been misinformed and the whole thing a misunderstanding. His main reason, however, had to do with the news Daniel Boone now worked for the Loyal Land Company which only recently made a trade with the Cherokee for territory in Kentuckee. He figured Boone would soon be bringing settlers in to the area to set up his own fort, a fact not of little importance to James and his planned settlement. Land now became a precious commodity and no doubt the wilderness way teetered on the verge of coming to an end.

James found Daniel at his homestead on the Yadkin in North Carolina. He reached his destination early one afternoon to find Daniel out in a small barn-like structure, cleaning rifles.

"Daniel! Howdy!" James yelled out as he walked to the small open-sided shed appearing to be a roof on poles more than a barn. The structure certainly became handy to work in out of the hot sun as well as rainy days. It was a nice set up, James thought as he walked on up to Daniel.

"Howdy James! What in the world are you doing in this part of the country?"

"Ah, being in the area on business I thought I would come by and visit."

"Not much happening around here, but I am planning another trip back into Kentakee."

"Seems I heard such news, Daniel. It's one of the reasons I stopped by to see you. Curious, I guess. Word is you are working for Henderson now and heading back west to start a settlement. Is that true?" James asked. He thought it was best to lay it out as he knew it.

"Yes, I'd say you're pretty much right, James. I have been hired by Richard's company to take a bunch of pilgrims to settle in Kentuckee. We have been trying to sign people up, sell them a piece of paradise. Same as you did, James."

"Have you picked a location yet Daniel?"

"Not for certain. I like up around the mouth of Otter Creek, at least that's what we call it. Henderson and his company made a deal with the Cherokee for land north and east of where I hear you have been camping regular. You ain't worried about not enough land to go around are you James?"

"Oh, no. Not at all. I just wondered if the stories I heard were true. We are doing fine right where we are located. We've not had a problem in the last few months with any warriors."

The two spent a couple of hours in the afternoon trading hunting stories. Daniel questioned James on the best ways in setting up the fort and settlement going, including information about some of the pit falls.

"How did you convince all those settlers to come into this wild country?" Boone asked.

"Good farm land, excellent hunting, and safe territory," James responded without hesitation.

"Well, it's a bit harder sell now the Shawnee have gotten riled up and especially after losing my boy," Boone noted with sadness in his voice.

"Yes, I'm...we're all sorry for your loss Daniel. Something you never get over, I reckon. Well, I can't even imagine how it would affect me, to be honest."

After their time together just before James said his farewell he finally put the question to Daniel. "There is a matter I've been wondering about Daniel. Back when we last met on the trail, the subject of a man named Swift came up. Do you recall?" James carefully worded his question. Daniel thought for a moment, trying to remember the conversation and wondered what James knew.

"Swift, ah, yes Swift. He was a hunter," Daniel stumbled for words.

"Funny you remember it like that Daniel, 'cause I don't recall the story exactly the way you just described it. Now I am not accusing you of, well, being less than up front on the matter but I'm pretty sure it was not like you say now. Don't you remember? Remember Lulbegruds from the book?" James pressed.

Daniel realized he was caught in a situation. "Your memory might have faded too, James?" Daniel responded curtly.

"Yes, there could be some truth in that statement. I was just confused because your men told my bunch a different story. I can't figure out why they would bother to make up a story," James said.

"The truth of the matter there was a John Swift. He showed up at our camp one day on my trip in with John Finley. He and old John were friends and apparently partners in a silver mining operation somewhere in the wilderness," Boone confessed.

"Oh, I see?" He thought that this was even more strange than the original story.

"It's true, James. John Finley told me so himself. He said he and Swift had a silver mine. He never shared the location of any mine but he showed me some of the silver himself he was carrying out."

"Why didn't you say that before?"

"I am truly sorry about misleading you James, but I couldn't trust all those other men who had become suspicious, I suspect of me and Finley. I should have taken time then to tell you the whole story."

"Have you been to actually see the silver mine?"

"No, as I said I don't know the location of the mine. Finley never told me. Well, he did tell me it was located close to where three streams come together. He never said another word about the mines and I can imagine there are several places with streams coming together. I am going back to look for the thing, though," Boone replied.

"Well, a good way to get plenty of settlers signed up to go into the wilderness with you for sure, hey Daniel?" James teased.

"How do you mean?"

"You know what I mean Daniel. If there is a silver mine somewhere in the wilderness, people can't wait to move into the region. All you have to do is get the message out and you can best believe a lot of folks will want to come with you into the rough country. Why you'll make old Colonel Henderson a rich man, indeed. Probably won't do too bad for yourself either."

"You're right I suppose. Silver would sure get their interest up, wouldn't it? Just let the word slip out and we can't keep them away. Of course I'd like to find the treasure mine myself," Boone said.

"Where is this John Swift now do you suppose?" James asked.

"I wouldn't have any idea and I have not seen John Finley either. I guess they are somewhere working their mines."

"I've got to be going, Daniel. I am glad you straightened me out on the whole mess and if you need any help when you do get your settlement started, get word to me. Reckon I had better go. I think I might become a silver prospector myself," James winked at Daniel, turned and headed down the trail.

"Me too!" Boone yelled after him.

Later the same month Boone visited with Colonel Henderson and discussed his plan to lead a party of settlers. He told some of his former hunters about the mysterious silver mine and it didn't take long and more would-be-settlers signed up than available space to make a safe trip. In time, Fort Boonesborough became established on the Kentucky River just west of the Warriors Path and a short distance southwest of the old Shawnee town and Camp Lulbegrud. Boone and his party selected the site because of its good location along the river and it was far enough east of James Harrod's settlement so no interference occurred between them.

After arriving back at the completed fort, Harrod could not get the mysterious mine off his mind. He would take off on long hunting trips, mostly east towards the mountains. He always searched for a place where three streams came together. If he found such a place, he thought, he would be in the general area of the silver mine and may possibly find his own. Daniel Boone had fallen into the same abyss. He had little luck in his search for John Swift's and John Finley's secret. Sometimes he would trek deep into the rugged mountains and steep cliffs that few people ventured. He reckoned this would be the area of the treasure.

James Harrod's fort became a westward expansion success. Now that land companies actively tried to sell title to land grants in the region, more people ventured into the great wilderness. There were level lands in every direction, with an excellent water supply from springs and a full flowing creek nearby. The strong fortress offered many settlers the security they wanted in a still hostile land. Though James Harrod never used the subject of vast riches to be discovered to sell people on coming to his fort and secure tracks of land, Harrod himself was keenly interested in the fabled silver mine. After confirming with Boone the reality of Swift, Harrod inquired to nearly every settler venturing his way and gleaned as much information as he could about the mysterious John Swift and his supposed silver mine operation. The story now had become widespread throughout the hill country of North Carolina and Virginia. Many came searching specifically for the treasure with no intention of homesteading. Tales of turkey tracks, haystack rocks, rock bridges and myrtle thickets had exploded. Some claimed a journal existed which Swift himself kept with accurate directions to the mines. There was even talk of more than one mine and that the treasure was near the forks of three big streams. Harrod knew very well the location of the three tributaries that came together in the mountains forming the big river that by now was being called the Kentucky

River. Harrod spent days on horseback and by canoe exploring the countryside, especially in the mountains. He also had made his way up and down all the major rivers in the area. James Harrod had become extremely knowledgeable of the land in every direction around his Kentucky fort.

Twenty-two:
38° North; 84° West

Jennifer played with her smart phone fascinated by the map and GPS tracking of their movement as Will drove around town. Ray watched Jennifer tinker with the device but had little to say.

"I'm going to pull in down at the River Park parking lot."

In a matter of moments the three were huddled over the GPS. The reading came back from somewhere in outer space, from a satellite to Jennifer's telephone. The display read 38°,10',59" N / 84°,49',59" W.

"Two of the numbers are the same as in the cave at the springs!" Ray excitedly exclaimed.

"Yes, and what if they represent latitude and longitude coordinates? If so, we are near, I mean very near, the place the rock map has been leading too," Will said.

"We could be near something," remarked Ray.

"Well, we could be at the forks of three streams if our idea of an ancient creek flowing where Holmes Street is today," Will noted.

"You say that Will, I'm not sure I understand. I believe you but the whole idea seems pretty far out there if you ask me," Jennifer remarked.

"Try to imagine you are straight up above us a few hundred feet," Will began to explain to Jennifer as he had done earlier with Ray. Will explained his ancient oxbow theory and how the remnants might have resembled a stream back in pioneer days.

"We are near coordinates matching the numbers at McConnell Springs. Well, maybe we are a little east of the exact spot. If I'm right, we are practically standing in the center of the giant turkey track, which in fact, is not a turkey track at all but a rough map of three streams coming together," Will said with some confidence.

"The GPS says we are 84 degrees and 49 minutes west. The numbers in the cave say 84, 50," Ray pointed out.

"Well that makes sense."

"How does that make sense?"

"This GPS system measures degrees, minutes AND seconds. Our little gismo says we are standing at 84 degrees, 49 minutes *and* 59 seconds. This means are just a little east of the 50 minute reading. The same for the latitude of 38 degrees. Looks like we are just a little south and east of the exact location."

"That would put the exact location a short ways up Benson Creek," Ray said.

"It's getting dark but we should scout the area out tomorrow," Will suggested.

The other two agreed. They had come too far on this adventure now not to at least see the quest through to prove it to be a hoax or they had just misread the signs. To Will Morrow the rock wall map they had discovered months ago meant something. They had found nearly every landmark indicated by the carving. This had led them to the fantastic discovery of the eye shape with what actually could be latitude and longitude numbers. It was better to start off fresh with plenty of daylight.

The next day the three made up their plausible excuses, called their places of employment and one way or another got out of going to work. It was more difficult for Ray because he was backed up in repair jobs already. Being one of the best mechanics in the business, he could pretty well get away with a day off every now and then. They decided the night before not to meet at their usual place in town to plot out their strategy. Meeting at the restaurant provided the chance to encounter Roger Hampton. He already was on to their secret and if he knew that they had found the cave with the markings at McConnell Springs, he'd follow them right to their target. So instead they picked another meeting place. They chose the little park area where Benson Creek flows into the Kentucky River. The stream confluence was the same location Will had made the rock carving connection with the idea it was representing three streams coming together. Ray arrived first, walked out on the old abandoned bridge now relegated to the city trail system. Ray examined every direction trying to picture in his mind the turkey track Will had described to him before. It was not actually a turkey track, but if viewed from directly above the point where Benson Creek flowed into the Kentucky River and the point the ancient oxbow met the Kentucky River the rough shape of a turkey track could be imagined. This was still difficult for Ray, probably because he remained confused on the oxbow effect. Will and Jennifer arrived together in Will's truck after a drive-through sausage and biscuit breakfast.

"So what's the plan?" Jennifer questioned.

"I say we head right up the road until we hit the longitude mark," Ray suggested. Will agreed.

"Can you get the map and coordinates back on your phone?" Will asked Jennifer.

"Sure."

As the three casually walked toward the parked truck Will tossed his keys to Ray.

"You drive."

Will observed as Jennifer accessed the GPS program. About half way up the long grade of U.S. Highway 421 North, the numbers for the longitude matched; 84 degrees and 50 minutes west longitude.

"That's it, pull over here, we have a match," Will announced. Ray immediately pulled to the side of the road.

"According to coordinates, if this thing is right we have to be close; the GPS still reads 38.11.03," Jennifer told the others.

"We're in the middle of a road, Will. That thing must be wrong or else you don't know what the hell you're doing," Ray unexpectedly lashed out.

"Take it easy Ray, I'm pretty sure I am working the thing right and the numbers say we are at the spot," Jennifer snapped right back.

"This doesn't make any sense Will," Ray obviously redirecting his conversation. The three had followed all the signs and had apparently figured out the map to come to a point in the center of a highway. Will was trying to figure a solution or explanation to the current circumstances. The excitement of coming all this way only to be confounded with a meaningless discovery was wearing down the nerves on all three.

"Maybe when the road was built whatever was hidden here on this mountain ended up removed," Will offered as an explanation.

"Have you looked over there? It's a straight drop off," Jennifer piped in.

"Come on let's see the situation," Will yelled stepping across the road and over the guardrail. Jennifer turned off the GPS receiver and turned it back on just to see if the same reading came up. It was odd, that the coordinates were here in the middle of the road.

"I don't get it, this is the place, the numbers are all matched," Will clung to a small gum tree which managed to root into the limestone cliff he had reached. A shear drop off stopped Will's advance down the steep bluff. He estimated a forty or fifty feet drop straight down to the first ledge. There was no direct access down at this point. Will could see more trees, leaves and generally a more gradual slope farther on down the road, toward town. Perhaps the better way to explore the place would be to climb up from below, Will figured.

"So now what?" Jennifer asked as she walked over to the guard rail Will had just stepped over.

"I don't know, unless there is a cave or something down in the ledges beneath us here."

"That might be the case, Will," Ray commented as he finally crossed the road after allowing a few cars to pass that had collected into a caravan coming to town over the winding road.

"If there is some kind of cave, it's too difficult to reach it from this vantage point."

"Why don't we drive up Benson Valley, cross the creek, and climb up from the bottom of the cliff."

"Good idea. Let's go." Upon this agreement they hopped in Will's truck and headed out. They drove about a mile up the Benson Creek road to a place they could see the steep cliff on which minutes before they were standing. Dark areas among the many ledges looked promising from this vantage point. Will wondered why he had never noticed the sheer size of the rock and there appeared to be cave entrances. He pulled off the road near the railroad tracks. The three modern explorers focused intently on the area across Benson Valley. It was nearly vertical in places with ledges and outcrops almost all the way from the top to the creek below. There were shadowy areas creating both excitement and speculation in the mind of the three explorers. Will, Jennifer and Ray stood absolutely still for a few moments pondering the potential of what lay in store.

"Do you really think there is something up there, Will?" Jennifer asked.

"I don't know. If that rock map and the signs are right and this GPS is correct, if there is something, it could be up there somewhere," Will answered as he pointed up to the cliff before them."

"Well, boys are we going up there and find it or are we going to stay down here and talk about it?"

"Let's go back over there and park along the road there about half way up the hill and walk around into that biggest ledge about mid way up," Will suggested.

"Sounds good." After the short drive back across the creek the three parked along the side of the road and started out around the hillside. It was a fairly long walk and started out gentle enough. The further they went, the steeper the hillside became. The ledge eventually turned more narrow and the walking got slower. After about an hour the three had reached a particularly dangerous and steep area. They found no sign whatsoever of a cave or prize of any sort.

"This is going to be a long, tough search. Even though the GPS has us on the exact coordinates we still have a pretty big area to check out. I don't imagine whoever carved the rock wall could measure any better than this anyway," Will said as he looked under ledges.

"Think about it. It would have to be hidden; something you wouldn't just accidentally find?" Ray questioned.

"Sounds reasonable," Jennifer said, while taking pictures all along the way, as they slowly trudged along the narrow ledge. She knew if they actually make a discovery she would want the photo documentation of the whole thing. Jennifer had photographed every place they had been so far. Some of the photographs were quite extraordinary and her interest from the beginning of this adventure trip had been to make yet another great photograph. As the day went on and the sun finally went behind the hills to the west the three knew the time had arrived to abandon their effort.

"We had better head back out. It'll be dark before long and we only have this one light," Will said.

"We for damn sure don't want to be up here in this ledge stumbling around in the dark. We can always come back tomorrow," Ray added.

"Did you guys see the dark hole up there?" Jennifer asked.

"Yeah, I see that. Perhaps it could be something," Will replied.

The large overhang was partially blocked by a monster, car-sized, boulder. Cedar trees and other shrubs clung to the cliff from nearly every crack and flat area on the cliff. The overhang went well back into the stratified limestone rock.

"I think we can reach that ledge from over there." Will pointed a little farther ahead of them. The many small cedar trees clinging to the side of the rocky slope provided something to steady their climb by hanging on to the fragrant bushes as they steadily moved up the hillside.

"Be careful where you step. You slip here and you'll have a long fall," Will told his companions as he started up the little access point. When they reached the car-sized boulder they had to negotiate through a tight squeeze between it and the cliff to get into the dark area behind it. It was a small overhang only about four feet high and about three feet deep. The shadows of the cliff along with the distance had deceived the explorers. The three sat there in the tiny ledge and peered out to the valley below and the many ledges below them.

"Funny, it looked bigger from below," remarked Ray.

"So what do we do now?" Jennifer asked. She had already begun snapping photographs of Will and Ray in the rock ledges.

"There are at least another dozen ledges here to explore," Will remarked. Ray was scratching around in the back of the shelter, when an unusual rock surface appearance caught his eye. Ray moved closer and examined the face of the rock at the very back of the shelter. A small section was completely smooth and was slightly different in color than the rest of the cliff face.

"Will, come here and take a look at this." Will turned and crawled over to Ray looking over Ray's shoulder. "Look at this," Ray pointed out the smooth, unusual surface on the cliff.

"That sure looks odd." Before them on the side of the rock, perhaps no more than two feet high and about the same across, was a smooth plaster looking surface. Will made his way over to the unusual looking rock and carefully examined the unusual outcrop, rubbing his hand over the smooth area. The other two adventurers gathered around Will and stared intently and with wonder the strange surface under the overhanging ledge. He rubbed his hand over the smooth surface. With the back of his fist he gave a knock on the strange surface.

"What the hell?"

To everyone's amazement a small hole about the size of his fist appeared revealing darkness and empty space. Will hit the plaster a couple of more times and though the material was more than two inches thick, it easily fell away producing a larger opening to a cave. The hole was just big enough to get through. Will crawled back into the darkness but could see nothing. The cave had not seen this amount of light in more than 200 years. The entrance immediately dropped off at a downhill slant. Will could not see anything in the dark void but enough outside light made visible a slope of dirt going down ten or twelve feet and then leveled off.

"Wow. We've definitely found a cave and at the coordinates!"

"Someone intentionally plastered over this entrance. That covering is not natural."

"No kidding," Jennifer added in a sarcastic yet humorous tone.

"I'm going in," Will announced.

"I don't know. Just be careful Will," Jennifer said.

"I am just going to slide down the slope and see if I can see anything. I do not trust this flashlight for caving. We need to get a bigger light if there is more to the cave than we can see here." Ray was standing on the edge of the ledge looking back down the direction they came. He thought he had noticed some movement in the brush in the distance. Ray felt a bit uneasy and focused his attention in the direction for awhile. Finally, satisfied that he must have been mistaken, turned and went over the large boulder by the tiny cave entrance where Jennifer was patiently staring into and talking with Will as he carefully slid down the incline into the darkness.

"Has he found anything?"

"He just went in, Ray."

"Do you see anything at all?" Ray yelled down at Will. At the bottom of dirt incline the cave did indeed level off. Will pointed his flashlight toward the direction of the largest passage which seem to be rather straight. He figured the little opening he had slid down was a small sink hole which connected to the bigger cave. There appeared, from what he could tell, to be three other passages going off in different directions. All four formations were different in size but big enough to get through. Two were high enough for someone to stand up in. The floor was dirt with a few rocks and boulders strewn about, probably dislodged from the roof and walls in years past. Will stood up and shined his small light all around the immediate area to get a layout of the discovery. On one side of the cave lay a large pile of river canes. He picked up one of the canes to examine. It was obvious that the canes had been left in that spot many years earlier because they were dry and brittle. He knew they had not been brought there by animals because the pile was much too orderly. This was the work of humans. Will's excitement grew with each breath so much he could feel his heart pounding in his chest.

"Ray! Jennifer!"

"We're here," Jennifer responded.

"I think I've found something down here!"

"What? What'd you find?"

"River canes."

"River canes?" Jennifer and Ray said nearly at the same time looking at each other with puzzled, confused expressions.

Twenty-three:
Finley and Swift Disappear

John Swift and John Finley met at the Falls of the Ohio in the spring as prearranged. Swift had contacted Finley in Pennsylvania and asked if he make another trip to the treasure cave. John agreed to meet at the Falls of the Ohio and they would head east on the old Shawnee trace to the cave. In recent days the vicinity around the falls had been transformed into a thriving business place. A person with money might buy or sell about anything. John chose the river route this time with the knowledge a mule or horse might be purchased at the falls to continue the trip and to carry out the silver. With two settlements in the area and several more people in the wilderness the two felt uncomfortable making a trip down the Warriors Path. The area had become Boone territory and common knowledge Boone covered the area pretty well. James Harrod and company were doing the same thing farther south. It was getting crowded in the wilderness and Swift was concerned.

Swift arrived first, but by only three days. He found a suitable camp spot upstream from the traders and the settlement. They knew the territory well enough to quickly find and follow the trail that headed east straight into the three streams valley and their precious treasure cave.

"Hello John Swift," John said as he arrived at the camp.

"Hello John. Good timing on your part," Swift responded.

"You been here long?"

"This is the third day. Done a little hunting south of here."

John could see and smell the fresh venison cooking on the quickly made hickory spit over the hot coals. John was hungry after the three days on the raft eating jerky and dry biscuits.

"The rafters held up a day waiting on another rider."

"You hungry?" Swift asked.

"As a bear." The two ate quietly though studying the many other encampments on both sides of the river at the Great Falls. There were more people and even some roughly made houses now standing at various places farther up the bank to stay out of the occasional flooding which sometimes happened in the spring. After they ate Swift noted from the sun the time to be a little past noon.

"I see you got us some mules."

"A trader down yonder sells 'em at a fair price. I figured these two would do the job for us. They're green broke so we might have to walk and lead them."

"So long as they can carry a heavy load."

"Ready to get going?"

"Yep." Swift packed his belongings, kicked some of the dry river sand on the cooking fire and began loading up one of the mules with his traveling pack. John loaded his pack on the other mule and they set out in the direction of their quest. Very little conversation went on between the two as they made their way east. By late afternoon they were into the flat grasslands that they knew would turn into rugged steep terrain and the eventual location of their cave.

"John, I heard something odd." Swift mentioned as they walked along briskly.

"And what did you hear that was odd?"

"I heard around and about from different people about a silver mine here in Kentucky."

"How would anyone know about a silver mine? Maybe George?"

"I am pretty certain it wouldn't be old George."

"Well, then who else would know anything even to tell?"

"What has come to my attention, and this is hearsay, Daniel Boone is hunting all over the place around the Warriors Path for a silver mine. Wonder where he got the idea there was a silver mine?" Swift commented.

"I wouldn't know, hadn't heard such a story. If you're thinkin' it's me...well, just get such thoughts out of your head, 'cause it ain't me," John replied. He was worried though, because he knew he had told Boone but he never dreamed Boone would tell anyone else. John thought this could be trouble.

The two reached the familiar creek headwaters then followed the shallow rock bottomed stream all the way down to the base of the cliff hiding their special cave. After a short rest and staking the mules they began the steep trek up the hill. The trip became routine over the years. Once on the creek they could find the cave with little trouble even though the hillside had become heavy with growth. They would approach from various directions and using different ledges in their climb each time to avoid developing a noticeable trail. Once the two reached the hidden entrance behind the large boulder they slid down the steep incline of dirt that collected near the entrance from countless rains over decades. Swift and Mundy had taken time on one visit to scrape up and pile on some more cave dirt to make the incline less steep.

For a few years they used a crude wooden ladder to get to the floor of the cave from the entrance. The wood tended to rot very quickly due to the continued dampness from the cave and surrounding limestone rock so the better alternative was to scrape up dirt and rock from the floor of the cave and improve the dirt ramp.

Near the bottom of the incline were the torches they had made and stored from the previous visit. The bundles of river cane lay stacked up on a small ledge that was faintly visible from the small amount of light shining through the tiny opening to the outside world. Swift struck the back of his knife on a piece of flint he always carried with him and produced enough sparks to ignite some dry grasses stored with the torches. One he got the fire going he lit one torch and another. With little hesitation the two men crawled down the main entrance until they could stand on the flat floor of the cave. They turned to the first passage on the right, which was narrow but high enough to walk freely. After the level walk of nearly thirty feet the passage opened up into a large chamber that was approximately a hundred feet long and about thirty feet wide. The ceiling was nearly forty feet high. Several large boulders lay randomly scattered about. The floor sloped upward across the giant room, to the opposite end. Stacked against the wall, on top of each other, on the boulders and even in the middle of the room were wooden barrels filled with newly minted English Crowns. Some coins were strewn about on the floor, dropped during previous visits as the men stuffed their sacks with as much silver as they could possibly carry. Near one large boulder was a ship's chest filled with silver bars and gold chain. Rough, crude log bins, made from nearby cedars that were placed to keep the hundreds of loose coins near the sides of the cave from being scattered about.

"Looks like everything is the way we left it the last time we were here," Swift commented.

"I've never asked you before, but I always wondered how you and George managed to get all this up here? My Lord, that must have been an awful feat?"

"Oh yes, a lot of work involved in this place. Like I told you it took us one whole summer to bring the silver from a hiding place much farther east of here. We used ropes and lowered down the barrels and containers, some in skin bags, to this ledge. Difficult for sure but look at what we have here, John."

"Let's get loaded up and back down to the creek and make camp for tonight. Like before, we shouldn't be up here too long." The two began to fill their packs with the crowns, grabbing handfuls at a time and throwing them in.

Back in Harrods Fort, folks had become used to James Harrod heading out from the fort on his 'explorations.' Most knew what James was really up to and some even grumbled about his absences from his responsibilities.

James Harrod leaned over and kissed his wife goodbye. "I should be back in less than a week. If not, send some of the men looking for me," James said.

"Where are you going, James?"

"I am going to hunt for that silver mine."

"Where will that be?"

"Up at the three forks of the river."

"Why do you want to chase after a silver mine, that is just a tale that Daniel Boone has come up with to get people to follow him to Boonesborough."

"Maybe so, but I believe there is a mine out there. And if it is, I am going to find it." With that, Harrod headed out the door of his cabin, and met up with Taylor Bridges, waiting for him at the gate and off they went. The two did not head east toward the well known three forks of the Kentucky River, but traveled northward. With the river only about five or six miles from the Fort Harrod and others always kept canoes near the river. After the walk they arrived at their canoes, boarded and started down the river. By the end of the day they reached their destination, the place where the three streams came together.

James guided the craft to a large sand bar at the mouth of the creek on the north side. This would make a good base camp and they could explore the valleys on all three streams and return to the camp in evenings. He reckoned they could do this in four or five days and then a full day, to get back to the fort: More than enough time to meet his self imposed deadline to return. Taylor immediately began to collect drift wood and started a fire. James secured the canoe and off loaded their supplies. The two treasure hunters gathered up longer pieces of drift wood and cut some of the canes growing on the river bank to fashion a crude shelter. They planned to be here for few days it was necessary to have shelter and traveling by canoe prevented carrying much supplies. They would live off the land, hunt small game and perhaps try to spear some fish in the shallows.

Harrod and Bridges settled in around the fire and watched the twilight turn to darkness. Unknown to the two, Swift and Finley, by pure fate, shared the same valley nearby.

Nightfall had arrived when Swift and Finley came out of the cave the moon provided enough light for the men to make their way down the mountainside. Both heavily loaded, started their careful decent down the steep cliff. They made their way by walking out one of the many ledges and finding a short jump down to the next ledge. The campfire on the mouth of the creek where it emptied into the Kentucky River was obvious.

"We've got company," Swift said.

"I see we do." John replied. They descended quietly to the creek where the mules stood motionless in the bare spots they had made as they munched the weeds and grasses around them. There was no evidence anyone had found the mules. Dropping their heavy packs of silver and ignoring their would-be campsite, the two began to follow the shoreline of the creek toward the campfire. John was troubled about the situation but Swift was downright angry.

"Wonder why they are here on this creek?" Swift whispered as the two carefully moved along getting closer to the fire.

"Could be hunters," John offered.

"Maybe, but I doubt it," Swift responded.

"You don't know they're not," John answered back. He hoped they were hunters anyway. The idea of someone searching for the treasure all because of Daniel Boone's big mouth was not a pleasant thought. The two, now within a hundred yards of the fire, slowed their pace, placing each step as not to make any sound. They heard men's voices coming from the fire but could see nothing.

"We had better make some noise to let them know we are coming or we'll get shot," John whispered. Quickly, Swift started whistling as loud as he could stopping long enough to loudly ask John how he liked his music.

Harrod and Bridges, startled by the sudden noise, grabbed their rifles and focused up the creek bank in the direction of the noise. At the same time both men moved away from the fire into the darkness, Harrod stepped behind a large sycamore tree that leaned out over the creek. Bridges moved into the tall canes growing along side their campsite. Each man, now ready for action, intently focused on the obviously intentional noise makers coming down the creek.

"Hello!" John yelled out as he and Swift came into view.

"Hello!" James Harrod yelled back, relieved it was not an Indian hunting party.

"I'm John Finley."

"John Finley, well, this is, uh, I'm James Harrod." Finley approached the campfire so Harrod dropped his rifle to his side and came from behind the tree to face him. After both Swift and Finley were by the fire, Harrod walked over to greet the two. Bridges then came out of the canes. The four men were face to face and John Finley knew the situation had become complicated. He just didn't know how bad.

"This is here is Taylor Bridges," Harrod gestured.

"This is John," Finley introduced.

"John Finley, well, we've never met but I heard you were guide to that rascal, Daniel Boone."

"Yes, I did guide for Boone awhile back but I haven't seen him in a few years now."

"I guess he is like us, out looking for a silver mine," James Harrod replied smiling.

"Say John, I didn't get your last name?" Harrod questioned Swift.

"Just you two in the party?" Swift countered.

"Yes, just us two Mr. ah ..." James Harrod paused waiting for Swift to fill in the blank.

"I don't believe John told you, but in any case it is Swift." At the same time he uttered his name, Swift raised up his rifle with one arm and shot James Harrod in the chest point blank. With his other hand he drew his side pistol and shot Taylor Bridges in the face. Both men died instantly. It happened so fast neither man had time to react. John was shocked by the act.

"What the hell are you doing?" screamed John.

"What do think I am doing? These men are within a half mile of our cave. They would find it John! And that cannot happen! Hell, the whole damn country is looking for it!" Swift shouted.

"Good Lord, you killed them. James Harrod is an important man in these parts. People will be looking for these men in a few days. My God, what have you done?"

"Come on John, we've got to close this camp down and get these bodies out of here," Swift sternly said. He was no longer interested in John Finley's shock.

Things had to be handled immediately. Swift moved down to the water's edge. Using a large rock, he knocked a hole in the bottom of the canoe. The canoe quickly sank after being pushed out into the main river. John sat and stared at the two dead men partly in a state of shock and partly in thought of what his own fate might be now. Swift dragged the bodies into a clump of bushes just in case there were others in the party that happened to be away from the camp. They sat by the fire and did not sleep. At daybreak each man quickly made a travois from saplings lashed together with rope that Harrod had brought. Travois were simple devices made with two long pieces of wood with shorter pieces as cross bars just long enough to hold the torso of the victim. The feet would drag behind, between the two long poles. Swift's experience on the high seas had taught him how to tie about any kind of knot and lash anything together. After erasing all signs of the campsite, each man hauled a body onto the travois then headed back up the creek to their own campsite.

"What do we do now?" John asked.

"First, we need to water the animals. Then we are going to have to climb back to the cave. We can put these bodies in there and they will never be found," Swift answered.

Each man led a mule to a much needed drink at the creek. Though they could go for a quite a ways without water, it had been the day before since the animals had quenched their thirst. After each animal drank its fill of the cool, sweet creek water the two mules were again tethered to a rope in the tall grasses.

"This fresh grass should keep them busy for awhile," Swift remarked.

Flies had already located the dead bodies in the hot sun and began the process of laying their maggot producing eggs. John felt sick and numb from the whole event and wanted to throw up. For the first time he was glad he had an empty stomach.

"Let's go, we need to get these fellers up to their resting place," Swift said as if the two murdered victims were relatives ready to be laid to rest.

"Why did you have to do this? They'll be looking for them and we might be hanged for their murder. You do realize that don't you?" John asked.

"John, I had to do what I by God had to do. Now, you are either with me or them, what'll it be?"

"I'm with you, of course. But I think the problem is only going to get bigger."

"Oh, how's so John? Listen, we drag these two back up to that cave, put them in one of those side passages and seal the cave entrance up the way we always have. Then we are coming back down here, load the silver on the backs of those two animals over there and get the hell out of this valley as quickly as possible. By hell John, the next time we come back for the treasure, half the people in this country won't even remember the these two anyway."

The climb was difficult and very slow going all morning. Climbing the ledges alone proved difficult but trying to drag a travois with a dead body became nearly impossible. With each advance to the next small ledge the men would look back down the creek and scour the whole area, looking for signs of another human. By noon they finally reached the cave and dropped the bodies down into the small, dark entrance. It was a simple matter of pushing them down the dirt incline to the bottom. Once this was done they quickly unlashed the temporary transport system and discarded the poles over the ledge. They climbed back into the cave, lit torches and drug the bodies to the back of the main passage, past the first passage on the right to the next turn out passage which was smaller but big enough for someone to stand up. They left the lifeless frontiersmen in this small passage. On the way out the two men went back into the large room that contained the treasure. They had no reason to do so other than it seemed natural to check to make sure nothing had changed.

"You killed two good men who had done nothing to you."

"Well, John, what would you have me to do? If you hadn't told Daniel Boone about our treasure we wouldn't have this problem, John." Swift laid it out on the line with John Finley. John knew this had become a problem far bigger than anything he had encountered before. The tone of Swift's voice and the two dead bodies made it clear to John he had reached a critical situation.

"What makes you think I told Daniel Boone or anyone?"

"Well it's pretty simple. I know I didn't tell and I know George didn't tell and you are the only other person in the world, alive who knows about it," Swift said.

"How can you be sure George didn't tell someone?"

"I know."

"Or what about your ships crew? They helped you bring the stuff into the territory, maybe one of them decided to tell.".

"No. Dead men don't talk."

"You mean you killed all of your ship's crew?"

"Had to. Well, George helped me."

John Finley didn't say anything. He was numb from the events of the past several hours. John understood he had reached the danger point of pushing the situation too far with Swift. John Swift was obviously ruthless. As ruthless as a person John had ever come across, and to his misfortune he was now the only living partner to John Swift.

"And George, you killed him too?" John asked.

"George Mundy was a fine man, loyal and trustworthy. I liked George and it saddened me when I had to, well let's just say, George changed and we had to part company."

John listened, watching Swift as he moved closer and reached over to pick up a hand full of crowns holding them out to John in a gesture in support of what he was about to say.

"George became greedy. He made several trips to this cave and carried out twice as much as we agreed to bring out. His actions surprised me, really. I never thought of George as going money crazy but he did. I figured it out when we were up at the same shelter where I healed you back together. George didn't deny the fact either. He owned up to his wretched ways. Well, let's just say o'le George will never return to the cave, we had an understanding." With everybody gone I still needed a partner to help me carry out the silver and help me fight off any Indians. You fit that part, John, so with some reluctance, you may recall, I brought you in. You agreed to keep this secret between us. You do remember agreeing, don't you John?"

"My God, this damn silver has made a killer out of you. If I had known this I'd never fell in with you. Lord what have I done?" John declared. If Finley had been numb before now he had become sick to his stomach of the whole situation.

"Now calm down John, we can handle this thing," Swift said as he put his right hand on John's shoulder.

"You have been a good partner, well, except for your big mouth. You never took more than was reasonable. Heck, I don't think you ever came here unless I was with you, but you could have. You helped me, just like you are now, carry out the silver I need, we need. All this is absolutely true John, I cannot and will not deny those facts."

"Listen, I did not tell anyone, anything about this place." John pleaded his case but at the same time knew he had told Daniel Boone. After being partner to a double murder, a lie would surely not send him to hell any faster.

"The problem here John, is I really don't believe you. Now you were with Boone and his bunch for a long time up near the Shawnee town and Pilot Knob. Not long afterwards comes along Harrod looking for my silver. Doesn't add up to anyone else, because I know who I've told. And John, you're the only living person in this world I've told and it's been that way for many years now." Swift had laid it all out nice and clear which made John far more uncomfortable than his ordeal back at the Shawnee town.

"We can figure this out, but we should get out of here now," John said in hopes of changing the tone of conversation.

"Yea, well, there is the problem, John." At that same moment without hesitation, Swift thrust his long knife deep into the chest of John Finley. John screamed in pain and terror. The strike was below the heart but landed deep, causing Finley's lungs to collapse.

John dropped the torch he carried surprised by the sudden feeling of faintness. He felt he was almost in a dream state, the point of drifting off to sleep. As his knee's began to buckle, Swift held on to him and gently lowered him to the cold floor of the cave. John now knew that he would never see the light of day again. He began to drift in and out of consciousness caused by the lack of oxygen to the brain as a result of his failed lungs. He would die in this very cave. Blood poured out the deep puncture, following the cold metal of the blade still in his chest. He was fading, the torches became dim. Swift pulled the knife from Finley's chest allowing the wound to bleed even more. Then, as suddenly as the first thrust, Swift finished the job with a second thrust directly into the heart of Finley. It was over. Swift, once again, alone knew the secret of his treasure cave.

Swift left the cave went back down the mountain to the creek, back to the hidden packs of silver. He rustled through Finley's belongings at the campsite and found a piece of deer hide among his camping supplies. He walked down to the bank of the creek and gathered up as much mud as he could on the deer hide, bound up the corners of the makeshift bucket and dipped the mud, deer hide and all into the clear waters of the creek. He figured the wet mud wrapped in the protective hide would remain moist enough for its intended purpose.

Swift began the long climb back up the ledges to the cave entrance. The trip passed much quicker without pulling the weight of a dead man up the hill. Upon arrival at the hidden entrance, he quickly stacked rocks of different sizes into the cave entrance making sure he could stack them as not to easily tip over. Broken rock fragments were plentiful scattered about the ledge. He finished up by dobbing the wet mud over the rocks he had just stacked until the entrance no longer was visible. He provided the final touch by gathering up handfuls of the lighter dirt and dust gathered under the dry overhanging ledge and throwing on the damp mud stucco he had just created. This, he figured, would provide some resemblance to the natural rock, at least enough to deceive any explorers.

Twenty-four: More Bodies

There simply was not enough light for Will to safely explore the passage ways. The small flashlight batteries had already begun to fail and he knew he had little time left. He could see around the immediate area the floor was fairly smooth and seemed to be hard packed. He scurried back up the dirt incline until he reached the small opening to the outside world where Ray and Jennifer waited.

"Well?" Jennifer asked.

"These dip-shit batteries are about dead. We need better lights or a lantern. I should have brought my Coleman."

"No problem, we can get new lights then check the place out good. If you think it is worth our time," Ray commented.

"It's most definitely a cave passage and worthwhile. Actually I think several passages might be down there. I didn't even get back far enough to really see anything other than it seems to be a fairly large sized cave."

"OK, I say we get the lights and come back as soon as we can," Jennifer recommended.

"Good deal. Let's go," Ray said.

"One more thing."

"What 'one more thing'?"

"People have been in the cave. I found river canes piled up. Some appeared to have been burned."

"Cane torches," Ray remarked as he began his careful decent down to the next narrow ledge.

"Cane torches?" Jennifer questioned, not sure of what Ray was talking about.

"Yes, cane torches were used by the Indians. They would tie a bunch of dried canes together in bundles and light one end of the bundle. The torch would burn for a good long time so the Indians could explore caves."

"Well, whatever, a big pile of dried river canes are laying next the wall down there, just as soon as you get to the bottom of the dirt ramp."

"Dirt ramp? What dirt ramp?"

"An inclined dirt ramp from just beneath this entrance extends out into the cave. It looks almost as if it had been purposefully built. In fact, I'm pretty sure it was built. Makes it very easy to get in and out of the cave."

"Any signs of Indians or anyone living down there?"

"I didn't get much further than the end of the dirt ramp because of this piece of shit for a light," Will complained slamming the light against his leg to emphasis his disgust for not being better prepared. The three slowly walked off the mountain retracing their steps carefully. The trip back took much less time than climbing up. They had to be careful and negotiate their way through a maze of small ledges that formed and petered out as they made their way down the steep hillside.

Roger Hampton was driving south toward town on highway 421 returning from just listing a new property in the northwestern part of the county when he noticed Will Morrow's truck parked along the side of the road. At least he thought this to be the same truck he followed to Pilot Knob. If it was the same truck he wondered why it was parked there, perhaps a breakdown he thought. Good enough for those crazy little farts, he thought, pleased with himself.

Two days later the truck was parked in the same place and the three were once again at the tiny opening of the cave. This time they had plenty of light and ropes should they need them.

After checking his new light, Will pushed his backpack through, and crawled in the small opening then slid down the dirt incline first. Ray followed. Jennifer decided she would remain at the cave entrance in case something happened requiring help. She was not thrilled about going into the cave to begin with and since they agreed someone needed to stand as lookout outside the entrance just as a matter of safety, she was glad to take the assignment. She sat with her back against the large boulder facing the opening. Jennifer fiddled and organized her camera case as she often did when she had to wait on the shot she was supposed to get on assignment.

At the bottom of the dirt ramp both men stood and examined the immediate area.

"Over there, Ray, are those river canes I told you about." Will pointed his light in that direction. Ray walked over to the pile of primitive torch material and examined them more closely.

"I'll bet these were torches for whoever used this cave. Look around and see if there is any flint scattered about. This might have been an Indian camp or something," Ray immediately supposed.

"Possibly, but I don't see any ventilation for a campfire. Where would the smoke go, not to mention the map coordinates? I doubt that Indians would be using latitude and longitude to locate their cave."

"You're right. But by using cane torches this is old I'll bet."

Both decided to follow the main chamber to get an idea of the size of the formation. They continued past three passages to their right and one to their left. The main passage they were in seemed most promising and they felt more secure exploring it before wandering off on any side passages. In about thirty yards, the main passage tapered down until it was gone leaving nothing but a stone wall. A small fist-size-opening was all that they could find and appeared to be the source of the water which possibly formed the cavern eons ago. Water moving through the limestone, contained acids which gradually dissolved the limestone hollowing out the cave. The floor was smooth with a few rocks scattered around.

"Nothing here, Ray."

"What about these side passages?"

"Let's go as far as we can. I am going to light the lantern."

Instantly the entire cavern filled with a soft glowing light.

"On the ceiling, Will," Ray said as he turned up the beam of the light he carried. Before them, plain to see, was a charcoal marking.

"It's another one of those eye shapes, Will, and it has *letters* inside this time." Instantly they recognized inside the eye marking the letters J S G M. The entire drawing was large, perhaps four feet across. Though crudely shaped, their significance instantly became recognizable. Apparently the letters were made by the blackened end of burned torches.

"Well, we are in the right place. We know that now."

"But what does it mean?"

"Don't have clue. I think we ought a check out this side tunnel now."

After following the main chamber as far as possible, they turned their efforts to the side passages. The first opening they started down was actually the last one on the right from the front entrance. In only a few steps the tunnel became very tight, so much Will could not squeeze through. The passage proved to be a dead end, not much of a cave at all. As Will retreated backwards, Ray also backed out into the main chamber they had already explored. They moved to the second passage which proved much easier to walk through. The floor was smooth with dirt just like the main passage. This one went for about 25 feet and widened a bit the farther they walked. This section was very dry and the dirt was like fine powder.

"Ray, over by that rock. Do you see it?" Ray swung his light in that direction then followed it directly to what appeared to be a rusty flint lock rifle. The wood stock had long ago rotted away. Beside the rifle were a few bones.

"Are those bones human?"

"They're bones all right." The bones appeared scattered, not in any particular shape, probably the result of rodents and animals over the years. There was no mistake however, as to the type of animal that once possessed these bones.

"They're human. No doubt about it," Ray confirmed, pointing to the two human skulls amid the scattered debris. A hunting knife and a few other rusty metal items lay amid the chaotic mess.

"No shit." Will quickly moved over to the pile of bones where Ray stood.

"One thing's for sure, we can find dead humans," Ray remarked.

"What's going on here? I mean, what do you think this means? Three dead bodies connected to the rock wall map that led us from one dead body to another. I don't know, Ray. We got us a little problem here, don't you think?"

"No shit, Sherlock."

"Do you suppose this is all about taking us to a burial site?"

"I do not see any kind of signs of a burial."

The two wandered around for a few minutes looking for other clues which could be important. They didn't find anything else.

"We had better go and check on Jennifer and tell her what we have found."

"You sure you want to tell her Will? She about freaked at Pilot Knob when we found the first skeleton."

"We've got to tell her Ray, she's in on this as much as either one of us," Will snapped surprised by Ray's sudden reluctance. He felt irritated with this attitude coming from his buddy Ray.

"I didn't mean anything, I'm just sayin' we should check it all out, that's all."

"Then what, Ray? Sooner or later Jennifer has got to know. She's gonna want to take pictures I would imagine, of this eye shape with the letters."

"I know, I know. It was just that, well…"

"Right. We fart around in the cave all day, 'till time to go and 'oh by the way Jen, we found more dead bodies down there? Shit, Ray! Come on, man!"

The two explores maneuvered back out of the side passage way into the main cave. When they were within only a few feet from the dirt incline and entrance, Will decided he would check the last passage.

"Ray, let's check this last one out before we go."

"You go ahead. I'm going out and get some fresh air, and a drink of water."

"Go on, I won't go far if this passage goes out a long way."

Ray acknowledged that he would return in a few minutes or bring Jennifer to the bottom of the incline now that they knew the main passage was safe. Ray quickly scrambled up the incline.

"Everything OK out here?" Ray asked as he surfaced into the brightness of daylight.

"Yeah, did you find anything? Where's Will?"

"He is still looking down another passage and sent me up to check on you."

"Oh, that's sweet of him but he shouldn't be down there by himself."

"Jennifer, we found some bones and the same eye-shaped symbol."

"Oh my God, did you really?"

"Yes, and inside the symbol were the letters *JSGM*."

"*JSGM*, hmm. No numbers, just letters?"

"Yep. *JSGM*, big as anything, right on the ceiling of the main passage of the cave. Will is still checking out what we think is the last passageway of the cave. Want to go have a look?"

"I sure do." Jennifer grabbed up her camera bag and moved over to the small opening in the giant limestone cliff.

"We believe the bones are human," Ray continued. Jennifer stopped in her tracks and turned to face Ray.

"Human bones. This is not good. Not good, Ray."

"Well, before you go and jump to conclusions, let's finish checking out the place."

"I think we need to report this to the police. These are not Indian burials, Ray. Did you ever hear of Indians using coordinates to find their burial site? This might be some kind of sicko serial killer getting his jollies. We have to report this."

"Now hold on Jennifer, just listen to me for a minute. We can go and report this when we get off the hill, but we need to get our stories together, because it's been months since we found the skeleton up at Pilot Knob. I would imagine the police might be more than a little curious as to why we took so long to report those bones."

"We tell them the truth, Ray. For God's sake, Ray! This is not anything to play around with."

"Just go see for yourself. Go ahead." Jennifer slid down the incline and into the darkness. Ray followed behind. The lantern still put out abundant illumination to the immediate area of the cavern. Ray showed Jennifer the pile of river canes next to the wall explaining how he thought they were used. Ray pointed up to the ceiling and Jennifer saw the symbols herself. She set up her tripod and attached the camera.

"I need a wide angle to get the entire eye in the photograph." Jennifer fumbled in her bag until she found the 28mm lens. "Wonder what this all means, Ray?"

"You mean the letters?"

"Yeah."

"I don't know. Maybe the *JS* means John Swift."

"You know those letters could be initials. In the Swift journal I read there was a partner to John Swift. His name was George Mundy."

"*GM*, George Mundy and John Swift. Could it be that simple?" Ray questioned.

"Where exactly is Will, anyway?"

"I last saw him going to go down that passage over there." Though Will Morrow was not far from Ray and Jennifer they could not see his light because of their own lantern was illuminating the main cavern.

"Where's the skeleton?" Jennifer asked.

"Off in a side passage up there. Come on, I'll show you." Ray led Jennifer into the second passageway to the small collection of bones. Jennifer stood over the discovery, carefully studying the details. She saw the area had been disturbed and some of the bones apparently were missing. Jennifer noticed the rusty knife blade and begun to snap photographs of the scene.

"Did you notice the rusty knife blade, Ray?"

"Yeah, we saw it."

"Ray, come over here and stand by the bones so I can get a perspective for my picture."

"Nah, you don't need me in the picture."

"Get over there Ray. I need you in the photo."

Ray reluctantly moved over near the bones and posed for the photograph. Ray was pretty sure Jennifer was going to run straight to the police with the information about two dead bodies they had discovered. Ray had just as soon not mention this to anyone and certainly did not want to be included in any discovery.

"We haven't found anything else in here. Will is checking out the last passageway now." In fact, Ray wondered what had happened to Will. He should have returned by now unless he was in trouble or found something.

"Sure is strange they are up here with the same symbol we found over at McConnell Springs with the right coordinates for this spot," Jennifer thought out loud. Ray began to move the bones around and looking for anything that might offer a clue as to whom the bones belonged. Ray was particularly interested and hoped that he would find some type of burial artifacts commonly found with Indian burials. He found nothing remotely related to prehistoric people. He found some metal buttons, a buckle and another rusty knife blade.

"Here is some more stuff. Buttons, I think, and another knife. I don't think this is an Indian burial."

"Looks like a murder victim to me, Ray."

Twenty-five:
The Discovery

Will walked along and gliding his hand along the wall through the passageway widening out at the same time the ceiling became much higher. He scanned the immense void with his light and decided he needed the lantern he brought. Once fully burning, he held the light out in front of him. The large chamber was filled with debris and rocks. As he walked through the rather large open room he noticed piles of small rocks almost all the same size. Will moved to one of the piles and picked up one of the round objects. Though dusty and tarnished with age Will held in his hand a coin. He was stunned as he gazed around the cavernous room. Before him were dozens, maybe hundreds of piles of these coins. Some were strewn about but most seemed to be in little mounds up to about a foot high up against the walls of the cave continuing all the way to the end of the passage way. Will walked around the entire room stopping at one of the piles of coins and retrieved a coin to compare to the last one he had sampled. The coins appeared to be the same. Will was certain they were silver. Time stopped. Will Morrow had found himself in an unreal world. At least one attempt to count the piles of coins was aborted simply because of the large numbers of piles. Will left the lantern sitting on a boulder in the room and with his flashlight retraced his steps back to the entrance of the passage. Ray noticed Will's light coming out of the passageway.

"Man, where have you been? We were getting worried about you," Ray scolded. More than an hour had elapsed since Ray had left Will to go outside and retrieve Jennifer.

"I've found something."

"Well, yeah, we figured out the letters in the ceiling too," Ray proudly announced.

"John Swift and George Mundy, I would suspect," Will replied.

"Oh, you're good Will. We don't know why anyone would put those initials up there, though."

"I do. Come on, I'll show you."

Will turned and led the others into the side passage with Jennifer practically on his back. Ray followed a few feet behind. The three made their way through the narrow beginning part of the side passage.

"What is it, Will?" Jennifer asked.

"You've got to see this for yourself. You won't believe this." When they entered the large cavernous room the lantern still faithfully illuminated the chamber. Will stepped aside to let Ray and Jennifer look at the situation. The soft glow from the light created shadows from the boulders as well as piles of coins throughout the cave.

"What is that?" Jennifer asked.

"Take a look for yourself," Will said has he grabbed a coin from a pile and handed to Jennifer. Jennifer examined the coin turning it over in her hand. Ray stepped to one of the stacks near him and retrieved his own to examine.

"Coins!" Jennifer exclaimed.

"John Swift's silver coins, I would imagine," Ray said.

"Guys, I think we have found it. We have found the mine!" Will shouted.

"You mean to tell me after hundreds of years of people searching for this silver treasure we're the ones to actually stumble upon it?" Ray questioned with excitement in his voice.

"It would appear the case, Ray."

"There are thousands of coins in here!"

"The entire chamber has these small piles of coins all along the wall and up against the larger boulders in the room."

"What kind of coins are these?" Jennifer questioned as she examined closer rubbing the dirt and dust off.

"I don't know for sure, but I would guess they are silver crowns."

"Well, the writing is English."

"Holy cow, there is a fortune in money in here," Ray concluded. The three spent quite a bit of time wondering about looking, and examining the room. Ray discovered more bones by one of the larger boulders in the room.

"Here's another body, I guess. So far this makes three we have found in this cave. I wonder if one of them is old John Swift. It appears like these silver coins had caused some killings." Ray commented. On the ground nearby lay the rusty works of a rifle. Ray picked it up for Will and Jennifer to see.

"This one has a rifle with it too. I think it is like the other one."

"This has got to be the Swift treasure mine."

"Oh wow, how amazing is this? I need to go get my camera and tripod. This is beyond comprehension," Jennifer said. She had left her camera on the tripod in the main passageway.

"Just think about the whole thing. We followed the map and found a treasure. Unbelievable," Will remarked.

"My God Will, what do we do now?" Ray asked.

"What do you mean?"

"Well, I don't hold the deed to this land, do you?"

"No. I hadn't really thought about it Ray." Will walked around the piles of silver coins reaching down and picking up handfuls at a time and checking each one. They were identical with the same markings and writing.

"This is a storage cave, kind of a warehouse. If Swift's journal is accurate and this is Swifts treasure, there should be a mine somewhere around here?"

"Will, what do we do now?" Ray questioned again, a little more persistently.

"I don't know. We need to take some of the coins and get them checked, identified or something. Then I guess we should ..."

"I'm going to do a story for the paper. This will make national news, no doubt," Jennifer interrupted.

"No. No. I don't think we're ready just yet," Ray responded.

"I kind of agree with Ray, babe. We need… we've got to think this thing through."

"Why? We've just made a fantastic discovery. We solved a puzzle and there must be millions in silver coins. Not to mention we found four dead people in the process. I say we have to let someone, the authorities or someone know about this."

"I do not agree with you on that Jen," Ray flatly remarked.

I don't care if you agree or not. This is a story and I should have the story before some other newspaper or TV reporter finds out."

Will saw things were getting a little testy between Ray and Jennifer though Will actually agreed with Ray taking time to make the right choices. Will felt they were instantly wealthy, perhaps, depending on how the situation was handled. After all, they had discovered the treasure; they should be entitled to some of it. Right now he needed to simmer things down a bit. The excitement of the discovery had ratcheted everyone's adrenaline and emotions up too high.

"Guys we don't have to decide anything just right this minute. This is major. I mean we've made a monumental find here. There is no need to fly off and tell everyone just yet," Will interjected.

"I agree with Will on this one." Ray immediately took Will's position.

"Oh I see. It's like that, is it?" Jennifer felt a little hurt and alone for the moment.

"For one thing, JENNIFER, how are we going to deal with all these coins?"

"Is it even ours, Ray?"

"Well, we found it."

"Not on our land."

"And there's my whole point, before we go off with some half-cocked bullshit, we've got to have a plan. We need to keep this between us for now, dead bodies or not. Whether we spill the beans on this today or two weeks from now will not matter one bit is the way I see it," Ray pointed out.

Will had dumped his survival items from his backpack to make room for some silver coins. Ray and Jennifer had developed a stand off and Will quietly put silver coins by the handful into his pack. Will pointed out to the others he was taking some of the coins in hopes of finding someone to identify them and perhaps place a value on them. With this information they could then develop their strategy. Both Ray and Jennifer agreed to this plan. Jennifer was concerned, but reasoned that a few hours wouldn't matter. Her conviction was still to report to the local police as to this discovery. She also wondered about whose property they were trespassing. Each person wandered about the large cavern examining the many piles of silver coins.

"The original wood boxes, barrels or whatever these were carried in here with have rotted. Someone sure had to do a lot of work to get all this in here."

"I'm amazed this has not been discovered before now."

"Apparently the only ones that knew about it besides us are those poor bastards whose bones we've been stepping on."

"I want to get my tripod and maybe go outside to get some air. The air is getting pretty heavy in here." Jennifer remarked referring to the disagreement she had with Ray. Ray saw he needed to make peace after he thought about it. In his mind, as long as no one jumped to conclusions until they all agreed to a plan, things could still work out.

"Look Jennifer, I'm sorry if I upset you. I understand and appreciate what you want to do. Heck, I would probably do the same thing if I was as talented as you," Ray began. In Ray's mind, he knew somehow this site needed to be kept a secret between the three of them. He was now convinced it was a bad idea to bring Jennifer along. If it had been just him and Will, there would not be a problem now, Ray figured.

"This is just about too much for us to even comprehend. Look at all those silver coins," was all that Jennifer could comment. She was still furious with Ray and hurt at Will for siding with Ray.

"Now that you two have made up I am going to explore farther back in this passageway to see if there is anything else."

"I'd still like to go get my tripod and go outside for a few minutes."

"Come on Jen, I'll go with you. I'd like some fresh air myself."

"I think I can find my way."

"I'm sure you can. Is it OK if I come too?" Ray politely asked.

"OK Ray, come on."

"You sure are worried about someone finding us. What's got you so nervous Ray?"

"Well, for one thing your truck is parked on the side of the road down there, secondly, we are up here on the side of a cliff on somebody's land without permission, need more?" Ray was becoming nervous and agitated with all this new-found wealth.

"Okay. Okay. Go on." Ray and Jennifer quickly exited the cave. Ray moved out and down the ledge away from the boulder that hid the opening in the rock to take a good look all around the hillside. Jennifer sat leaned up against the limestone cliff near the tiny cave entrance, soaking in the beautiful sunlight and breathing the evergreen scent of the cedars scattered about the ledges. Ray had not come back up from his observation spot.

"Ray, come on. Let's get back in there." Jennifer climbed up from behind the large boulder and came around to see Ray standing on the next ledge down focused intently down, the mountainside.

"Ray. Come on."

Twenty-six: Boone Bewildered

Several people now occupied the town and fortress Boone established on the banks of the Kentucky River. He had disappeared from the fort, captured by the Shawnee. The incident happened at the Lower Blue Licks while on a salt gathering expedition with others from Ft. Boonesborough. The natives descended upon the men with intent to capture or kill but Boone negotiated the release of the others in return for submitting himself to capture.

Daniel Boone had garnered high respect from the various tribes of the region but none more than the Shawnee. After his capture they conducted a purification ritual and named Boone Sheltowee or Big Turtle. During his captivity he was free to go about his business of hunting and exploring. Boone knew somewhere in the wilderness, south of the Ohio River, remained the treasure mines his good friend John Finley told him about while they were camped on the creek near Eskippakithiki. Boone, under the watchful eye of a couple of Shawnee warriors, scouted through the rugged mountainous terrain extensively searching under promising looking rock ledges or any other sign of mine workings. On one occasion, Boone and some Indian companions spent several weeks in one particularly interesting area. Boone even fashioned a crude hut to remind him of his days of living in a cabin, though his captors preferred to stay in the open area of the rock shelter. From this location Boone scouted valleys and ridge tops for miles in every direction. Sometimes it seemed to Boone that his old friend John Finley had outright lied to him. Still, there was the pack full of freshly minted crowns Finley had lugged back to camp. This knowledge drove Boone onward in his search for the mine.

Boone finally escaped the Shawnee on one of his expeditions and returned to Fort Boonesborough. Daniel Boone was accused of treason but overcame those charges due to the testimony of his salt gathering companions who had been released. During his long departure, his wife and family, thinking he was dead, returned to their lands on the Yadkin River in North Carolina. Boone went to his old home, gathered up his family and returned to Kentucky. Boone did not return to his fort, however. Instead he chose to live on a small creek farther west than Fort Boonesborough, on the very edge of the wonderful levels of Kentucky. From this family fortress the famous hunter would spend days exploring north and south along the Warriors Path. He claimed to be hunting but his secret objective was to find the mysterious treasure he thought to be somewhere in the wilderness. Though sometimes frustrating, he knew the very whispers of silver in Kentucky brought more and more people seeking a new life. He had not heard of anyone finding any mines. Boone was also obligated to the new state militia to protect the Kentucky County that Virginia now claimed. Due to the efforts of Daniel Boone and others, the Kentucky wilderness was being settled at an ever increasing rate. Settlers arrived from Boone's now famous trace to the south and by the Ohio River from the north.

On one of his outings Boone again visited the banks of his now famous Lulbegrud Creek, near the old Shawnee town of Eskippakithiki. He wondered about the beautiful levels of the fine Bluegrass Region. On this trip along the Warriors Path he met up with one of his original hunting party members, William Cooley. Cooley was heading south on the path loaded with all the deer skins his mule could carry.

"What are you doing up this way, Daniel?" Cooley asked.

"Just doing some hunting. Always did well in this particular area," Boone responded.

"Yes, well our famous Lulbegrud Camp is just over there, isn't it, Daniel?" Cooley noted and gestured toward the east.

"Well, I reckon you're right Cooley, maybe a half mile in that direction," Boone pointed.

"That's where we met that Swift fellow and heard about his silver mines, right?"

"I don't know nothin' about any silver mines."

"Now, come on, Daniel. It's common knowledge all over the country about those mines of Swift's. Did you ever actually find them?"

"Don't know of any mines Cooley. You've been listening to a bunch of crazy talk."

"Maybe so, but I was with you at the camp and I know for a fact you and John Finley brought a man named John Swift back to camp one night."

"While that's true, there never was anything said about any silver mines."

"Daniel, I don't know who really started that story. I always heard it was you. All I know is there are a lot of people, including your old buddy James Harrod, hunting for those mines."

"Well, I don't know how all that got started. But I can tell you a lot of fools are wasting a lot of time if they are looking for silver in this country."

"That's fine, Daniel, whatever you say. I'm just going on what I've heard. You would know."

"Well, that is the place. I mean the Camp Lulbegrud."

"I knew it was, Daniel. Do you still have a station down river from the Fort?"

"Yes sir. Me, Rebecca and the rest have us a nice place down there. Nice tobacco land and didn't have to do much clearing. We have a clean, steady water supply and plenty of game. Yep, we're in pretty good shape. What about old John Finley? You haven't run across him anywhere have you?" Boone asked.

"No. I've not seen him or that feller Swift. I've not even talked to anyone that's seen either one of them. It's just like they disappeared. Maybe them two are living it up back east on the coast or in Europe. What with all them silver mines and stuff, you know."

"I told you Cooley, there ain't no silver mines, never was."

"Well, I have been all over this country around here and I ain't seen no gold nor silver mines. I also heard you and your boys made that up anyway just to help old man Henderson sell this Kentucky land," Cooley said.

"Well, that's not true, either. Where do you hear all this stuff anyway, Cooley? Good Lord man! Can't people just leave things alone and go about their business?"

"Okay Daniel. You're a good man, in my book anyway, and if that is the way you say it is, then that's the way it is. I know you treated me fairly in our first hunt in this country. Well, anyway, good luck on your hunt."

"Thanks, good to see you again Cooley. Good fortune on your endeavors, too. If you are ever down my way stop in, we'd be glad to see you."

"I'll do that, Daniel. I'll do that. By the way, Daniel, why did you call the camp Lulbegrud? You never called it that the whole time we camped there."

Boone was not prepared for that question. Boone just stared at Cooley. Cooley never said anything else, turned and headed down the Warriors Path.

Boone continued on north and Cooley headed south. He hoped that he would run into his good friend John Finley again and even had hopes he would be in and around this area. He wasn't though. Boone wondered what had happened to John Finley over the years. He had not talked to anyone who had seen him. Boone was aware James Harrod came up missing and never returned from a trip searching for the legendary Swift silver mines.

For the next few years Boone worked his small farm, moved further north up the Warriors Path and searched for the thing that haunted him the most.

Twenty-seven: Loading Up the Loot

Will sifted through coins searching for any that might be different. The backpack was filled with hands full of silver crowns in practically no time. He continued to explore the room while he waited on Ray and Jennifer to return. He could hardly comprehend the situation. Here he was in a cave, with thousands of silver coins, not more than 300 feet from a heavily traveled highway. Will wondered if he and his friends had made the discovery some people spent their entire life fortunes in search of, the lost silver mines of John Swift. At the same time he realized the only thing they found so far were silver coins indicating this might indeed be Swift's mine. Will scanned the walls and the floor of the cave looking for signs of minerals or workings of a mine. If this was the silver mine there should be some evidence of mining activity, Will figured. He moved to the nearest wall and walked carefully, stepping around and over piles of silver coins. He found absolutely no sign of any kind of mining activity. Perhaps this was some other treasure left recently by some nearby residents. However, the old coins, pioneer weapons with the skeletons seemed to indicate otherwise.

Swift's journal spoke of mines as well as counterfeiting crowns. Will wondered if these could be counterfeit. He had no concept of time but it seemed to him Jennifer and Ray should have returned by now. He was virtually in a dream. Walking back across the large room he took time to examine the bones of the body in the floor. Could you be John Swift, he thought. There were no objects in particular with the body except a couple of buckles. Everything else had either been removed or decayed long ago. Nearby, almost underneath a large boulder, lay a knife and a flint lock rifle. This confirmed, in his mind at least, that this was the work of pioneers and there was no evidence that anyone discovered this place since this poor fellow was last alive with the treasure.

Silver coins in the thousands. "This is not happening," Will kept saying to himself under his breath. "No way." Several minutes had passed and his thoughts returned to Jennifer and Ray. Shouldn't they be back by now? Will thought as he picked up his light and started to head out the passageway. He could see the light flashing as his partners returned.

"Did you think we weren't coming back?" Jennifer asked as the two arrived invigorated by their brief exposure to the fresh air outside.

"Are you kidding? You would leave me with all this treasure to myself? I knew you would be back."

"You got that right," Ray added. Both Will and Jennifer exchanged expressions of puzzlement at Ray's remark.

"Look here guys." Will led them to the bones and pointed out the same long rifle Ray had already picked up but lost interest in when they first entered caverns.

"I see a knife here too. I'd be safe in saying this poor fellow didn't climb up here last year. Do you suppose he might be our Mr. John Swift?"

"How would we ever know?"

"I guess we won't for sure. I've looked through what's left of the old boy, and I can't find anything identifying this poor loser."

"Why do you call him a loser?" Jennifer asked.

"Are you kidding? A cave full of silver treasure and this poor bastard is dead as a door nail. I'd say his karma was definitely off that day."

"What about the other bodies?" Ray questioned.

"I know, it appears something terrible happened in this mountain. Three bodies in one treasure cave. Pretty bad," Will concluded.

"That's the point, Will. We already found the one skeleton at the cliff by the map which led us here to this cave and now this? We find three more dead people. What are we going to do?" Jennifer asked, bringing everyone's thought back to the fact of what was undoubtedly foul play.

"Anyway, I think I'll take some pictures of this place," Jennifer added.

"You're not thinking about selling these pictures are you?" Ray questioned in a serious tone. Jennifer was busy unloading her rather bulky camera case and glanced up at Will casually as she answered, "Why no, don't be silly Ray. Why would I do that?"

"Ray, what the hell? Why are you so edgy and worried. You think we are going to try to screw you out of your share?" Will scowled. Will had become agitated at Ray for vaguely suggesting Jennifer would reveal this secret.

"No. No. I just. Well, I don't know what I think right now. This is such an unbelievable discovery! Ah, I don't know what I am thinking. This is just too much for me in one day. My God, we have found a fortune here," Ray simply stated.

"I know. It is unbelievable."

"How much do you suppose these coins are worth?"

"God only knows. Let alone the historic value, these are nearly pure silver. They're worth a small fortune, I'd bet."

"What about the mines?" Ray asked. It occurred to him the Swift story was all about silver *mines*.

"Maybe the mine was nearby and this was used as a storage place, a sort of warehouse for the silver," Jennifer suggested.

"Then there should be some type of smelting operation in order to make these coins. You know, a furnace and molds, stuff needed to mint coins. That would mean these are counterfeit coins just like Swift's journal described," Will said.

"We have been in all but one passage of the cave and didn't find anything except two dead bodies."

"And we need to check out the last passageway on the other side of the main entrance passage." By this time all three were filling their backpacks with the silver treasure. It occurred to Will that anywhere they took this silver would create a major situation.

"You know, we must make some long lasting decisions before we take even one piece out of this cave. Wouldn't you guys agree?" Will questioned.

"Of course we do, Will, I've been trying to tell you guys all along?" Jennifer remarked. "And at the top of that list, we need to go directly from here to the police," she added.

"Umm," Ray groaned.

"Think about it, Jennifer. I don't think we could just take these down to the bank and cash them in for their value," Will concluded.

"I'm pretty sure a lot of decisions, as well as explanations, will be made once my story hits the newspaper."

"Gee, when you think about our situation, we either tell the whole world our story or keep the secret between us," Will reckoned. It was becoming increasingly clear to Will that their lives had gotten much more complicated than they had ever been before. They had found a huge treasure potentially worth millions. He knew for sure before they took anything from this cave and went out into the world they needed to establish a clear and concise plan.

"Not to mention the fact we don't even know who the hell owns this land, but it sure and hell doesn't belong to us. We are trespassing, for Christ's sake. Wouldn't you know it? We find the damn richest and most famous treasure in the history of Kentucky and we don't have a clue whose land the thing is on," Ray surmised.

"We've got a situation. That's for sure," Will said. Now they stopped filling their packs and thought about their unusual predicament. The whole thing confounded them, though overjoyed with making this discovery. They were deep in the reality of the 'barking dog chasing the car' scenario. Several minutes passed before anyone made any comment.

"All right, how about this. Instead of packing out a lot of these coins, we take out one or two and take to some antique coin dealer and get an expert opinion. We'll know then what we have here and maybe then figure out what to do," Will suggested.

"What about the dead bodies?" Jennifer asked.

"What *about* the dead bodies?" Ray retorted. Will had thought about them as well. He figured the question would arise again and he also knew Jennifer was going to want to report the bodies to the police. He saw he was going to be in the middle on this issue.

"I've been thinking about that too."

"And what are your thoughts on the matter?"

"It seems to me these bones are old. Just looking at the old flint locks with them suggests they could be very old. What I'm trying to say is these are not recent murders and such. It seems to me, anyway."

"Still, they are remains of humans. It just wouldn't seem right not to report what we've found."

"And I don't disagree with you on the point, I'm just not so sure we have to be in any hurry."

"Why would we want to wait? This is a fantastic find and sooner or later we're going to have to tell. The longer we delay, the more explanation we will have to provide."

"We will report it, I agree, we have to. A day or two will not make any difference and would give us time to talk to someone we trust on how to handle this situation."

"I agree. One thing is for sure, we are three rich assholes now!" Ray blurted out.

"Shit Ray, I am serious. We've got to approach this carefully. You can't mouth off to anyone, I mean anyone, Ray. Do you understand?" Will asked Ray looking right at him. Ray didn't quickly respond.

"Do you understand, Ray?"

"Yes, Yes. There won't be another Roger Hampton mess like I caused before. We should go back outside and check on things. It's getting late in the day."

"Are we all in agreement on this? We tell no one about any of this until we can take a couple of coins to someone and find out what they are."

"Hell, Will, we know the silver alone is a fortune. We just need to figure out how to get the shit out of here and sold."

"No, Ray we don't know anything. We're not even sure they *are* silver."

"Let's just take a few coins out, seal up the cave and find out what we can before we start carrying out the loot by backpacks full," Will suggested.

"I thought we agreed to report this in a couple of days, I never agreed to sneaking out of here with bags of coins. Will, these coins, this stuff, doesn't belong to us just because we found it," Jennifer flatly stated.

"Finders keepers, losers weepers, I always heard," Ray happily interjected.

"OK, OK, OK," Will shouted.

"Like I said before, let's just take out a couple of coins, find out what the deal is and take it from there. One step at a time. I know this is not ours, but we did find it and if it is what we think it is, well, someone is going to be rich, even if it's the county. I'd like to believe we'd get something for our discovery."

"Who's going to do the deal?" Ray asked as if he already knew the answer to his question.

"Do what deal, Ray?"

"Take the coins and have them checked out."

"Shit Ray, I don't care. If either one of you wants to, be my guest."

"No, you should do it, Will. You know about geology and stuff. If anybody can find out about these coins it will be you," Jennifer noted.

"Well, I'm going outside to get some fresh air. I'll be outside," Ray announced.

"I'm going to check out that last passageway. I should be out shortly."

"I think I will go out with Ray." Ray, followed by Jennifer, headed toward the entrance. Will, determined to finish his exploration of this mysterious cave, proceeded toward the final passageway before joining them outside.

Twenty-eight:
Ray and Roger Fight

The sun was settling near the western horizon. Dark shadows had already fallen on the valley below until the scene was almost colorless, where only thirty minutes before was radiant in varied shades of green. Ray stretched out his arm and made a tight fist. Squinting one eye he noted it would fit exactly twice between the sun and the horizon.

"About an hour 'til sundown," Ray yelled back to Jennifer as she emerged from the mountain side. Ray often used this primitive estimation to determine the amount of time left in the day. Standing at the outside edge of the giant boulder he gazed over the entire area around them. Only an occasional pickup truck traveled the road far below. He did hear the continuous traffic on the road nearly directly above them. Jennifer moved up to the boulder on the other side which faced east. The mouth of Benson Creek, the Kentucky River, part of Frankfort and the Capital, all could be seen from her vantage point. Jennifer concluded this would be a good photo opportunity so she retrieved her Nikon camera from its protected carrying case and began to take a few shots.

Just as Ray started to turn back to move to the entrance he caught a glimpse of something moving in one of the ledges below him. He froze and watched. Then, only about out a hundred yards down below, was another climber. He scrambled to the edge of the ledge.

"Quick, get behind the rock, Jennifer!" Ray whispered as he started to move out along the narrow strip of rock supporting him. He wasn't sure if the person following them had seen them or not.

"What is it, Ray?"

"Someone is climbing up the hill. We've been followed."

"Well we are trespassing on someone's land Ray. Maybe it's the land owner, who lives down there and is coming find out what we are doing up here."

"I wouldn't be surprised if this is state highway right-of-way we are on, we're practically under the road."

"What do you mean the road right-of-way?"

"That is exactly what I mean. We are standing in a ledge underneath the road. I think the right-of-way extends beyond the road and this cave sure as hell goes underneath the road."

By now the intruder had moved up several ledges and was only about a hundred feet below. Ray studied the lone visitor and scoured the valley again looking for any other would be hikers. Ray had just left a cave full of silver treasure and it was about to be jeopardized by this character. Ray flushed with anger.

"Can you tell who it is, Ray?" At the same moment Ray recognized the intruder.

"It's that damn Roger Hampton snooping after us again. I am going to kill that son-of-a-bitch. Stay back behind the rock and don't let him see you. Maybe I can get him to leave," Ray declared, mumbling while hurriedly climbing down the ledges to meet Roger. Ray was trying to divert or whatever desperate move he could manage to keep Roger from finding the cave entrance. Roger had already seen Ray climbing down the ledge as well as a glimpse of someone else, now hiding behind a large boulder.

"Hello, Ray," yelled Roger Hampton.

"What are you doing here, Roger?" Ray demanded an answer.

"Same thing you are Ray, searching for that treasure." Both men reached the same dangerous ledge high above the ground. The two men were standing on a narrow strip of rock about four feet wide with a few scrawny cedar trees.

"I tell you what Roger. You can turn the hell around and get your dumb ass off this hill and you won't get hurt," Ray bristled.

"This is not your property and you don't have any more right to be here than I do. Did you and your little buddies get permission from the person that owns this place? Do you even know the land owner? I'll bet you stupid asses just blunder on up here. And how do you know I didn't get permission? Don't mess with me Ray or you'll get in over your head."

"I don't give a shit. You had better get out of here now or..."

"Or what Ray? Or what? What are you going to do about it? I have as much right to be here as either of you. Where are your little partners, anyway? I know the three of you are up here, 'cause I followed you here."

Ray was about to boil over into one of his insane rages he had been known for as a young boy when he was bullied too much. Blind rage would overcome him and he would lash out without thought of consequences. Roger Hampton had pushed him nearly to that point.

"Roger, you had better get your ass off this mountain, now."

"I told you Ray, I am in this deal with you, whether you like it or not."

"No, by God, you're not!" Ray screamed and stepped right up in Roger's face. Roger never backed up and attempted to brush past Ray. This insulting act provoked Ray and he snapped. Something was happening Ray didn't understand. Everything around him went out of focus except Roger Hampton. He exploded and shoved Roger backwards. Roger grabbed onto a small bush but his foot slipped on the edge of the narrow ledge and his body dropped. The full weight of Roger Hampton hung down below the ledge. The small cedar bush bent and yielded to Roger's weight, but clung steadfastly to the rock outcrop. Roger held his grip on the bush and grabbed at the bare rock ledge with his other hand. Ray watched as Roger Hampton dangled over the edge of the cliff. Although there were dozens of jagged outcrops and ledges below him, it would be unlikely any of them would do any favors if he let go.

"Help me Ray! I'm slipping!" Roger screamed.

"Give me your hand."

"Help me Ray! For God's sake, I'm going to fall." Roger Hampton was digging at the rock wall holding on with one hand. He tried to swing his leg up but could not get his heel to reach the top of the ledge. Jennifer heard the loud talking and decided to peek out from behind the boulder down to the ledge on which Ray and Roger stood. She was shocked to see Ray standing over Roger Hampton, clinging to a bush. It was a terrifying site almost not believable. Ray suddenly began kicking and smashing Rogers's hands as hard as he could with the heel of his boot breaking Roger's fingers. The pain was too much and with broken fingers Roger lost his grip and fell away screaming. Ray watched as Roger hit, tumbling from ledge to ledge like a rag doll, coming to rest landing on his back with one leg folded underneath his body. Roger lay still the instant he stopped falling. Ray looked around the countryside, up and down Benson Valley to see if anyone by chance happened to be gazing in this direction. Ray studied every direction, over and over, searching for any movement. Jennifer screamed in horror, breaking Ray's concentration. Ray turned and looked toward the cave entrance and saw Jennifer disappear behind the large boulder. She scrambled to the cave entrance and slid head first, shocked and terrified by what she had just witnessed.

"Will!" Jennifer yelled as she landed at the bottom of the now familiar dirt incline. There was no immediate response.

"Will! Where are you?" Jennifer called out in the near darkness, with only the light from the small opening above. Sobbing and terrified, she had to think clearly. Will had intended to explore the other room. Jennifer did not know which room it was, but she did know which room contained the treasure and had light from the lanterns. Feeling her way along the wall she wished she had grabbed her flashlight outside. The terrifying sight of Roger Hampton falling from the high ledge to his likely death kept conquering all other thoughts in her mind. Jennifer reached the entrance to the treasure passage and began to see dim light. She kept her right hand sliding along the rock wall and stumbled along over broken rocks.

"Will!"

"What? I'm in here," came the answer from the large fortune cavern.

"Oh my God! Oh my God!" Jennifer screamed as she entered the chamber and ran to Will.

"What is it? What's happened?"

Jennifer grabbed Will and held on tightly, sobbing and shaking.

"It's Ray. I think he's killed Roger Hampton."

"Killed Roger Hampton? What are you talking about?"

"Ray! Roger Hampton fell off the cliff and I think Ray caused it! I think he's dead," Jennifer managed to get out between hysterical sobs.

"Where's Ray?" Will asked trying to get a fix on their present situation.

"I'm right here, Will." Ray said as he entered the large chamber.

Twenty-nine:
Ray Goes Nuts

"What's the problem?" Ray asked.

"You tell me, Ray. What happened out there?" Will firmly asked. Jennifer had her face buried into Will's chest and continued to whimper. Now terrified of Ray, she could not face him.

"Nothing happened," Ray calmly answered.

"Don't bullshit me, Ray. Jennifer came in here screaming that you killed Roger Hampton."

"She did, did she? Well, Ms. Jennifer may have got it all wrong. She might have thought she saw me kill Roger. Heck, I tried to save him."

Will sensed Ray's calm tone did not seem quite normal. He also knew he had a major problem. Jennifer, always level headed, wouldn't be this hysterical if something sinister hadn't happened. Will concluded in an instant, right or wrong, he would challenge Ray as to the validity of his statement.

"Ray, you're a liar. You killed him. He was hanging over the cliff and I saw you kick his hands free as he begged for you to help him. You killed him," Jennifer blurted out, half talking and half crying.

"Is that right, Ray? Is that the way it happened?"

Ray remained quiet and stared intently at Jennifer, burning laser beams into her. Just as calmly he turned his stare directly toward Will.

"Will, we have a situation here," Ray calmly said, glancing back at Jennifer so that Will could see.

"Whoa, wait a minute here, Ray. You may have a 'situation.' For God's sake Ray, what did you do?" At that moment Will realized they had a serious problem, several problems for that matter, and nothing ever would be the same again.

"I did what I had to do."

"You didn't have to push him over the cliff. Christ! Did you even go and check to see if he is dead?"

"Oh, I'd bet your farm he's dead. He fell two hundred feet from ledge to ledge, " Ray sinisterly answered.

"You're a murderer, Ray," Jennifer sobbed.

"Shhh, Calm down," Will softly whispered to Jennifer. He had a tremendous problem on his hands and Ray acted much too calm about the matter. He didn't like the predicament and had to do something pretty fast. Ray had started to walk around in a small tight circle, mumbling to himself.

"Let's all calm down and figure out our situation here," Will said.

"What is our situation here? I'll tell you our situation. I think I may have killed a man and we have a shit pot of a treasure now only three of us know about. Now I can go down there and drag that dead bastard up here and leave him in this cave with other the poor dead bastards and we can walk out of here rich. Or…."

"Or what, Ray?"

"Or I don't know, I need time to figure this out."

"Damn it Ray! We don't have a whole lot of time here, we have a big problem."

"They're going to find out sooner or later Ray, YOU murdered Roger!" Jennifer screamed at him. "I just want to go home now."

"Well we can't do that just yet can we, Jennifer," Ray rebutted, more agitated than ever.

"Yes we can, Ray. We just walk out of here, go to the authorities and they'll know what to do. It's simple Ray," Jennifer pleaded.

"Yea simple. Right. Simple to you maybe, but from my view it's pretty damn complicated, wouldn't you say old buddy? Ray turned away from his glare at Jennifer and glanced at Will.

"Ray! Stop!" Will demanded.

"Oh, kiss my ass. No Will, I will not stop. Tell her to shut the hell up and quit whining. It's done and now I have to figure out what to do." He pulled out a gun from underneath his shirt.

"Ray, what are you doing?" Will demanded noticing the gun was the one he kept in the glove box of his truck. He felt foolish. He should have kept the gun with him in his pack instead of just leaving it in the glove box.

"I'm not crazy, Will. I just need for everyone to calm down and let me figure this thing out." His hands shook as he held the gun pointed at his two friends. Jennifer, even more terrified, broke into uncontrollable sobbing.

"Ray, before you do anything else that you will live to regret, give me back my gun and let's walk out of here right now. We'll go check on Roger. Maybe he is alright. Then we can go explain to the police it was an accident." Will tried to reason with Ray, although he had no intentions of reporting a murder as an accident. In the current state of affairs, lying was not an unreasonable option to Will.

"No, no, we can't just walk out of here now. I think Roger may be dead and you two don't sound to me like you would be on my side. And here we are with a million dollar treasure."

"We're friends here. You and I have been friends since we were young boys. Listen, we can get out of this hole, check out the situation with Roger, go to the police, and keep the cave a secret until after everything settles down."

"Who're you trying to bullshit? You know damn well the police will be all the hell over this hillside. Give me a break. Do you think I'm that stupid, Will?"

"No, you're not stupid, Ray. That's why I suggest let's just calm down here, get a grip and sort this out. We can go to the authorities and say we found Roger's body, that he must have fallen, or some story like that. What about it Ray?"

"Hell no. You and her will be rich while o'le Ray rots in the pen because you turned him in, is the way I see it. No, No, that ain't happening, the way o'le Ray sees it." Ray became more agitated as the conversation continued. Will was not sure about his next move and was about to suggest that they should all go down and check on Roger Hampton. That would at least get them outside the cave where Will thought they might have a better advantage. Will did not like being in the cave with Ray holding a gun, his gun, pointed toward them.

"What do you plan on doing then, Ray?" Jennifer asked. She had finally calmed down a bit but still clung to Will as they both looked at Ray intently. Will cringed at the question and wished she had not asked it. Jennifer, however, became convinced Ray was going to finally lose control and shoot both of them right there in the cave. She imagined for a split second their bodies would be just additions to those that had already succumbed to the hidden treasure.

"Sit down on the ground," Ray shouted.

"Ray. Don't do this," Will pleaded.

"I am going to tie you up and you can stay here for a little while until I check out the Roger Hampton situation. I need more time, that's all. You two will be just fine." Although not a good situation, at least this bought them a little time. Ray grabbed one of the packs lying nearby and fumbled through it until he found the brand new roll of duct tape Will kept in his pack. He watched Ray's every move wondering why was he so careful to pack his backpack but not enough to check the damn glove compartment in his truck to make sure his gun was there. He always checked.

"Put your hands behind your back. I am just going to tie you up for a little while, like I said. I will be back for you in a bit. Don't worry."

"Don't worry! Ray, you're tying us up here in a cave! Come on. Don't do this," Will pleaded.

"Got to." Ray had already wrapped Will's wrists and feet tight with duct tape and now proceeded to do the same with Jennifer. After the awkward task was completed he left the cave.

"Is he gone?" Jennifer asked after a few minutes.

"I think he's had enough time to reach the entrance. At least he left the lantern lit so we don't have to be in the dark."

"What are we going to do?"

"We need to try to get loose from this tape and get out. He'll be back soon and will have to make up his mind on how he is going to handle this mess he's made."

The whole affair seemed surreal to Jennifer. How could Will's best friend suddenly become this way Jennifer wondered. She was frightened more than ever before. The cave seemed colder to both Will and Jennifer. The flickering light of the lantern drew Will's attention. It was definitely getting dimmer and Will knew it was only a moments before the last of the fuel in the lantern would be burned and leaving them in total darkness. Will knew he had to do something quickly.

"Jen, can you move your hands at all?"

"A little, they're pretty tight."

"I'm going to try and cut this tape against that sharp rock over there if, I can get to it." He had noticed a sharp-edged protruding from one of the large boulders that was a few feet from them. There were piles of silver coins scattered all around the boulder but the silver was not important to either of the two at the present time.

"If we don't do something we are going to run out of light."

"What!"

"The lantern is getting dimmer. It's about out of fuel. We'll be in the dark soon."

Will rolled over and over in the dirt across scattered silver coins until he reached the boulder he had spotted. Sitting up and situating himself he braced against the rock and with his hands securely fastened behind him and felt around for the jagged edge. Once located he began to rub the tape back and forth. The effort was hit and miss. Sometimes instead of rubbing the strong strands of duct tape he would gouge his hands. He felt the blood running down his hands as he cut and slashed blindly at the tape holding him. Jennifer had hopped closer to Will now. With her hands bound tightly, Jennifer could offer little assistance in Will's desperate effort to free himself. He knew time was running out. So did Jennifer. Minutes seemed like hours as he continued to use a back and forth sawing motion, slipping off his intended mark almost every other stroke. Ray had wrapped Will's wrists tightly with several layers of duct tape, the same tape he carried everywhere with him on his outings. The tape was tough in the cold damp air of the cave which had become a prison. The lantern dimmed more and then pulsated brighter indicating the fuel was nearly exhausted. Will sawed and yanked. Finally, the tough tape broke free, separating his bound wrists. Will grabbed and pulled at the tape from his ankles and then went to Jennifer. She turned instinctively for Will to unbound her, which he did using his pocket knife.

"What are we going to do?"

"I'm not sure. Our concern right now is Ray and what he is up to."

"I'm scared. I want to get out of this place. I'm calling for help as soon as we get out of here. Ray has gone nuts!" Jennifer had retrieved her cell phone from her camera bag, but didn't have a signal in the cave.

"That's not the Ray we know, for sure."

"We've got to get out of here and get some help before Ray comes back."

As Jennifer spoke, Will had already grabbed up his pack. She saw Will preparing to leave and was glad.

"Come on, Jennifer we don't have much time. We've got to get out of here now!" Will declared. It was already too late. He saw the faint glow from Ray's flashlight from the main passageway, although he did not hear anything.

"Shhh, quick, get over by the rock and put those duct tape pieces around your ankles," Will whispered to Jennifer.

"Oh my God, no."

"Just do it Jennifer! We need Ray to think we are still tied up. The light became brighter as Ray turned into the passage way where his two prisoners awaited his return.

Thirty:
Tragedy

Will and Jennifer hadn't noticed the time but more than an hour passed since Ray left them tied up with duct tape. They heard Ray making his way down the main cave passage way. By now, they heard the strained breathing and occasional grunt as if Ray was trying to move something. Ray was moving very slow and was dragging something heavy when he entered the main treasure room.

"You two all right?" Ray asked as if nothing had happened.

"Ray is that Roger Hamp...? Will started to ask.

"Hampton." Ray finished the sentence.

"Yes, it's Roger Hampton for sure! And I'm afraid folks, o'le Roger is dead as a door nail."

"You just can't drag him in here and leave him Ray! People, his family, the police will be looking for him."

"Well, they ain't gonna find him. They sure as hell won't find him in this cave after it's all sealed up."

"This is not right Ray, the way you're behaving. Let us go right now." Jennifer demanded.

"Can't do that, *Jen*. No, I can't do that." Ray spoke in a crazed tone.

"Listen Ray, you need to settle down and get a grip. Think about the treasure and what the three of us can do with all the money we've found." Will said slowly and softly. Jennifer gave Will a look of complete shock and surprise. Will glanced at Jennifer, raised one of his eyebrows and tilted his head slightly the moment Ray was distracted looking at one of the piles of silver coins. Jennifer quickly grasped Will's subtle body language and backed off to see where he was going with this tactic.

"You see, my problem is what to do about you two."

"There's no problem here Ray, believe me. There *is no* problem."

"Oh, I think there is and you know it the same as I do. Roger Hampton fell off the ledge of sorts and killed himself and Little Missy there is screaming I did it. Now let's see where that leaves old Ray at the end of the day after we get off this mountain. Oh, of course, his ass will be in Franklin County Regional Jail out on Coffee Tree Road."

"Look, we're friends, partners Ray, for Christ's sake."

"Nope. You're wrong, just plain wrong. We *were* partners, but I, uh, I'm afraid you two will turn me in for killing Hampton and, well, you two get the loot and old Ray goes to the pen. We wouldn't be partners anymore anyway." Ray became more crazed and agitated. He drew out the gun he'd taken from Will's truck. Ray knew time was running out. He moved over to Jennifer and pointed the gun at her.

"You're all wrong about the situation. If you'll just calm down and get a grip we can sort this out until no one goes to jail and we all share in the loot," Will explained even though he was lying. He had already come to terms there would be no good ending here.

"Move over there by Will. Go on! Hop over there. You can hop can't you *Jen*."

Jennifer hopped and stumbled but managed to right herself by the boulder. Ray didn't notice that the duck tape was gone from around her ankles. Will knew he had to do something now. Jennifer made the first move; she bolted and jumped behind the big rock. This caught Ray by surprise and he chased after her momentarily disregarding Will. This provided the opportunity Will needed. This likely would be the only chance to get out of this situation although he wished it had not happened this way. Jennifer was running, stumbling from boulder to boulder. Ray could see her and fired the pistol at her. Will picked up a rock and smashed Ray's lantern and the cave light diminished to the spurting single lantern. Ray turned toward Will and fired the pistol. The sounds of the shots were deafening inside the enclosure. Ray turned and fired a third shot at Jennifer.

Will had been spared the bullet. He ran toward Ray while Ray was firing at Jennifer. Jennifer screamed as she felt the sting of the bullet when it hit her side and she fell to the rocky floor. She was surprised by the actual lack of pain from the bullet and was still moving. But in the darkness of the cavern and the shock of the injury she quickly became disoriented. She gasped, confronting the obstacle of pulling enough air in her lungs. Not having any idea of her location in the chamber she became even more confused, stumbled and fell to the ground. Breathing became difficult and at the same time she felt dizzy. Jennifer's fall landed her between two rather large boulders and by chance, separated her from Ray. This location hid her breathing so he lost track of her approximate location.

The only remaining illumination was Will's failing lantern and it's lighting power weakened, like a collapsing star after a supernovae. Even though in the dark environment of the cave, even a small light provides enough illumination to see objects near the source of light. But spread out across the cavern were numerous boulders and, of course, millions of dollars in piles of rare coins. Ray abandon his search for Jennifer and turned his attention on Will.

Will already had reached the edge of the main wall, crawling along the way, trying to make his way toward Jennifer.

"Were the hell are you Will? Come on out, I won't hurt you buddy."

Will had made his way into the middle of one of the fallen piles of silver coins that at any other moment in the history of his life would be a fantastic place to have wound up. At the present time, however, Will knew his and Jennifer's lives were in grave danger. Will picked up one of the silver crowns and threw it toward the back of the cave. Ray instinctively turned and fired in that direction.

"You lying son-of-a-bitch!" Will yelled out in absolute anger.

"That was an accident Will, the gun just went off. I didn't mean for that to happen," Ray spoke with some sarcasm.

"Accident my ass." Will hollered as he crawled long the wall to another boulder. Ray honed in on the location of the voice and began walking in that direction. Will had to move quickly because he was the next target. The sputtering, empty gas lantern finally quit. It was a great miracle, Will thought, the lantern had finally extinguished. Or perhaps not, since the lantern by his estimate, should have diminished five minutes ago. Either way, they were now in total darkness and neither of the three could see anything. Will remembered the direction of the exit of the passageway into the main cave passage. He listened for any sounds from Jennifer. Ray listened for any sounds from Will. Will was certain this was the worst possible situation he could ever be in. He knew, beyond a shadow of a doubt, he had to get out of the cave for help.

Will had taken time to memorize the layout of the cave passages. Even though there were irregular rock piles, once Will reached the side wall of the cave, he felt a sense of direction. The silence of the darkness was broken up by an occasional stumble by Ray as he also moved toward the cave exit.

"Where are you Will?"

He would not answer but Ray's voice gave Will some idea of his approximate location. Will kept his breathing low and duck walking and sometimes crawling toward the exit while continually reaching and touching with his left hand the relative smooth cave wall that was serving as his guide to freedom. Will stopped frequently and listened for any sounds from Jennifer but heard nothing. He figured she may have made it out of the cave. After what seemed like hours Will reached the narrow passage that was the way out of the treasure room. He could hear Ray behind, not far it seemed, stumbling through one of the piles of silver coins.

The metal, tingle sound of coins being strewn about, filled the cave and for the brief moment provided a cloaking noise for Will to make an exit from the chamber. He hoped Jennifer had already made it to safety and if he could get out they would make a mad dash over the ledges and find a place to hide from Ray. Reaching the main cave entrance passage way, he saw the light in the distance and ran for the bottom of the dirt incline the three, once fun loving partners, had become familiar with. Now he could only think about getting to the dirt incline and getting up out before Ray killed him. He reached the dirt ramp and scrambled, digging and clawing his way up the smooth ramp and squeezing his way through the tiny opening. He heard Ray behind him and thought for sure Ray would shoot him in the back as he made his escape. As soon as he stood up in the fresh twilight air he frantically was trying to formulate a plan for the eminent danger nearing the bottom of the dirt incline. He looked for Jennifer, scanning the ledges that lay below him. She was not there. He could here Ray yelling for him, climbing up the ramp. He knew he was trapped. By the time he could get to the second ledge below him Ray would be standing where he stood now. He would be an easy target. And where was Jennifer, he couldn't leave her he thought.

Ray hesitated as he reached the opening before climbing through. Wary that Will might be waiting just outside the entrance ready to jump him he carefully peaked through the opening inching out little by little. He did not see Will anywhere so he completed his exit and stood up scanning the rock ledge all around him. Ray started to follow the animal path around the large boulder that hid the cave entrance and led to the small drop off to the next ledge. Will was on the opposite side of the boulder hanging on to a cedar bush. He was as far down as possible and had Ray taken the time to look left around the boulder, he would have found him. He assumed Will had moved down the mountainside. The tiny spot Will found was hardly big enough to balance himself on. Ray reached the ledge he had pushed Roger Hampton from and could see on down the cliff side. He figured since Will was nowhere in sight he didn't have enough time to get very far. He realized Will was behind him so he turned and climbed back up the ledges. Will had moved out from behind the boulder and stood in front of the cave. He could see Ray coming back up the rock ledge. Will instinctively picked up the large rock lying on the ground near the cave entrance and stepped out from behind the boulder to confront Ray.

"Ray. Stop right there. Don't come any closer."

"There you are old buddy. I must have missed you." Ray kept on climbing ignoring Will's demand to stop. He knew Will didn't have any weapon except his pocket knife since he had Will's hand gun. "I'm warning you Ray. Stop right there."

"Oh what the hell are you going to do? Throw rocks at me?"

"Hells bells man! You and I got a real problem to sort out here Will."

Will raised the rock over his head and flung it at Ray. It missed its mark, as Ray ducked. Time was running out and if he didn't receive some sort of a miracle, Ray would kill him right then and there in a matter of moments. His only option was to move back behind the boulder for protection but Ray was within a couple of yards of being in reach. As soon as Ray made it to the boulder he saw Will diving head first behind the other side of the boulder. Determined to kill him Ray lunged behind the boulder only to realize his mistake. Will had grabbed the cedar bush and swung his body around clinging to the little tree to keep from going on over the ledge. He was hanging out over the ledge, feet dangling and if the little bush wasn't rooted deep enough, he would fall to his likely death. Ray was not aware the ledge ran out just past the boulder and he had nothing but dirt and rock to try to cling to. He had not bothered to check behind the boulder when they first arrived, something both Jennifer and Will had managed to do. Ray clawed and grabbed but it was no use.

He slipped over the edge right beside Will hanging on for his own life. He fell nearly seventy feet to bottom of the cliff.

A strange quietness settled on the cliff side with only the light breeze rustling through the small red cedars growing out of the face of the cliff at every possible place they could establish a root system. Will listened to hear any sounds from Ray below. There was only silence. Will clung to the small miracle of finding the strong little cedar tree. He needed a miracle and the tough little tree provided it, he marveled. Will pulled himself back up from the small ledge and thought about his predicament. After a few moments Will reasoned Jennifer might still be in the cave. The evening sun had already dropped below the horizon and darkness would be arriving soon. If he could find his way back into the cave and find his pack which contained extra lights, he would be able to help Jennifer. Will once again entered the dark cave, sliding head first down the now well worn dirt incline. With the faint light of twilight, he made his way to the entrance of the treasure room passage. Following along the wall, Will moved slowly down the passageway until he was in total darkness. Rather than depending upon the safety of the cave wall, Will moved straight forward guessing his way to the approximate center of the cavernous room. He knew his pack was somewhere in the general vicinity where they were tied up and Ray didn't bother to take either Jennifer's or Will's packs. He felt coins occasionally under his feet as he carefully moved through the darkness. He kicked around in all directions feeling for the pack of resources.

"Jennifer. Jennifer! There was no response. Will stopped to listen for any sound. In the total darkness, the only sound Will could hear was his own breathing. His foot finally made contact with something. He felt down in the darkness and picked up Jennifer's camera case. His pack was nearby so he expanded his search and found what he had been looking for. He pulled open the flap and felt inside until he found the emergency light stick. He always kept a couple of light sticks because he never trusted flashlights since the batteries would always go down with time. Will concluded years ago to only keep emergency equipment that would not expire with time. The single firefly colored glowing stick instantly lit the immediate area when he cracked the tube and shook rapidly. In fact, the entire treasure room was faintly illuminated by the small device and for a brief moment Will was surprised by this event. He scanned the room in wide arcs looking for any sign of Jennifer. He saw a shoe just beyond a rock about twenty five feet from the entrance of the treasure room. Will ran over to find Jennifer lying face down and motionless.

"Jennifer!" Jennifer did not respond as Will grabbed her and rolled her over onto her back. He saw the dirt beneath her was stained with blood and her clothes were bloody. A quick check for a pulse yielded nothing. He placed his ear next to her mouth to see if he could detect any breathing. He didn't. She was dead he reasoned. Ray had killed Roger Hampton, now he had killed Jennifer and failed in his attempt to kill him. The events of the day were beginning to pile up on Will. He couldn't focus, perhaps it was shock, he wondered. He felt nauseous and turned to throw up but nothing came. He leaned against the cold boulder trying to think clearly. It was difficult.

Over and over in his head he replayed the events of the last few hours. He couldn't sort this out but realized he needed to get help and fast. He grabbed up his pack heavy with the coins he had inserted before the whole day turned upside down. Not taking time to unload the pack he headed for the cave entrance. Once outside, he headed down the ledges holding his light directly toward the ground as much as possible so not to be noticed and see the ledges he must negotiate. He needed to check on Ray but finding him in the darkness could take all night and Will was suddenly very weary and very tired.

Thirty-one:
Swift Returns to the Cave for the Last Time

John Swift climbed up the rocky face maneuvering himself from one rock ledge to the next at a rapid pace. He and his now absent partners made the trip enough times to know the correct path to take in order to avoid any dead-ends. There were many such ledges and Swift knew how to navigate and climb from one ledge to the next. After several minutes of hard climbing, Swift reached the boulder hiding the entrance and saw the cave entrance was left intact. It remained walled up, just as he had left it during his last visit more than 15 years ago. He stopped at the cave entrance bracing against the boulder and looked out over the valley below. He was always careful to see if anyone had followed him to his secret location. From this high vantage point he could see his horse and pack mule tied up near the creek. It occurred to him this might be his final trip into the wilderness. He intended to carry out enough silver coins to purchase a new ship and sail on to Cuba. He longed for the warmer climates having spent so many harsh winters in the wilds of Kentakee these years past. Besides, big changes were underway back east and things had changed here for that matter.

The new nation of the United States had formed and any curiosity about his shipping activities had long been forgotten by the British Navy. This once grand, wild country now known as Kentucky was being settled by families seeking to be land owners.

Swift took his knife and carefully began removing the rock and clay seal of the cave entrance. Once the stucco like material was removed the hidden access was revealed. The dirt incline he and George Mundy built when they first moved the silver into the cave awaited his decent. It was a massive undertaking as Swift recalled as he slipped down the incline into the darkness of the cave.

At the bottom of and beside the ramp he found the cane torches he and John Finley had left from one of the previous visits. The two had made the torches from river canes they collected on their way to this cave. The torches were made Indian style by bounding a dozen canes together in a tight bundle and securing with a piece of leather, cloth, vine or whatever was handy at the moment. The torch ends were then lit and provided excellent light for several minutes. A cane torch could easily last long enough to explore all the passages of this particular cave. With the help of some dry tender, a piece of flint he always carried with him and his knife, he started a fire. The dry canes caught fire quickly and provided excellent light in the cave. Swift grabbed up three of the bundles and headed straight for the area with the amassed amount of treasure.

Once in the treasure room he saw his treasure was still safe. Kegs and piles of minted silver coins were stacked along the walls, near boulders and along the beaten path that ran generally in the center of the room. Silver and gold coins remained scattered loosely on rocks once used as tables to count and sort out coins. Swift wondered to himself how they ever got this much silver this high on the mountain. Each keg and sack full of coins had to be carried by him and George Mundy up through the ledges and down into this cavern. It took them months, Swift recalled, but along with the help of a couple of trusty mules, they managed to move the entire treasure into this final resting place.

Swift glanced without the slightest remorse at the bones of his old friend Finley whose life he ended here. In the other room remained the bodies of James Harrod and his traveling companion leaving a mystery for all the folks that long ago gave up their search. He and Finley stashed them in the cave, never to be found by anyone. Swift thought of the past only momentarily then began loading up sacks with coins. He gathered up nearly all the gold coins and gold bars. During the course of the day Swift made five more trips up the mountain and carried out a small fortune by anyone's measure. He figured he would not be back for a long time, if ever. As far as he knew the treasure cave still kept his secret and only he knew the location. Just in case he ever got confused about the location, Swift had taken careful measurements and wrote them down in another secret location all of which he had indicated on the rock map left back at the high knob along the Warriors Path.

On his last trip back up the rock cliff, Swift took with him a good amount of clay he had obtained from the creek bank. He took his water pouch that was on the ground by his staked horse and mule, filled it with water from the creek and along with the clay headed back up the mountain. He would use the water to mix the clay into a mortar. The cave floor was a dry and powdery offering nothing usable. When he had finished carrying out all the coins he required, he put out the cane torches, left them at the bottom of the dirt incline and exited the cave. He then began to mix water with the clay, adding broken and crushed bits of limestone and dust he found eroded away from the main cliff and lying about the area around the boulder. The limestone dust and small pieces would change the color of the mud to look more like the natural rock around it. First, Swift stacked small rocks much like building a stone fence to fill most of the cave entrance. Then over the rock foundation he rubbed on the clay mortar mixture filling the gaps in the rocks and sealing over the cave entrance until it looked just like the rest of the cliff face. Swift figured the entrance had been made invisible and unless someone knew the exact location, it would continue to go undetected.

John Swift felt this could be his last trip to the cave. People had begun moving into the territory. Hunters and now settlers had set up stations, sometimes called homesteads, as close as the big springs half way between the cave and the mountain. Someone sooner or later would see him and track him to the cave and put and end to his secret treasure, Swift thought as he carefully made his way back down the cliff to the valley below. He planned to spend his remaining years among the islands of the Caribbean. This bounty would provide for him well. It had taken him all day to haul the valuable silver coins down to very base of the cliff were the animals grazed lazily about to the length of their tethers. Resting only occasionally, he hoisted and secured the heavy sack of coins onto the mule for the long trip back east. He moved out from the site as soon as he cleaned up any signs of the campsite. He crossed the river at the Buffalo crossing and followed one of the trails eastward camping off the trail along the way until he reached the Warriors Path.

John Swift made his way up to the Warriors Path and headed north until he reached a trail that headed east. The route went through the mountains but the now well-worn trails from continued use by explorers and settlers were all over the place. The Shawnee and every other tribe had been forced farther north and to the west so Swift met no hostile natives on his trip. Once he arrived to the lands now considered established Virginia proper, he felt more at ease. A captain of the seas, he missed the ocean and was determined to sail and enjoy the warmth of the tropics before he got too old. He planned on purchasing a sailing vessel, perhaps one of the smaller, faster vessels now being made in America. His purpose would be more for joy than profit. After all, he still had untold wealth stored back in the wilderness only known to him. He was comfortable in that knowledge.

Upon his return to the coast, Swift purchased a fine schooner and named her Quicksilver. He signed on a small crew and sailed south. He returned from time to time to ports along the coast of the Carolinas. He brought goods from Cuba and Dominica but each time he remained careful only spending a few days in port. The seasons came and went and Swift eventually never returned to the east coast. Kentucky had been established as a state separating from its mother-state of Virginia. Swift had disappeared. No one knew of his whereabouts. The treasure cave lay undisturbed with a few randomly scatted clues that no one had put together to solve Swift's magnificent treasure.

Thirty-two: Will's Turmoil

The darkness seemed evil and harsh as Will made his way down the steep cliff from ledge to ledge using the tiny glow light held close to the ground. Several times he almost took the wrong step. It was an ordeal making the trip slow and painful. He had just lived through the most horrible thing in his life and he still was on the mountainside. All he could think of was getting out and finding help. He stumbled and tripped down the ledges until he found the path that led to is truck parked on the side of the road. Jennifer, Ray and Roger Hampton were all dead. He could hardly keep his thoughts straight and felt like he was about to pass out. Once he got close to the road he put the glowing light stick in his pocket and sat down. Now in darkness he listening for any sound of Ray yelling for help or moaning in pain. The woods and cliff above him remained silent. He could see the lights of Frankfort but darkness engulfed him. An occasional car would pass by on the road. This was the worst mess he'd ever gotten himself in and he wondered why he didn't die like the other two up there in that cave.

"Damn it to hell! This is one hell of a mess!" Will spoke out loud even though there was no one to hear him. After a few minutes of collecting his wits, he climbed up the shallow bank to his truck. It was right where the three left it earlier in the day. Parked right behind it was Roger Hampton's vehicle.

Will began to think about his present situation. He should go straight to the police and report this tragic event. He fumbled for his keys while mulling over the horrendous last few hours and wondered how he could explain this whole matter to the police. Maybe he would just call from his cell phone, which was still in the truck. If he had brought the phone with him, Ray would have taken it away just like he did Jennifer's when he tied them up in the cave. Will drove without thinking the direction he was driving but he did not go to the police station. Instead, Will found himself headed out of town toward home. He pulled into his drive and went into the house. Once inside, Will sat down in the chair by the back door thinking about his situation. Ray had his gun, if the police find the gun and there are no fingerprints, then he himself would be a prime suspect in the triple murder. He needed to find the gun and Ray for that matter. His gun killed Jennifer. What if the police thought he had murdered them, he considered. He needed rest, just a couple of hours of sleep. He hoped he would wake up from a bad dream. He knew it was no dream. Will moved to the couch, flopped down and sleep came almost instantly from pure exhaustion.

Sometime after midnight Will awoke and went outside to the truck and grabbed his pack and opened it just to verify the pack contained old silver coins. Jennifer and Ray are dead upon that cliff and so is Roger Hampton. He realized he was the only witness and when he reported the incident two things would happen for certain. First, he would immediately become the prime suspect. Without any living witness, this will be most difficult to explain all the events leading up to yesterday. Secondly, though now not as important, the treasure would be lost to whomever, but certainly someone other than himself. He needed a plan, a way to approach this sensibly. Will realized what he might have to do.

The thought of leaving everything behind was not pleasant. The farm would go to his sister in Wyoming. The animals would have to be cared for. How would he manage their care? He figured the horses have plenty of grass and water in the pond, they can go the rest of the fall. The dogs will hang around but will eventually go down the road to the neighbors for food. They already performed such acts on occasion. The chickens can be turned loose. Will went inside and looked through the house, grabbing up a change of clothes and some snack food. He checked his sock drawer for the emergency cash he'd stashed away. He always kept five hundred dollars in twenties hidden there just in case he needed quick cash. He couldn't go withdraw money from the automatic bank machine. In fact, he couldn't be seen by anyone for the rest of the night. He poured out enough dog food to last several days and opened the chicken lot gate. He headed for his truck.

Will drove up Benson Valley to the parking lot for the marina that was located on the deeper waters of Benson Creek. This seemed like a better parking place than along the road side and likely delay authorities from finding his truck a little longer. This location would require a longer hike up the creek and across some open fields to get to the bottom of the rocky hillside he needed to climb. Dawn was breaking when he pulled into the empty parking lot. He had to move fast or take a chance on someone spotting him. He jumped out of the truck and stuffed the food, bottles of water and clothes into his already heavy pack and locked the truck. With no relatives and no ties no one would immediately be looking for him. Besides, he knows where a cave full of silver treasure remains undetected. Will walked back through the fields along the bank of Benson Creek until he arrived at the closest point to the cliff the cave is located. Though a long walk, the fields he crossed were flat pasture land making for an easy hike. He climbed up the ledges using his flashlight hoping that no one noticed the strange light. When he reached the big rock hiding the cave entrance he slid in behind the massive boulder bracing himself. He would wait until sunrise and figure out what happened to Ray. Will dozed a little and ate some snack crackers with a bottle of water he'd brought along. When daybreak arrived enough to see, he crawled carefully around the rock to the place he clung to save his life. Ray foolishly slipped over to presumably lose his. Peering over the edge he only saw a small section of the ledge where he figured Ray landed. There wasn't any sign of Ray. With a plan now beginning to come together he climbed back down the route he came until he reached what he estimated would be the best route to take to get to the place Ray landed. He left his pack and everything back at the big rock near the cave entrance. After an hour of trial and error routes to reach the ledge he found Ray Deevers' body lying in a contorted heap on some rocks. Ray's head had hit a rock and killed him, probably instantly. He checked for a pulse and found none. Ray was dead from his own doing. Will searched around for the gun but could not find it. Damn, the gun must have slid on over the cliff to another ledge, he concluded. Will knew he really needed to find that gun. After a considerable amount of time he figured the gun simply slipped into a crevice or under leaves. Again, no breaks coming his way, Will contemplated.

By mid-day, Will had carried, dragged mostly, the stiff body back up the hillside to the cave. He noticed the buzzards had already picked up the scent of decaying flesh and circled the valley. He pushed the lifeless heap through the cave entrance and it tumbled down the dirt incline. The body came to rest very near Roger Hampton's body which Ray had dragged into the cave earlier in the day. With a light containing fresh batteries retrieved at home, he went back into the cave treasure room just to check on Jennifer one more time. She was still lying in the same spot though Will couldn't recall her exact position. He didn't think she'd moved and nothing had changed. He checked her pulse once again. She's gone he thought and sobbed for the first time since the whole ordeal started. There was nothing he could do for her other than go get help. He left the treasure room and scrambled up the now worn dirt incline to the outside. His backpack remained in the same spot near the entrance. He had already planned on closing back the cave entrance the way he found it which seemed to be a clay mud, probably from the creek below and bits of limestone from the cliff itself. He needed to try to find his gun first. Once again he climbed back down to the location where he had retrieved Ray's body, he searched much slower and systematically this time. Still he could not find the gun. The weapon must have slid on over perhaps to one of the smaller ledges below. Will made his way down and looked around. Another two hours of searching failed to yield any sign of the gun. He had to get the cave sealed back to the condition in which they discovered it.

Will set out for the bottom of the cliff and the stream below. Once at the creek, he wandered along the bank, searching for clay mud or some other material that nature offered he could use as a type of stucco. In a matter of a few minutes he found the dirt bank that was a mixture of rock and clay. He searched around for some way to carry the clay dirt. He found a short, broken board that had floated up the creek during backwater flooding from the Kentucky River. Will scooped up the clay by the handful and slapped it on the board. In short order he'd filled the little board with all the clay he could carry. After quickly dipping the board with its load of clay into the shallow running water of Benson Creek, he heaved the load up on his right shoulder and headed back across the field to the awaiting hard climb. When he reached the boulder and the tiny portal he began gathering up any loose rock and gravel and chunks of the stucco mortar material. With the largest rock he could hold in on hand, Will began bashing the materials into a powdery grit then added fists full of the crushed stone into the clay. He figured he could use this material as binding and hardening materials for the clay mixture. It also gave the filled-in cave entrance a natural rock appearance. He needed more water for making the putty so he grabbed the two remaining bottles of water in his pack and poured them into the clay and grit. He kneaded the muddy mix just like bread dough. Satisfied the mixture was consistent and tacky enough to stick, he stacked rocks filling in the bulk of the small opening. Then he pressed the stucco-like material over the rocks. Pressing, smoothing, and placing small rocks into the mixture, he managed to give it the textured appearance of a rock wall. He spent the better part of an hour later completing his task. The clay nearly dried before it was finished. Unless someone stood right there looking for it, the now hidden cave entrance would not be discovered. It was a miracle they found it and now he was sorry they did, Will thought.

The sun was setting in the west, and Will realized that he had spent all day on this mountain side. Most disturbing was the fact that he had just sealed his girlfriend up in a rocky tomb. Not sure why but certain he had to, the idea of leaving her made him sick and terrified at the same time. He was scheduled to work at the bar today but figured since he didn't show up, the manager most likely called in one of the other bartenders. There would be little concern for Will's absence. Ray sometimes played hooky from work so missing a day didn't draw much attention there either. Roger Hampton's absence was probably causing a bit of commotion already, Will thought. Jennifer's parents would be calling but not become concerned until tomorrow or the next day. He needed to be out of Frankfort no later than tomorrow adding yet another problem to work through. All he needed was time to think but he had very little at his disposal. Only a few hours ago, he and his friends were oblivious to time. They had all the time in the world to have fun, explorer, and follow dreams. Now alone, his time is running out fast and he could do nothing about it.

With a final check to see the outside cave area appeared as he, Ray and Jennifer had found the place, Will climbed out on the narrow strip of rock and slid down to the next one below. He proceeded along a path made by animals in the opposite direction from the way they came to this cave. He moved from one jagged outcrop to another until reaching one leading into the woods. The tree cover provided him protection from being discovered. Though this was a steep area there were plenty of trees to grab and pull himself up to get up the mountain. He climbed up the slope he figured would lead him to the road over top the hidden treasure cave. In a short time he stepped over the guardrail and crossed over highway 421. With his pack slung over his right shoulder he started walking north bound. By now evening had arrived and the heavy traffic from the workers heading home had already ended. He looked back at every car coming to make sure he didn't recognize anyone before he stuck out his thumb to hitch a ride. Several cars and pickup trucks passed him by. One truck did stop, and a gruff looking fellow yelled out.

"Where you going?

"Eminence," Will replied.

"Going as far as Pleasureville, hop in," the driver said. Will did not know the gentleman and tried to not make eye contact. This guy might identify him if he saw his photograph in the paper, he figured. He looked out the window and thought they never would arrive at Pleasureville. When they arrived at their destination Will exited the truck offering his thanks and began walking northbound. The less contact with anyone, the better for now. In a less than fifteen minutes another truck stopped. Will hopped in and began to put more distance between himself and the nightmare he left behind. This time he made it to Madison, Indiana. By now darkness had draped the countryside. His ride ended on the north side of Madison. This was farm country offering few houses along the way. He found a suitable barn far enough off the road he figured no one would find him. He felt pretty sure sleeping in a barn, in the middle of nowhere, could offer safe accommodations for the night. Exhausted beyond anything he'd ever experienced he collapsed on some of the bales of hay and fell into a sound sleep.

By four in the morning, Will was awake and on the road. He figured people at home would be concerned by their absences by the end of this day. He needed to get as far away as possible. He caught rides all day, mostly rides for short stretches. Will offered little conversation to his ride hosts, though some would make the attempt. All he thought about was Jennifer lying in that cold cave. Why did I leave her, he thought. Maybe I should go back and try to explain everything to the police played over and over in his mind. Once stopping at a service station/food mart, he bought some coffee and something to eat. He cleaned himself up a bit, then changed into his only other pair of clothes in the restroom. As luck would have it, he managed to catch a ride on into Indianapolis. Will found a pay phone, called a taxi and made his way to the bus station. He had completed formulating his plan of disappearance. He now knew he was about to give up everything and everyone he ever knew. His Jennifer was gone and he would almost certainly be pinned with the triple murder and lose the treasure as well. The treasure and the bodies would most likely remain a secret for another 200 years for all he cared at the moment. At the counter he requested a ticket to Detroit. Not yet burdened with the hardships of terrorist screening, purchasing a bus ticket was a simple matter.

"That will be eighty three dollars and ninety five cents," the clerk stated.

Will handed him the money while the clerk typed in information that would eventually show up on the ticket. He actually thought the process would be more difficult than it turned out. He was not at all sure about this purchase, but he needed to get to Canada or somewhere away from here. From there he could decide where and if he should go somewhere else. In Canada he would be safe and missing just like the others. And then it came, the question.

"Your name sir?"

Will, paused for a moment, staring at the older gentleman. The long delay in response prompted the old clerk to glance up from his keyboard with suddenly more interest in the customer.

"John, uh, the name is John," Will fumbled out.

"Last name," the clerk droned out as if Will were an idiot.

"Swift. John Swift."

Final Note

This book is a work of fiction. With the exception of historical figures, all characters are fictional. Inspiration is obtained from many sources. Some of the inspiration for this story is from early writings of Kentucky history. In the Filson Club Quarterly Lucien Beckner describes John Findley as the first path finder of Kentucky; R.S Cotterill in his wonderful account of pioneer Kentucky published in 1917, offers a concise review of events unfolding in the late eighteenth century. John Filson, wrote the first book ever about Kentucky in 1784. It was from Filson's work that much of the legend of Daniel Boone was derived and revered today. The collection of Appalachian stories and Swift information by Michael Steely provides a wide array of treasure tales. Of course, the late Michael Paul Henson, who published the first works including variations of the famous Swift Journals, perhaps offered the greatest source of inspiration by both his books on the subject and many hours of personal discussions I personally had with the author.

While no direct quotes are attributed to any of the above mentioned sources, they all provided meaningful understanding to me of both the characters and time period. Other inspired moments come from stories, tales, and encounters over the years with some amazing people. Some spent many hours of their lives in pursuit of solving the long running mystery of the John Swift lost silver mines. I've had the good fortune to meet a few of these folks, to listen to their findings as well as share their dreams and hopes on the mystery.

Locations and places in this work are mostly real. Businesses are fictional and are not intended to reflect a specific private business entity. There are two exceptions however: The Kentucky Coffeetree Cafe in downtown Frankfort and the Ale81 Bottling Company in Winchester Kentucky both graciously allowed the use of their names. All non-historic characters are purely fictional and any resemblance to real persons is coincidental.

For more information on Swift visit:
edhensonbooks.com

Visit online:
http://www.kentuckycoffeetree.com/

http://ale8one.com/